Content Advisory: Although this book falls within the young adult genre, it does contain some violence and foul language and is intended for readers 16+.

I0596014

REIGN OF BLOOD

THE FERAL SENTENCE – BOOK 1
BEASTS OF PREY – BOOK 2
PRIMAL INSTINCTS – BOOK 3
REIGN OF BLOOD – BOOK 4
GAME OF DEATH – BOOK 5

Shade Owens
www.shadeowens.com

Edited by Nikki Busch
www.nikkibuschediting.com

RED RAVEN PUBLISHING

ISBN: 978-1-7775422-6-9

PART ONE

PROLOGUE

I'd tell you my name, but you already know it. That's a comforting thought; some days, I feel like I'm on the verge of forgetting it.

I've been through hell this last year, or two... I can't keep track of exactly how long I've been living here. I've seen more violence than anyone should ever have to see in a hundred lifetimes. I've been beaten and starved over and over again by my captors, the Northers.

The good news, though, is that I managed to escape them. People died trying, but many of us got out. Quinn, a friend I met during my imprisonment, led half our group to a safe location in the jungle. A lot of other women and I went onward to locate the Cove with a promise to return for Quinn and the others once we were certain everything was safe.

The thing is, we aren't safe. Here I am... in another shithole.

This was supposed to be our freedom, or at least, a semblance of freedom on an island miles away from home.

The Cove was supposed to be a replica of the Village—a society in which women equally contribute their skills and prior real-world education for the betterment of our society. Instead, I've come to what can only be described as a campground.

There's no order.

Women go about as they please, fighting each other over fish carcasses, cheap wooden jewelry, and filtered water.

Sure, over a hundred women now view me as their leader for having saved their lives, but what about the people already living at the Cove? I can't change their minds... I can't get them to work together to rebuild the society we once had. Who am I to them? The woman who freed prisoners from our sworn enemies? Maybe. But that isn't enough to get them to obey orders.

To make matters worse, Hawkins, a heinous woman, has taken charge of half the Cove.

She's a criminal mastermind who I at first thought to be some low-life, emotionally driven killer.

The truth is she's clever, relentless, and hardheaded, which I've come to realize will benefit my people and me.

How? She wants Rainer's head, and so do I.

To top that off, she somehow managed to bring a military-grade communication device onto the island. So, what's in it for me? Well, our deal is simple: I tell her everything I know about Rainer and the Northers, and once Rainer's dead, Hawkins gets my friends and me off this godforsaken island.

I believe we can do this—I have to. Hawkins is our one chance at getting off this island alive. So, I've told her everything I know about my captors, and I'm ready to fight. What bugs me about it all, though, is that a rotten feeling sits in the pit of my stomach... Am I in over my head?

CHAPTER 1

"You realize you've put yourself in this predicament," Hawkins said, twirling a bone hunting knife in her fingers. She made it look so easy—almost as if she'd been practicing the trick since childhood.

She walked with her broad shoulders pulled back, looking fearless. Her messy blond hair was tied into a bun at the base of her skull, revealing her worn trident tattoo down her neck. Hawkins wasn't old, but she wasn't young, either. She looked like the type of woman who'd spent years behind prison bars, succumbing to the *kill or be killed* lifestyle.

Her chest, large and robust, was covered in wooden armor that looked like it was constructed by an amateur. Had Coin been staring at it, she'd have cringed at the poor handiwork.

Hawkins cleared her throat, hacked, and spat out a glob of mucus into the sand.

"Hawk, please," the woman in front of her begged.

I hadn't caught her name, but I'd seen enough

to know that she'd broken one of Hawkins's rules—something about stealing from someone else. It appeared Hawkins didn't much care to get involved in personal conflict, especially physical, but when it came to theft, she had some strong opinions about it.

I wasn't sure why. Maybe it had something to do with having been robbed in the past. Or, maybe she viewed thieves in a certain light; in her eyes, thieves were perhaps the lowest of the low.

Wanting to look away, I clenched my fists. Why couldn't I look away?

Two women with shaved heads grabbed the pleading prisoner and dragged her to the sand, toward one of Hawkins's wooden tables. A small crowd had begun to form, but Hawkins didn't seem to mind it. In fact, it was as if she welcomed it; she wanted to make a point.

"Everyone here knows the rules," she said, now flipping her knife into the air and catching it by the handle. "You steal from your fellow comrades, you steal from me." She then tilted her head and smirked at her victim like a cat toying with a half-eaten mouse. "Come on, Kat. You know this." She bent down to stare Kat in the face, her frightening gray eyes looking more colorless than ever. "But you must have forgotten."

"She... she owed it to me!" the woman, Kat, pleaded.

Poor Kat. Although I couldn't interfere, I felt awful for her. She'd gotten up early to take a basket of fruit away from an Asian crew. According to her, she'd given them several ounces of hemp a few days earlier in exchange for something, but they'd never repaid her. So, obviously, she'd taken matters into her own hands.

Chances are I'd have done the same thing.

"Business is business," Hawkins said. "If someone doesn't pay you, you force them to through brute force or threats." She glowered down at Kat as if she were a bowl of rotting lemons. "You don't get *sneaky*." The last word came out as if it nauseated her.

Hawkins quickly raised an eyebrow at her henchwomen and together, they forced Kat's hand down onto the wooden plank by Hawkins's knees.

Kat jerked from side to side, trying to free herself. "No, please!"

But the two henchwomen grimaced, their muscles bulging as they pushed down harder.

"It's no use fighting," Hawkins said.

Her calmness was what disturbed me the most. How was she so placid in a moment like this? Without so much as moving her mouth, she clicked two fingers, and out from the crowd came Collins.

Looking at her made me cringe. She walked with a smirk, and her AOP tattoo—a large black X with a circle around it—looked darker than ever. It was like she was proud of it; she elevated her chin as if trying to get the sunlight to land right on it. I didn't understand how anyone could be proud of a symbol that encouraged the Age of Progression; it was a symbol of extremism that promoted terror. My mom described it as comparable to the swastika during Hitler's reign.

Every time I saw it, I had a compelling desire to punch her in the face.

I couldn't do that, though.

The one reason I was here, by Hawkins's side, was to use her as my weapon against Rainer. As a bonus, Hawkins's had promised me a way off this island.

I'd simply have to bite my tongue.

Rubbing her shaved head, Collins handed Hawkins a small pouch. Hawkins snatched it from her hands, opened it, and without even dipping her finger inside, sniffed the pouch's opening. A light gray powder dusted her nose, and she wiped it off with her index finger in a hurry, then spread it into her mouth and over her teeth.

"Ahhh." She breathed out, smiling up at the sky. Within seconds, her features changed as if possessed by a different soul. She wiggled her pinky finger at her two henchwomen and tossed one of them her knife. "All right, on with it."

"No, Hawk, please! I won't—"

But it was too late.

At first, I heard a crack and a tear, but the sound of Kat's screaming masked any other sound that followed as the tallest of the two henchwomen pressed the knife down on Kat's pinky finger, severing it from her hand.

Blood pooled around her hand and her finger rolled into the sand. The two women holding her down let her go with an unnecessary jerking motion—an aggressive push that said something along the lines of, *Take that, bitch*—and walked away.

Kat's face was swollen, red, and wet with tears. Her mouth, a dark abyss, hung open so wide her tonsils were visible. She sat in the sand, clutching her bloody wrist and screaming at the top of her lungs.

CHAPTER 2

"You still think teaming up with Hawkins is a good idea?" Fisher said, staring toward the shore with a sour look on her face. She removed her hair tie, shook her dark matted hair, and tied it back up into her usual tight ponytail. "We could hear that woman screaming from here."

Coin cracked open a nut with a wooden tool she'd made and I cringed at the sound. "Yeah, man. That was pretty nasty."

"She was only trying to enforce her rule," I said.

Fisher and Rocket scoffed at the same time.

"Enforce her rule?" Fisher said. "What makes her think she can make the rules around here?"

She leaned her head against the cliff wall and rubbed at her scarred leg as she did every morning. It was clear the pain from her wound still affected her even though her leg appeared to be healed. Every time she rubbed it, I did my best to look away—but not because the pink tissue disgusted me in any way. Every time I looked at her leg, it brought me back to the day the crocodile attacked her, and I had enough traumatic memories as it was.

"I already told you," I said, "Hawkins is our best chance at taking Rainer out."

I hadn't told anyone what Hawkins had promised me—freedom. What if she wasn't being honest? What if she didn't hold up her end of the bargain? I couldn't allow the people I cared about to get excited over something that might not happen even though deep down I hoped to God it would.

Ellie, in particular, had a hard time understanding why I'd team up with someone she'd come to refer to as a *monster*. So now, I was the one who looked like the monster. Was my revenge on Rainer worth getting involved with the Cove's most dangerous woman?

My friends didn't seem to think so.

"Rainer doesn't know where to find us," Rocket kept repeating. "So why bother going after her?"

Even Tegan, who over the last few weeks began enunciating somewhat complete sentences, had warned me against Hawkins.

"S-s-she's bad, Brone," Tegan had told me several nights ago. "A... A real criminal. The kind who isn't... isn't afraid of anything. Whatever reason you're doing this for... It isn't worth it."

Then, she'd continued crumbling her Lupacho leaves—the bright hot pink leaves she'd picked up on our way here that apparently held powerful healing properties—to make a tea. I was happy to see she was getting back to her old ways by brewing up concoctions, making soaps, mixing lotions, and giving advice to the women about all kinds of health issues they were experiencing.

In truth, it wasn't only about our escape—it was about Murk and about removing our most dangerous threat once and for all. Why live in constant fear of being attacked by the Northers when we had someone willing and able to neutralize that threat? Two weeks had passed since Hawkins and I had made our deal, and now, it was a waiting game.

When would she ask me to leave with her? I'd promised to show her the way to Rainer's territory.

"Hey," came Ellie's voice.

I glanced up and smiled, feeling guilty. Although looking at her often calmed me, it had stirred up a pang of guilt these last few days. I'd be leaving her again soon, and she knew it, too. I patted the sand next to me and she pulled her hemp dress up, sat down, and leaned her head on my shoulder.

"You okay?" she asked.

I'd learned to offer an automatic response to Ellie. "I'm good."

Almost every day, she asked me this same question. It was as if she believed that I was one incident away from snapping or breaking down. I understood where she was coming from—I'd been through a lot, and she was no doubt waiting for the other shoe to drop.

"See what I started?" Coin asked, pointing a thumb out toward the cliff wall.

Along the wall were two small shacks constructed of dry wood. She'd even left the bark on the sides of the cabin for a cottage-like feel. It looked great. The entryways, two doorframe-sized openings, weren't all that tall but they were large enough for the average person to fit through them. Biggie didn't seem too impressed with Coin's design.

She scoffed and slapped the air in front of her. "Girl, you a sizest."

"Sizest?" Coin asked, curling her upper lip high enough for her gold tooth to make its usual appearance.

"What you did there ain't fair. How am I supposed to get inside?"

Johnson smirked, the countless freckles on her average-looking face spreading like sand in the wind. I could tell her brain was conjuring up some smart-ass remark seeing as insulting people seemed to be her specialty.

"You're big and strong," Johnson said. "Lift it and put it over you."

Biggie's fat bottom lip stuck out and she stared at Johnson without saying a word.

Coin winked at Biggie. "Don't you worry, girl. I'll make one for you."

Hammer, who was now half of Biggie's size since she'd lost all her weight, beamed and ran a hand through her short curls. "Hey, I'll actually be able to fit."

Then, Rocket pulled her dreadlocked hair back and tied it into her usual bun at the base of her skull. She kicked out her stick legs and lunged up to her feet, breaking our little morning circle. "All right, ladies. Some of us have actual work to do." She reached down, grabbed her bow from the sand, and threw it over her shoulder.

At the same time, Elektra came running out of the Cove's cave with a spear pointing straight in front of her.

"Elektra!" Rocket hissed, and Elektra stopped dead in her tracks. She pointed the spear upward, bowed her head, and walked at a slow pace—obviously, this wasn't the first time Rocket had scolded her for running with a spear the way a mother scolds her child for running with a pair of scissors.

"Sorry," Elektra mumbled.

I couldn't get over how much older she looked. It was as if she'd aged several years over the course of a few months. Although still scrawny and small-framed like Rocket, she was growing tall and awkwardly so.

"We're going hunting," Rocket said. Then, her narrow green eyes rolled my way. "You wanna join, Brone? For old times' sake?"

I was about to get up and say yes when out of nowhere, the air around me became cool and I realized a shadow was blocking my sun.

"Got a minute?" Hawkins asked.

I clenched my fists, wishing she hadn't come to this side of the Cove.

Hawkins never came to this side—it was almost an unwritten rule that ensured my women and her women stayed apart even though we shared the Cove. There were, of course, a few strays in the middle who didn't associate with either side.

But the truth was, there were sides.

My side had somehow put me in charge, even though Fisher had seniority. And now my women— the ones I'd helped escape from the Northers— always kept an attentive eye on me.

Jack was the first to come waddling our way the moment Hawkins made an appearance. She stood by me, stocky and puffy-chested as always, and glowered at Hawkins. Her short hair sat so messily atop her head it looked like she'd dunked it into the ocean and a gust of wind had dried it upside down. She crossed her arms and sucked on her rotten teeth.

This didn't seem to bother Hawkins—in fact, she smiled at Jack and, in an instant, raised two eyebrows as if to say, *What's up?*

Jack placed a fist in her palm and made her knuckles crack. Although her intention was probably to look tough, it was embarrassing. By now, everyone knew Jack was a bit crazy, but crazy didn't beat craziest. Hawkins was twice her size and too calm to be overlooked.

Red-faced rage was frightening, but calmness during a chaotic event was far more terrifying.

When Jack didn't back down, Hawkins let out a sigh and planted her hands on her waist. "Relax, kid," she said. This seemed to piss off Jack even more. "I'm here to talk to Brone."

"Whatever you have to say to her," Fisher said, "you can say to us."

I waved a hand. "Guys, it's okay. Thanks for the concern, but I got this."

Fisher, struggling against Biggie's shoulder, pulled herself up onto both feet to stare Hawkins square in the face.

"You better fuckin' watch how you treat my girl," she said without blinking.

Hawkins's smile didn't fade. It was as if nothing in this world frightened her, which made her all the more dangerous. I glared at Fisher as a way of saying, *Let it go,* but she didn't back down.

In a split second, Hawkins wrapped a firm arm around my shoulder and pulled me in close against her side.

Both Fisher and Jack tensed up at the same time, but no one moved.

"What's all this tension for?" Hawkins said. She shook me playfully with her one arm, then planted a kiss on my cheek. Her breath smelled of three-day-old fish and toasted seaweed. "Brone and I are friends. Ain't that right, kid?"

I forced a smile, no doubt looking uncomfortable pinned up against her side.

"Let's take a walk," she said. "What'd'ya say?"

CHAPTER 3

The idea of being alone with Hawkins wasn't all that appealing.

But what choice did I have? She wanted to talk in private, and to get what I wanted out of her, I had to cooperate.

"Your friends seem a little uptight," she said, dipping her feet into the shore's shallow water.

"They're protective," I said.

She tilted her head back, and with eyes closed, smiled up at the sun. Had she been wearing pants with pockets, no doubt she'd have slid her hands inside of them to stand with a relaxed, laid-back posture. As the sun hit her face, I noticed a small, uneven scar on her chin with a dark gray dot in its center that looked like it had been caused by a pen or pencil stab. Being that she was likely twice my age, it made sense that she'd been around before pens and pencils started disappearing from stores. Chances are it had happened in prison.

Today, she let her hair hang loose over the wooden plates on her shoulder, which wasn't common for her. It was straggly and greasy-looking, with natural highlights over her entire head. A few strands of gray hair sat near her roots, but they were barely visible. It was her crease-filled skin that gave her age away; crow's feet sat at the corners of her eyes and became even more prominent every time she smiled. Around her lips were cigarette lines that shot out in every direction. Her nose, neither big nor small, was a bit crooked, which made me think she'd received her fair share of punches in prison.

Hawkins wasn't a model by any means, but she wasn't ugly, either. Although slightly rough-looking, there was a uniqueness about her I couldn't quite put my finger on.

Maybe it was the gray eyes that looked like something only colored contacts could produce. As she squinted up at the sun, she let out a long, satisfied breath.

"Beautiful, isn't it?"

I didn't respond.

Instead, I stared at the horizon, watching gentle waves disturb the flat surface. The sound is what I enjoyed most of all—the crash of the bubbly froth spreading across the sand. Overhead, a flock of seagulls flew in a circle, almost as if trying to warn me about something.

Don't get involved with Hawkins kept popping into my head as if on some annoying repeat cycle.

But I shook my friends' worries out of my mind

and reminded myself that this was the only way.

The enemy of my enemy is my friend, I told myself.

"I want to attack," Hawkins said as if asking for something as simple as a cup of coffee.

I hesitated. "When?"

"In three days."

I knew her plan of attack would come on as a bit of a surprise, but I hadn't expected it to arrive so soon.

"Why are you telling me privately?" I asked.

With her face still aimed at the sun, she tilted her face sideways enough to crack one eye open away from the sun's hot rays. As the sun blasted on her face, the gray around her pupil looked white. She didn't blink, and instead, waited for me to clue in.

But I didn't clue in. What was going on? If she was planning to attack in a few days, why weren't they gathering weapons, water bladders, food? Why weren't they creating arrows?

When I didn't say anything, she sighed through wide, flared nostrils and scratched at the pen scar on her chin.

"Brone, Brone, Brone," she said, closing her eye.

How was it that she always made me feel like a child? Like someone far too juvenile to take part in adult matters? It was as if this fight between her and Rainer was out of my reach—as if I should allow the adults to fight and sit from the sidelines.

"You're a smart kid," she said, and I wasn't certain whether to take this as a compliment or as an insult. So I did neither and waited for her to finish. "I've been thinking long and hard about everything you've told me... About Rainer's location, about the mountain... the gates. The Orphans. All of it. While I'd love to attack full force, I feel like I'm out of my depth."

Shocked, I crossed my arms over my chest and turned to face her. Was Hawkins seriously admitting to being unable to defeat Rainer?

This time, she grinned at me and I took a step back in the sand.

"The truth is, my women aren't fit to fight against these"—she rubbed the air in front of her face the way one does to symbolize money—"*Orphans*. They've been training for years under the rulership of some crazy, emotionally driven mother. They've also spent their entire lives on this island. And my women?" She breathed out and bowed her head. "They're a bunch of low-life criminals. Sure, some of them can handle a gun, others a knife. I may be forceful and fearless, Brone, but I'm not an idiot. We aren't a match to fight these... *Northers*." The last word came out with so much hatred I could have sworn I felt a wave of heat come off her body.

She had to have a plan, right? Or, was she about to back out of our deal? Was she about to tell me that the fight wasn't winnable and that we'd have to get used to living on the Cove with her as the top dog, or whatever it was called?

I swallowed hard, my heart beating fast.

Would she at least have some decency and get us off the island as promised?

Before panic could set in, Hawkins patted me on the cheek and lowered her head as if prepared to puncture my eyes with her invisible horns.

"Over the last few years, I've learned something..." she paused, either for effect or because she was reliving her past. "There's always a rat." She bent her knees and slowly lowered herself into the sand. "Have a seat."

I did as told; I'd come to learn that so long as I listened to Hawkins, we remained on good terms.

"You think someone's been giving information to the Northers?" I asked.

How was this even possible? We were isolated at the Cove. The only people I ever saw leaving the Cove were Rocket and her Hunters. And besides, if there was a rat, why hadn't the Northers attacked us? They had to know where we were.

It didn't make sense.

"I can't be sure," Hawkins said, "but I'd be willing to bet on it." She shrugged as if she didn't have a care in the world. "It's okay, though. This rat is going to get me what I want."

I stared at her as a way of saying, *What're you talking about?*

She crossed her fingers together over her knees and sucked in a long, calculated breath. "You know... I've dreamed about attacking that Rainer bitch ever since I got here, but now I realize... sometimes there are better ways to take someone down."

What the hell was she talking about? Why wasn't she spitting it out already?

"So, like I said, in three days, we attack," she said.

"But you just said—"

"We won't make it far," Hawkins cut in. "And that's exactly what I want. If I'm right... If there's a rat in my group... The Northers will be waiting for us."

I almost shouted, "Are you insane?" but kept my mouth shut. Although calm on the outside, I was panicking inside. If I got caught by the Northers, they'd kill me on the spot. I was the reason more than half of their prisoners escaped from them—Rainer was no doubt on the hunt for me herself.

"Relax, Brone," she said, most likely realizing how suicidal her plan sounded. "It all makes sense up here." She tapped her temple with her index finger and winked at me. "If we can't destroy them from the outside, we'll destroy them from the inside.”

I'd heard about this at school—in History class, we'd learned about the Trojan horse attack in ancient Greece. Was that what she was planning?

"A Trojan horse?" I asked.

She winked at me again.

CHAPTER 4

"It's insane," I hissed, my voice carrying up the sea cave's walls and out through the large opening overhead.

Ellie let her feet dangle from the ledge, swirling them in the clear green water below. Although Hawkins had ordered me not to tell anyone about the Trojan horse plan, I couldn't *not* tell Ellie. Hawkins had told me because she knew I couldn't possibly be the rat, and that was precisely how I felt about Ellie.

I trusted her more than anyone, and I had to tell someone. Did that make me stupid? Maybe. But I didn't care.

She'd brought me inside the depth of our sea cave, where we often went to be alone.

"I don't get it," Ellie said. "Didn't the Northers kill Trim for being the leader last time?"

I nodded, trying hard not to let the vivid memory slip into my mind.

"So what makes Hawkins think they won't kill her?"

Kicking water into the air, I shrugged. "I think

she's crazy. It's like she doesn't think about consequences. But then again, she said she's been thinking about this attack for weeks and she doesn't believe we'll win if we attack. So, it's clear, she isn't entirely reckless."

Ellie sighed. "I don't like it, Brone. Can't you tell her you're out? I mean, if there is a rat, the Northers already know where we are. But no one's come for us, so none of this adds up."

"Or, maybe they're waiting for us to come out so they can attack us in smaller groups," I said.

Ellie smiled. "Or, maybe there's no rat at all."

I wiggled my toes in the water again, the warmness of it making the rest of my body feel cold. Then, Ellie covered my hand with hers and, in an instant, a sense of calm washed over me.

"Please don't do this," she said.

How could I tell her I had no other choice? If I wanted a life with Ellie off this island, I had to do this. If I held up my end of the bargain, Hawkins promised to hold hers. This was the one thing I hadn't told Ellie, and I felt guilty for it. But the less she knew, the better—at least for now.

"I'll be okay," I said, feeling like a liar.

How did I know I'd be okay? The truth was, this whole Trojan plan felt like a suicide mission. No way was Rainer going to let me live after what I'd done.

But if I didn't go, I'd spend the rest of my life on

this island. I didn't want to become Murk; I didn't want to be here in forty years from now, welcoming teenagers onto the island.

She shook her head, pulled her hand away from mine, and stared into the water. "You don't know that."

"No, I don't," I admitted. "But you have to let me try. Please, Ellie. I have to do this."

She didn't answer or look at me. Instead, she inched off the edge of the rocky ledge and slipped into the water, her head entirely submerged. When she resurfaced, she smiled up at me with wet eyelashes and flattened hair. "You coming in, or what?"

CHAPTER 5

It was like staring at floating rocks in the distance. The clouds were so thick and lumpy they didn't resemble clouds at all. The last time I saw a sky like this, a powerful storm had hit Kormace Island, tearing down trees in the process and forcing us miles away from shore.

Even the ocean seemed to be bubbling like a pot of boiling water. A cool breeze swept toward us, dragging with it a thin wall of sand.

Shivering, I wrapped my arms around myself.

"Well, this sucks," Coin said, throwing a handmade mallet into the sand. "Damn storm better not ruin my work."

She'd been working so hard at building shelter for the women—I didn't want to imagine what would happen if the storm tore it all down.

Now, everyone was so busy staring at and talking about the approaching storm that no one spoke about the attack to come. I'd told them what Hawkins had told me; we were attacking the Northers in three days' time, and whoever wished to join was welcome to do so.

Deep down, I hoped most of them would stay behind. They didn't deserve to be part of this secret Trojan horse plan and be imprisoned again. But if I said anything, Hawkins would have my head, literally—she'd threaten to cut it off with a sharpened piece of wood, if that was even possible.

"You guys better get inside the cave," Fisher said, leaning on her walking stick.

Her message had been intended for everyone nearby—everyone on our side of the Cove, that is. The strays, as Fisher and Rocket called them, bundled up at the center of the Cove, heads turning from side to side, trying to figure out where to go.

There were five secluded groups in total—African American, Hispanic, Asian, Native American, and a small group of older women who wanted nothing to do with the rest of us. I hated that segregation was occurring on the island, but there was nothing I could do about it.

What were they going to do? Sit in the sand and pray they'd survive? What if a massive wave came crashing down over the entire Cove? They were being unreasonable. Surely, no conflict in the world was worth putting your life at risk.

We had the cave—they didn't. And neither did Hawkins and her women.

It was only a matter of time before they came crawling our way seeking shelter.

"Come on," Rocket said, wrapping an arm around Elektra's shoulders.

Elektra bounced up and down, pointing at the terrifying sky. "But I wanna see!"

"Trust me," Rocket said, "you don't want to see it when it gets here."

Pouting, Elektra refastened her bow around her shoulders and followed Rocket into the cave. Fisher had ordered everyone to go as far back as possible, which meant they were all to hide out deep inside the sea cave—*our* hideout.

"You comin'?" came Jack's voice.

She stood stiff as usual with two hands planted on her curvy waist. Her hair resembled a wild animal in the wind, which was in part her fault for having allowed Elektra to cut it for her. I'm not sure what possessed her to think a child could cut hair, but she seemed to enjoy the process. Maybe before coming to the island, she'd had a child of her own.

Then again, she'd admitted to killing her own husband; it was a bit difficult to imagine Jack as a mother.

"I'll be there soon," I said, still gazing out at the horizon.

The wind began to pick up, flipping large palm tree leaves upside down. The sound, a deep and fast-approaching rumble, made me feel insignificant. It was the same sound that had preceded the storm after the fire—the sound of

Mother Nature's wrath, a force capable of taking countless lives.

"Come on!" I shouted to a group of three women in the water. They giggled, trying to splash water at each other. Every time they brought water up into their palms, it was swept away by the wind. It seemed to amuse them. Why were they acting like a group of irresponsible preteens?

"Now!" I ordered, and the youngest-looking of the bunch turned to me, her smile disappearing. She shouted something to her friends over the sound of the heavy winds, and they all came running my way.

"Sorry."

"Sorry, Brone."

"Yeah, sorry, Brone."

They jogged past me and made their way inside the cave.

I pointed at a few other members of our group and signaled them to get inside the shelter.

It was eerie seeing the Cove like this—empty and lifeless. The stray groups that often cluttered the center of the Cove were all lined up against the back wall, no doubt hoping the water wouldn't reach them.

Hawkins, too, had taken shelter under a tree at her side of the Cove. Her women surrounded her, almost as if acting as human shields.

What were they thinking?

I glanced toward the cave to find Fisher staring at me. She threw two arms in the air as if to say, *What's the holdup?*

Sighing, I stuck one arm in the air with my index finger pointing upward—the universal sign for, *Hold on a minute.* I knew that what I was about to do next would piss her off, but I couldn't stand around and let people die, even if I hated them.

Maybe subconsciously, I didn't want Hawkins to die, given that she was my ticket out of here. Would I have let her die if she was of no use to me? I hoped not, but at the same time, it wasn't far-fetched to think I would after everything I'd gone through.

What was the harm in letting nature take care of a bunch of criminals?

But as I stared at them—at their bodies huddled together and at the way they shivered in the cool wind—I didn't see *criminals.* I saw women; I saw human beings.

As I took a step toward the first group, the small crowd of Asian women against the back of the cliff, Hawkins and her women started walking across the Cove and toward the cave.

What were they going to do? Demand entry? I'd been about to offer it to them, but it looked like they wanted to take it instead. Both Hawkins and I reached the cave's entryway at the same time, where Fisher waited, arms crossed over her chest.

"The fuck do you want?" she said to Hawkins.

"Safety," Hawkins said, and Fisher laughed in her face.

"You expect me to let you inside after the way you've been acting around here? Taking charge and making rules as if you own the place?" Fisher's voice carried through the cave, and I wondered if women far down could hear the altercation. "And don't think I didn't hear about your attack plan." I swallowed hard, and Hawkins's cold eyes rolled my way. No way did Fisher know about the true plan. I hadn't told anyone but Ellie. Had she overheard us? My heart raced. "You think you can get a bunch of survivors to fight against Rainer? It's a suicide mission, and you fucking know it. You aren't going to win."

Hawkins smiled and I caught my breath.

"I don't give a shit what you think," Hawkins said. "We're coming inside."

Fisher tore a knife out from her belt and threw her walking stick to the ground. "Like hell you are."

It was obvious that standing was painful for her, but she wasn't allowing the pain to stop her from putting up a fight.

"You can sit out here and let the storm kill you for all I care," she said.

Hawkins clenched her fists and grimaced at Fisher. Although scary when she smiled, Hawkins was even more terrifying when she didn't. She took a step toward Fisher and I jumped between the two of them, hands raised by my face.

"Okay, relax," I said to them both.

They stared through me, refusing to break eye contact with each other.

"Look, Fisher," I said, turning to her. "There's plenty of room inside. We shouldn't be casting anyone out in that storm. Imagine if that was you—"

"Well, it ain't me!" Fisher shouted, saliva splashing in my face. Her face, now as red as a fresh beet, was inches away from mine. For a second, I thought maybe she'd turn on me, too. "And I can't believe you're taking her fuckin' side!"

I felt awful. The last thing I wanted was for Fisher to think I was taking sides. It wasn't about sides—it was about doing what was right.

"I'm not taking sides—"

Fisher scoffed. "Yeah, you fuckin' are."

"Look, I'm sorry, but I can't simply let people die–"

"*You* can't let them, huh, Brone? 'Cause this is your decision, right?"

I didn't say anything. In fact, I didn't have to— as she said that, Jack and four other of my women appeared behind Fisher with balled fists. Fisher must have heard them coming; she turned around, and when she realized she was outnumbered, she let out a laugh so forced it sounded like a cough.

"You've got to be kidding me."

"Fisher—" I tried.

She stuck a flat hand in my face. "Don't even."

I parted my lips to try to apologize, but she walked away, storming into the cave. How was I ever going to be forgiven for this? Fisher wasn't the type to forgive, especially not when she felt betrayed.

Had I ruined my friendship with her? Over Hawkins?

Hawkins, standing taller than everyone, patted me on the cheek. "Good girl."

And as she did that, I slapped her hand away so hard the sound echoed around us. "Don't fucking touch me."

Out of nowhere, Collins wrapped her fist around my collar and raised me up. If she was trying to intimidate me, it wasn't working. I'd potentially lost one of my best friends to save their lives. Now, my blood was boiling. Grunting, I shoved her as hard I could and she fell into her women with her lanky arms swaying over her head.

Fucking idiot.

Everyone stiffened at the same time, and Jack, being the first one to always have my back, pointed a small shiv at Hawkins and her women.

"Whoa, easy," Hawkins said. "We're all friends here."

She gave me a rotten smile and moved passed

me. With shoulders drawn back and arms swaying too far away from their bodies, she and her women marched their way into the cave. The strays must have been watching the whole ordeal from the beach; one by one, they ran toward us, arms folded in front of their faces as the strengthening winds swept their hair into the air.

"C-c-can we?" one of them asked.

I nodded and pointed at the cave. "Get inside. All of you."

CHAPTER 6

I sat at the edge of a rocky surface with my knees bent and my forehead resting on them. In most cases, I enjoyed dipping my toes into the water, but as the storm picked up outside, it sent a gust of wind into the cave, making the air around us damper and cooler than usual.

At the center of the sea cave, where a beam of sunlight typically warmed the water from overhead, was dull, gray water—something I would never dare jump into. I peered up to where moss and countless trees decorated the cave's circular opening, all I could see were dark clouds and a fuzzy mist caused by a light drizzle.

It was only reaching us now—any moment, the storm would fill this space with heavy rain from overhead, and the women at the center, swimming about as if nothing was happening, would come rushing out of the water.

"Get over here!" one of them shouted, slapping at the water in front of her.

Her voice carried up the walls and echoed several times. Most of us, including Hawkins and the bulk of her women, sat on the rocky platform surrounding the pool of water. And despite our bodies being so close to one another, no one spoke—no one but a few of Hawkins's women whispering in the corner.

"Shut up," Hawkins hissed, her voice reminding me of a snake rattle.

At once, the two women fell silent, and everyone seemed focused on the three Asian women in the water who appeared to be having the time of their lives.

In a sense, I hoped that having everyone confined in one place would eliminate trivial conflict. We were all in this together, weren't we? So why was everyone pouting as if they'd rather have stayed outside and faced nature's wrath?

I glanced at the far back of the cave, where darkness dominated. Somewhere within the blackness of it all, I caught a glimpse of Fisher's face—or at least, half of it. The one eye I could see was narrowed into a resentful slit and aimed right at me. To make matters worse, she sat alone as if everyone had abandoned her.

Where was Rocket? Flander? Biggie? Proxy? And then I heard Proxy's voice.

"Actually," she started, and although she was mixed up in the crowd, I was certain she was pointing her index finger up toward the sea cave's ceiling, "hurricanes can travel up to speeds greater than 160 miles per hour."

"Hurricane?" someone shouted, their voice an explosion amid the silence.

"Most likely," Proxy said, matter-of-factly.

"That's—" the same person started, but she let out a grunting noise and fell silent. Someone must have elbowed her in the ribs to get her to shut up.

"Did you know that September 22, 2065, is known as National Reporter Day?" Proxy said.

A few scoffs were exchanged as if the idea of a National Reporter Day were even more stupid than a national cheesecake day.

"To commemorate all the reporters—" Proxy started.

But then, someone shouted something and a crack resonated around us.

"What the fuck!"

"Get off me!"

Another crack, followed by a whimper.

"Enough!" Hawkins growled, and the two women quarreling let go of each other, though their eyes remained glued to one another.

"Well, that was unnecessary," Proxy pointed out. "I was only trying—"

"None of you bitches has the right to laugh at that date," said the woman who'd thrown the first punch. "Lost my fucking house. My kids. My husband. My parents. Everything."

A heavy silence weighed down on everyone.

* * *

September 22, 2065

"More devastating proof that global warming is—" the news reporter shouted over the blowing wind. She pressed two fingers up to her ear, opened her mouth, and closed it again as a wall of rain came pouring down on her.

The screen switched over to a man wearing a blue collar, a black tie, and a Red Cross pin. He was so clean-shaven and well-groomed that it wasn't hard to imagine what he smelled like—crisp aftershave with a hint of citrus.

As I sat in my room, playing the historic event online, chills ran down my back as if I were standing right there with the news reporter. It must have been terrifying for everyone all those years ago.

"Allison? Allison?" said the news anchor. He cleared his throat and stared intently at the camera. "We seem to have lost connection. We have reports coming in that Hurricane Winston has set a new record in the United States as being the deadliest hurricane in US history. The death toll is expected to reach over 50,000 American citizens, though we won't know until the devastation is over. If you're anywhere near what remains of Miami, you're asked to leave as soon as possible. Now, if you've been following us these last few weeks, you know Hurricane Winston is the fourteenth hurricane to hit us within the last ten days. Meteorologists are describing this phenomenon as beyond catastrophic and attributing this streak of destruction to the rapid progression of global warming. Despite reports flooding in on the matter, President Reed has yet to change his decision about cutting government funding for global warming research. Have a look."

The screen flickered to President Reed standing at what looked like a rally. I wasn't born when President Reed was in power, but Mom told me he was President Seth's father, and that although less cruel than Seth, he was as equally ignorant, stubborn, and unfit to be president.

The old president—a round-faced man with light brown hair combed backward, overly-long sideburns, and skin so sun-damaged it looked like he'd spent his entire life on a beach—stood tall with his arm wrapped around a thirty-year-old version of future President Seth.

Cameras circled him and reporters yelled questions his way.

"Is it true, Mr. President, that you're unwilling to reverse your decision regarding cutting funding for global warming research despite a decade of profound advancements on the subject? Water-fueled vehicles are about to be released to the general public. Millions of citizens are prepared to make lifestyle changes in support of—"

Arrogant as always, President Reed raised a stiff-fingered hand. "I understand your concern, I do. But the truth is, global warming isn't to blame for this. Our problem is bad people. Wars. Chemicals. It's obvious, God isn't happy with the way we're doing things, and he's punishing us for it. We need to put our government funds to better use."

Young Seth rolled his eyes, and although no one knew it at the time, it was his hatred for religion that made him so irritable. The moment he became president, he illegalized any form of public practice. I'm certain that if his father had been alive to see it, he'd have wondered where he went wrong.

"Are you suggesting—" the female reporter continued, but President Reed raised his famous hand and turned away.

"Thank you, thank you," he said, offering a rancid smile.

The screen switched back to the blue-collard news anchor whose expression remained flat.

"And there you have it," he said, smacking his hand on his desk. "We have more coming later this evening on the new Aquastone vehicles, which have been placed on hold. Please stay with us as we continue to report live on Hurricane Winston."

* * *

I'd turned off the video clip soon after that, but I

did remember seeing the final death toll in other videos that were released several weeks following the devastating event: 75,893. I wasn't often good at remembering numbers, but I'd seen the number so many times that it became glued in my mind.

After that hurricane, several more hit—they weren't as deadly, but in comparison to hurricanes from the early 2000s, they were catastrophic.

I stared at the woman who'd thrown her fist at the few laughing women. I couldn't imagine how much she'd suffered during that time. Was that why she was here? On Kormace Island? Had she snapped and gone after someone following her loss?

She pulled her knees up to her chest and wrapped her arms around them. Then, I noticed the marks. They ran from her palms all the way down the insides of her forearms. It didn't take a genius to know she'd attempted suicide, and chances were it was more than once.

Whatever she'd done to get here, she'd probably done it in a moment of impulse. How was life so unfair? This woman had lost everything, while others seemed to have everything yet did nothing but complain about the few problems in their lives.

She caught me staring, so I looked away and turned my attention onto Hawkins. She sat still— quieter than I'd ever seen her before—with her legs crossed in front of her and her head resting against the dark gray stone wall behind her.

Was she thinking about her plan in three days' time? Maybe it wouldn't happen. Not if the weather persisted or damaged all of their weapons. Oh God... How long was this storm going to last? Were we even safe in here? If extreme, the storm could very well flood the inside of the cave. What would we do? Swim to the top opening? Best case, the rain would be over within a few hours. Worst case, it would last several days and destroy the Cove.

"Hey," I heard.

I turned to find Flander, slowly crouching down beside me. She looked exhausted and weak. Was it her age? Was it catching up to her at long last? Her silver locks, still wet from the rain, hung in waves on either side of her saggy-skinned face. The first time I'd met her, her hair had been short and cut into messy spikes. She must have grown too tired to groom.

"You okay, kiddo?" she asked.

I shrugged.

"You know..." she said, "if ya ever wanna talk about what happened out there, I'm here, okay?"

What did Flander have to offer me as life experience? She'd told me how she'd landed on Kormace Island—she'd spent all night drinking at a bar and left with her keys only to wake up in the hospital the next day; she'd driven drunk and killed two little girls and their mother.

But as I looked into Flander's eyes and at the hundreds of wrinkles on her face, I knew she'd endured far more than she'd initially revealed.

What was her story? Why did she drink so much?

She smirked at me. "World War Three," she said, watching my curious eyes.

My jaw dropped. We'd learned all about it in school—it had occurred from 2042 to 2051, and it was even more devastating than the first two world wars with over 100 million casualties. The majority of the deaths had included innocent citizens killed by Korean and Chinese nuclear missiles. The one reason America came out of it alive was that Russia got involved.

"I was in the marines," she said. "Got captured and tortured... Pretty ironic, ain't it? That I'd end up on a remote island after all that bullshit?"

It all made sense now—she'd probably been abandoned by the government after her years of service and forced to live off lousy funding.

"Ya know," she went on. "I know now that I shouldn't'a been blowin' the tiny pension I had on booze, but what else was I supposed to do?" She shook her messy-haired head and sighed. "I was miserable. The things I've seen, Brone... The things I've been through..."

For a moment, she disappeared. But not for too long, undoubtedly because she'd trained herself not to dwell on such violent memories.

"So, if ya need to talk about it..." she said again, patting my thigh.

Although I didn't want to talk about any of it, knowing I had someone capable of understanding reassured me. "Thanks, Flander."

CHAPTER 7

Over twenty-four hours had passed since we'd all rushed inside the cave—at least, I thought it had been a whole day. Without clocks, watches, and even the sun, it was impossible to know. Had the sun been shining, it would have resurfaced through the cave's overhead opening.

All that came through that opening, however, was rain.

Rain, rain, and more rain.

The water levels had gone up, reaching halfway up the cave's ledges. If this continued for another day, we would no longer be able to stay dry.

Fisher had barely moved, other than to urinate in the water. It grossed me out—everyone was doing their business in the water, and although they'd go down the cavern toward the entrance to do it, it would end up in our shelter's circular opening at one point or another.

How were Ellie and I supposed to enjoy our time in here knowing hundreds of women had urinated and possibly even shat in the water?

"This is bullshit," someone said, shifting from

side to side.

Without a doubt, she was sore, like everyone else.

The surface beneath us was hard and cold, and most women had resorted to sitting against each other to keep warm, especially overnight. A few sat by themselves, like Fisher, preferring to freeze over being touched by anyone.

Nightfall was approaching again, and women shivered in the darkness. The clouds were still so thick overhead through the cave's opening that not even moonlight entered, making it difficult to see anything at all. So I closed my eyes and attempted to block the noise of women whispering, snoring, and shifting their positions.

I barely slept at all that night.

By the time light entered the cave again, my eyes were dry, my lips were cracked, and my stomach was so empty I was nauseous.

When would this end? Women became restless, oftentimes snapping at one another over nothing. Several times, Hawkins and I shouted at women to stop fighting, and every time, we'd glance at each other, no doubt sharing the same thought—*who's really in charge?*

I supposed the crowd was an even split: half the women looked to me for guidance while the other half looked to Hawkins. In this case, however, the cave was my territory, not hers.

"I'm fucking starving," someone said over the downpour.

It splashed hard at the center of the cave, making the entire pool look like boiling water inside a witch's cauldron.

"Shut up," someone responded. "We're all starving."

Without warning, a woman was pushed so hard that both arms flailed above her head. She took several steps backward until she stepped into nothingness and fell into the water. But there was no plunging sound—instead, something loud cracked, and everyone nearby stood up, necks craned like a crowd of city folk around a dead animal's carcass.

"Where is she?" someone hissed.

"She fell right there!"

Several women pointed down, where a hidden, ragged-edged platform protruded from the wall. The rocks looked sharp—sharp enough to split someone's head open.

Fuck.

"That was Allister! Go get her!"

"You go!"

I hesitated, staring at the blackness of the water. What lurked deep down was anyone's guess. How deep did it go, anyway? The longer I stood there, the farther she'd sink.

Why wasn't anyone jumping in?

"Fuck, fuck, fuck," someone said, pacing back and forth.

I glanced toward Hawkins. She sat at the opposite end, playing with her bone-carved knife without a care in the world. The flat look on her face said, *Clean up your own mess.*

What a bunch of cowards, I thought, glaring toward Hawkins and her women.

Swallowing hard, I pushed my phobia away and dived headfirst into the oil-like fluid, chills running down my back the moment I slipped into the water. The water was unusually cold, causing my muscles to tighten.

Just find her.

But how could I? It was pitch black. I blinked several times in the water, and I saw nothing.

My heart pounded so hard I was certain the entire pool of water was vibrating with every beat.

This was the worst feeling ever, but I couldn't focus on that. This was about saving a life. I dove a bit deeper, kicking my arms and legs out in hopes of making contact with this woman, Allister.

Where was she?

I swam sideways, then the other way.

Nothing.

The pressure in my ears felt like my head had been put in a vise.

How deep was I going? I looked upward—or at least, I thought it was up—and saw a widespread lightness I assumed was the surface.

I was running out of breath. I had to go back.

But, I also had to find her; I was afraid that if I swam back to the surface, I'd jump out of the water in a panic and refuse to come back inside.

I pressed my legs together to make myself as straight as possible and descended a bit farther. That's when something slimy touched my foot.

Fuck. A shark? An eel? It had felt like silky skin.

My heart racing, I almost launched myself all the way back up to the top. Any second now, some giant mythological sea monster would awaken and its eye would split open right in front of me.

You're being ridiculous, I told myself. It had to have been seaweed. Then, I felt something hard and slimy beside me. A wall? It was definitely a wall.

I touched it, grimacing. It was cold—colder than the water itself—but it was hard and covered in algae.

She wasn't here.

My lungs began to ache, causing my panic to worsen.

I had to get out.

I kicked hard against the wall to launch myself up, when a dark shadow appeared out of nowhere, blocking the subtle light of the surface. At first, I cringed and pulled away from it, but after blinking my irritated eyes several more times, I realized the shape had a head, arms, and legs.

Allister. I'd dived right past her.

I swam hard, wrapped my arm around her waist, and continued my way up with legs kicking like a frog.

The surface seemed too far away. My chest ached so much I wondered if I'd die of a heart attack before reaching it.

I'm so close.

The moment my head penetrated the water's surface, I sucked air in so hard it must have sounded like a bark. Footsteps shuffled nearby and a dozen hands reached down to grab me and Allister.

"Brone!" came Ellie's voice.

I lay on my back, breathing hard.

"Get outta my way, move!"

Someone shoved their way through the crowd and knelt down by Allister. They breathed in, then out, and then another sound followed—it was the sound of something squishing wet material.

Compressions? Mouth-to-mouth?

"Hang in there, kiddo," came Flander's voice. "One, two, three..."

"Brone?"

Warm hands cupped my face. I blinked hard to find Ellie's silhouette floating above me, resembling an angel.

"One, two, three..." continued Flander.

A loud, barking cough blasted out beside me

and bounced off every wall inside the cave.

"There ya go," Flander said.

Allister coughed as her friends circled her.

Turning my head sideways, I caught Flander's stare.

"Thanks," I breathed, watching Allister sit up and rub her head.

Flander looked at me as if I was the one who'd hit my head. "Didn't do much, kid. You're the one who saved the girl."

Slowly, I sat up with Ellie's help, and something rather unexpected happened next. Everyone in the cave, including most of Hawkins's women, started clapping, their wet hands sounding like rubber hitting rubber.

CHAPTER 8

"If you expect me to thank you for saving her life," Hawkins said, "you can fuck off."

Why was she so upset about it? She'd stormed out of the cave after everyone thanked me, and I'd come out to find her standing near the entrance.

"I came to check on the storm," I said.

She scoffed.

What was her problem? Was she scared I'd win her women over? That she'd lose her power here at the Cove?

Water trickled all around us, forming little waterfalls around the cave's entry points. The wind had subsided, but the rain came down as if prepared to flood the entire island.

I stepped through the wall of rain and found myself on the other side, in the mud. Mist and fog floated over the entire Cove, making it impossible to see anything. How were Coin's cabins doing? Had they been destroyed?

Probably.

Then, I realized something.

Hawkins's radio.

I rushed back inside with a hand over my head to block the rain, which felt like little nails stabbing my skin.

"Isn't your—" I started.

"Relax," she said, no doubt thinking the same thing as me. "I already told you. It's waterproof."

Waterproof, or water resistant? I wanted to ask. But I kept my mouth shut. Surely, Hawkins knew what she was talking about.

"You better hope we can get to it," she said.

Get to it? What was that supposed to mean?

"Or that it wasn't dug up by the wind and swept away," she added.

Was she trying to stress me out? Why would she have been so stupid? Why would she have left the damn thing behind in a storm?

Maybe she was lying—maybe, the radio was hidden somewhere in the cave.

She moved closer to the wall of rain pouring off the rock shelter. Had I known any better, I'd have assumed she was about to lick the water. But she didn't—instead, she stood there with misty water sprinkling across her face and onto her eyelashes.

"I want your women," she said at last.

Was this some sort of joke? Did she honestly expect me to hand over the people I'd saved? My friends? And did she think they'd follow her aimlessly? If she did, she was delusional.

Standing still with my mouth hanging open, I

didn't respond. How was I supposed to?

She turned to face me, her cheeks glistening, and without smiling, she said, "I'm done with this two-team bullshit. We're one people. Not two. And you and I both know I'm a more capable leader."

I almost scoffed in her face, but kept my mouth shut instead.

More capable leader? Who had saved hundreds of women from a life of slavery from under Rainer's rulership? Who had just saved one of her women? How the fuck was she more capable? All she did was snort drugs and teach people lessons through violence and intimidation.

The Cove was a shitshow.

What had she done to fix it? Nothing. At once, I felt stupid for having turned against Fisher by taking Hawkins's side to protect my own interests.

She stared at me, eyes hollow and pale face resembling that of a lifeless carcass. The moisture on her face was surely a combination of rainwater and sweat. Over the last day or so, I'd noticed something different about her—a sickness.

Was she withdrawing? Her hands, now planted on her waist as if this stance would somehow intimidate me, trembled as if she'd consumed ten cups of coffee.

Pathetic, I thought.

I must have made a face; at once, her lips curved downward with disgust and she stormed straight at me. I didn't move or flinch, which may have been idiotic of me, but if I'd learned anything over the last year, it was that fear didn't get you anywhere.

So we stood face-to-face, the tip of her nose touching mine.

"It wasn't a request," she said through clenched teeth. When I didn't respond, she let out a hard breath, making me hold mine—aside from a decaying body, nothing smelled worse than an empty stomach combined with rotting teeth.

Wanting to push her away from me, I took a step back.

"You already told me everything I need to know about the Northers," she said, a venomous smile creeping up. "I don't need you anymore."

I couldn't believe it.

Fisher was right.

She'd used me.

She'd fucking used me and she wasn't going to hold up her end of the bargain.

"We made a deal," I growled.

She threw her head back and laughed, though the sound died within the loudness of the rain.

"I promised to hold up my end of the deal the moment I kill Rainer. Do you see Rainer's head anywhere?" She extended two long arms and twirled in a circle like a madwoman. The one thing missing to make her look like a real psycho was blood between the cracks of her teeth. "I need your women if this plan's going to work."

"For what?" I said. "You can't seriously expect all of them to walk right back on Norther territory. Not after what they've been through."

"Whatever my plan is doesn't concern you," she hissed.

"Yeah, it does!"

She raised a solid fist above her head, and I clenched both of mine, prepared to take her on. I didn't want to, but if I had to, I would. I glanced down at her belt, where her other hand hovered over her famous knife—a knife she'd used to kill several people on the Cove.

Maybe this was my shot.

What if I took out Hawkins? What if I killed her? Wouldn't I be doing everyone a favor?

But then, I thought about Rainer and the Northers. The only way to fight them was to send someone like Hawkins after them. Besides, Hawkins had a weapon and I didn't. There was no guarantee I'd win the fight.

She caught me staring at her knife and a sadistic smile spread across her face. Then, like a cat toying with the bloody remains of a dying mouse, she tilted her head. "You wanna try me?"

"Brone?"

I swung around to find Ellie approaching us from inside the cave. Her eyes rolled toward

Hawkins, and then to me. "Everything okay?"

"It's fine," I lied. "Go back inside. I'll meet you in a minute."

She hesitated, her gaze fixated on Hawkins who straightened her stance in a hurry and placed both hands behind her back.

"Please," I begged.

Ellie parted her lips, but nothing came out. Instead, she nodded and turned around, disappearing into the darkness. The moment she was out of sight, Hawkins leaned forward, the entire upper half of her face darkening. "Well, well, well."

"Well, what?" I snapped.

Quickly, she plucked her knife from its holster, but not in a threatening manner. Instead, she twirled it between her fingers and started pacing across the rock platform again.

"The grieving heart regrets decisions not made," she said as if reading out of some poetry book.

"What the fuck are you talking about?" I asked.

"You have two options here, Brone."

I didn't like the way it had come out of her mouth.

She stiffened up, poked the tip of her tongue with her knife, and breathed in enough air for the lungs of three people. Then, she drew its sharp tip along her cheeks, her jaw, and up to her temples.

"You either give me your people, or your little girlfriend wakes up without eyes."

CHAPTER 9

"Fish, we need to talk."

"Fuck off," Fisher said, her face masked by the darkness of the cave.

"This is important," I pressed.

"I said... Fuck. Off."

I shuffled toward her and sat down against the cave wall. The moment my hand accidentally touched her thigh, she flinched and moved away with aggression.

"Look, you don't understand," I hissed. "I'm sorry about earlier, but Hawkins made me a deal I couldn't refuse."

Fisher scoffed. "Like what? Freedom? A life off this island?"

How did she know? Had someone from Hawkins's crew spilled the information? When I didn't respond, Fisher threw her head back and a gentle *clunk* sound filled the air. "Jesus Christ, Brone. Are you fucking kidding me?"

And this was why I hadn't told her—I knew she'd freak.

She lowered her voice even more. "I was saying

the most ridiculous thing I could think of. And you're saying I was right? That's what she fuckin' offered you?"

"I didn't say anything—"

"You didn't have to!" she growled.

"Stop—" I tried, but she must have known I was about to tell her to keep it down. Women weren't too far from us, and the last thing I needed was for anyone to hear our conversation.

She inhaled slowly, then whispered, "Hawkins is a lunatic, Brone. She doesn't have the means to get you off this island or anyone one else for that matter—"

"She's communicating with someone on the outside," I cut in.

Fisher fell silent.

"Fish?" I asked.

At long last, she said, "What do you mean?"

"She has some sort of radio device. She checks in with the guy every few hours. She promised to get me and you guys off this island once she kills Rainer. Can you see my dilemma? I want Rainer dead, too. We all do."

"You're in way over your head, Brone," she said. "Hawkins isn't your typical murdering criminal. She's *loca*... a goddamn psycho." Although I couldn't see Fisher, I imagined her twirling a finger around her head as a way of saying, *crazy*. "Look, I get why you took the deal... Honestly, I do. But you can't trust her. The fact that she wants to go after the island's biggest badass means she wants to take over. You seriously think she's gonna let you and a bunch of us go? She wants power."

"She wants you guys," I said.

"The fuck is that supposed to mean?"

I swallowed hard. I felt awful for dropping all of this on Fisher when Ellie was supposed to be my go-to, but Fisher was good at saying it like it was. She was a no-bullshit kind of woman, and that was precisely what I needed. Ellie, as much as I cared for her, would no doubt try to make me feel better about the whole situation.

Besides, I didn't need her knowing about Hawkins threatening to hurt her—I didn't want her to stress out.

"She wants to be the leader of the Cove," I said.

Fisher chuckled, but it wasn't a fun kind of laugh. In the darkness, she was probably shaking her head and slapping her forehead.

"It's already happening," she said.

"What is?"

"She's using this thing... this communication device shit... she's holding it over you."

Fisher was right.

But how was I supposed to get out of it? She'd threatened Ellie. I couldn't risk Ellie getting hurt.

"I don't have much of a choice," I said. "She threatened to go after Ellie."

"There's always a choice, Brone."

"Like what?" I said. "Run?"

The sound of clothes chafing against rock came before she spoke—a shrug, I assumed. "Why not? Why stay here, anyway? Didn't you say you have a friend waiting for you?"

Was she insane? How were we supposed to run from the Cove? The rafts were our one way out, and there were only a few of them. Each raft, at best, could hold up to ten people. Last I'd counted, there were over a hundred of us.

"Even if we leave, that isn't gonna stop Hawkins from going after Rainer. She'll take care of that problem for us whether we're here or not. Man, it's not like she's gonna hold up her end of the deal, right? You can forget getting off this island. The one decision you have to make is to either stand up or let her win. So, unless you're willing to hand us all over, I suggest you get ready to fight or run. Your choice, Brone."

Why did everything have to be so complicated? How could I have been so stupid? Hawkins didn't care about me or my people. She wanted to win no matter the cost. She sure as hell wasn't going to pull in resources to get us off the island after she'd already gotten what she wanted.

I didn't want to fight, but at the same time, Hawkins's women were far more willing to fight to the death than we were. Every day, they trained onshore, battling with sticks, arrows, spears, and shields.

What were we doing? How had we been spending our time? Building shelter, clothing, and weapons which, without question, would be taken by force by Hawkins's women when the time came.

So where did that leave us?

Right where we'd started—on the run.

CHAPTER 10

Ellie smiled down at me, brushing the back of her hand along my cheek.

Ellie!

I sat up in a hurry and looked around.

Where was everyone? The cave was empty. With the back of my hand, I rubbed my eyes.

"W-what's going on?"

"Storm's over," she said.

Without saying anything, I threw both arms around her neck and pulled her in. She fell on top of me and giggled. What she didn't know was that I wasn't being playful—I was beyond relieved that she was alive and well right here next to me.

I hadn't yet given Hawkins my answer, and although I knew taking my time was a risk, I hoped she'd at least give me a bit of time to decide.

"What's it like out there?" I asked, my lips pressed against the pulsating artery of her neck.

She pulled away from me and gave me a solemn look. "Not good... Everything's turned to mud, and the winds destroyed everything. The shelters, our food station, our clothes... everything."

I should have known this was going to happen. Why the hell would anyone seek shelter right by the water? It was idiotic.

"There's another problem—" she said, and I jolted upright.

"What is it?" I asked.

She sighed, patted my thigh, and got up with a grunt. "Come on. It's better if I show you."

Before we even made it outside, I could hear women shouting over top one another. It sounded like they were arguing over something—like everyone on the Cove was arguing over it. What could be so important that everyone was fighting about it?

Was it Hawkins? Oh God. Was it a fight? Had both sides finally turned on each other?

"Relax," Ellie said, tugging her hand out of my clenched fist. "No one's hurt."

That was a relief.

The moment we stepped out of the cave, hundreds of eyes turned our way. Half of the crowd—my women—threw their arms in the air almost as if to say, *There she is.*

But I couldn't bring myself to acknowledge them—instead, my eyes were focused on the massive beast lying in the shallow water behind them. From a distance, it resembled a giant rock, but as I moved closer, its silky skin glistened under the clouded sun, and its dark eye shifted from side to side, no doubt terrified of every human in sight. Although still a bit wet from the rainfall and from the shallow water pooled around its body, it was apparent by the blotchy skin discoloration on its exposed side that it was starting to dry out. Its height reached the shoulders of most women, and it stretched out over at least thirty feet. As it moved gently with the water, hundreds of grooves were revealed under its belly—beautiful lines that resembled artistic carving.

Was it a blue whale?

I moved forward, awestruck by the devastating sight.

What was everyone doing? Why were they standing there, clueless? And what had they been fighting about?

Then, out from the crowd came Collins holding tight to a spear over her shaved head. Her eyes, two bulging balls of anger, popped out of her skull. "It's fucking meat!"

Jack lunged in front of her with a hand palm up in front of her face. "Back off!"

Women copied Jack and formed a protective wall in front of the whale.

"Brone, do something!" Johnson shouted.

That's when I caught Hawkins staring at me. She stood farther away from the crowd as if nothing more than a bystander, waiting to see how the situation would unfold. Why wasn't she stepping in? Did she encourage the idea of her women killing the creature?

"You're being fuckin' stupid!" shouted another one of her women. This time, a rock came hurtling through the air, hitting Flander underneath the eye.

"Hey!" I shouted, and the woman who'd thrown the rock smirked at me.

I'd left my bow and quiver in the cave, so it wasn't like I was prepared to threaten her by aiming my shot at her face. Rocket, on the other hand, was prepared. She and her Hunters, including Elektra whose skin was so red it looked like she'd been sunburned, stood stiff with their bows drawn and their arrows pointed at Hawkins's women.

Were they seriously waiting for me to make a decision? Why was it up to me? And why was Hawkins looking at me like that? I knew what this was—it was a test. If I stood up to Hawkins, she would accept that as my refusal to hand over my women.

"Did you know?" Proxy said, pointing a wet finger in the air. When no one turned to listen to her, she raised her voice. "Did you know the blue whale is the largest animal to have ever existed?"

Several women scoffed at her.

"Bullshit," someone said. "Dinosaurs were bigger!"

"Actually, blue whales are larger than prehistoric dinosaurs." She shot her arm straight into the air and everyone looked at her. "Ironically enough, they eat tiny krill despite their massive size."

Someone opened their mouth, but Proxy cut them off. "Krill are like shrimp. And an average male blue whale can eat up to 36,000 kilograms of krill per day. Do you have any idea how much that is? That's the equivalent of eating the weight of six African elephants."

Collins shifted her weight onto one leg and a wave of water crashed up against her knee. She held her spear at her side, tilted her head, and gave Proxy a look that said, *Why the fuck are you telling us this?*

"Blue whales," Proxy continued, "are incredibly intelligent animals. Why kill such a beautiful creature for food that is going to go to waste? In fact, even if you killed it for its meat, you would never be able to consume all of it before it rotted on the shore."

"Yeah," Biggie cut in. "This is bullshit. This thing's a beast. And the longer y'all stand here bitchin' about what to do, the more you're makin' it suffer!"

Glances shifted between Hawkins and me.

This was it—I had to make a decision.

Although Fisher had remained at the back of

the Cove, against the cliff wall, I could feel her eyes on me. I didn't look back at her, but I pictured her leaning the weight of her body into her staff, waiting to see what I'd do.

"Brone," Hammer said. She moved toward me gently, arms swaying from side to side with intent. Her hair barely moved in the wind because she'd let someone cut it—though I didn't know who—which made her look more like the Hammer I'd first met when arriving at Kormace Island. The difference between now and then was her weight, which she seemed to be regaining at a gradual pace. "You can't let them kill a helpless creature. Look at it."

Its eye slowly rolled toward me, almost as if it were capable of understanding what was going on.

Maybe it *did* understand what was happening. Who was I to judge?

I smiled at Hammer, though I didn't mean to. Were we, a bunch of murderers, seriously considering saving the life of an animal?

* * *

"Honestly, serves them right," said the old woman.

She leaned sideways in her electric wheelchair, and with her wrinkled hand, she plucked the newspaper off its shelf. It read: "Kormace Island—New Prison for Female Convicts." Underneath the headline read another headline: "Krimos Islands Save Government Millions of Dollars."

It was the only newspaper on the shelf. The government had shut down hundreds of newspaper companies.

"We live in an era where paper is no longer necessary," one politician had declared.

These islands, I remembered thinking, must have been pretty damn important to be on the front page of the only newspaper in town.

The Department of Justice had finally come forward and announced two of their new locations; Kormace Island, the land reserved for female convicts, and the Krimos Islands, a collection of islands reserved for the most notorious and violent of male murderers. A lot of attention was focused on the Krimos Islands because of the heinous crimes committed by the male convicts.

Who would end up on Kormace Island? I'd never heard of female serial killers. Although, surely, they existed.

"Bunch o' punks," the woman said.

The old man standing next to her smiled sweetly as if seeing her for the first time. He laid a gentle hand on her shoulder, revealing a wedding ring around his finger.

The woman slapped the magazine on her lap and laughed. "Aren't you glad we led a straight life, Alex?"

The man chuckled with his wife, shaking his

head. "Good on the government. We don't need people like this leeching off our system."

"Exactly!" the woman exclaimed. "I hope they all kill each other on those damn islands."

"Jessy," the man hissed, his eyes darting around the convenience store.

It was obvious he didn't want anyone hearing them trash-talk criminals. I looked away before he caught me staring and went on to the chip aisle. On the other side, they kept going, now chuckling like teenage lovers.

"If you're gonna take someone's life, then you're nothing but a piece of shit," the woman said. "Those criminals have no souls, Alex. None. They're evil. I'm telling you. I bet they aren't even human."

* * *

Hammer stared at me, her eyes pleading. "It's innocent and helpless," she repeated. "This isn't right."

That couple was wrong, I thought to myself.

We are human.

And humans make mistakes.

I watched, mesmerized, as countless women crossed their arms in front of the whale to protect it.

We aren't evil or heartless.

And this island wasn't about things being black and white.

It was possible, I realized, to become hard

without losing my humanity. It was possible to want to kill someone while wanting to save another. I didn't have to be *all or nothing*.

I wanted Zsasz dead, but I wanted this innocent whale to live.

Did that make me a bad person? Did I even care about good and bad anymore? Maybe there was no such thing—maybe everything sat on a fuzzy gray line.

Glaring toward Hawkins, I too, crossed my arms over my chest. At first, she raised her chin and an arrogant smile distorted half her face. But when she realized what was going on, she glowered at me.

Leaning into Rocket, I whispered, "Can you go get me my bow?"

She nodded and bolted through the mud like a professional athlete.

If Hawkins wanted blood over this, she'd get it, because I knew this wasn't about wanting the whale dead—this was about power, and I wasn't willing to play her game.

The moment Rocket came back, I drew an arrow, stretched the elastic of my bow, and pointed the arrowhead straight for Collins. With a hunched posture and with water splashing up to her knees, she spun her spear in her fist as if preparing to launch it straight at me.

Several women shouted, some with balled fists

and others submissive with their hands almost shielding their faces.

"Whoa, come on!"

"Fuckin' shoot and see what happens!"

"Is this what you all want?" I shouted. "War? Because that's what Hawkins wants."

It took everything in me not to release my arrow. I was so angry at all of them. Most of Hawkins's women, if not all of them, had once been Murk's people. What had gone wrong? How had they gone from living in a civilized society to acting like a bunch of animals?

Several of them exchanged glances, clearly contemplating which side to take.

If looks could kill, Hawkins would have torn me apart into countless bloody bits. In silence, she stood away from everyone, squeezing her knife as if trying to draw blood from its handle.

She hadn't expected this.

Neither had I.

What was I doing? These were *my* people, I thought. I'd gone through hell and back to protect them. I wasn't about to let them go to some psycho bitch. And it wasn't about power, either. I didn't want the power or the fame. All I wanted was for these women, myself included, to have a semblance of a normal life.

I was so sick of the fighting, the violence, and the petty wars.

Finally, I understood what Murk had fought so hard to maintain.

"Let's get the whale back in the water," I said, staring at Hawkins.

With a venomous scowl, she aimed her knife at the whale. "Kill it."

The moment Collins raised her spear, I fired my arrow through her thigh. She shouted so loud that everyone around her fell silent. In seconds, I drew another arrow and aimed it at the woman next to her who'd also moved toward the helpless creature.

"If you any of you touch that whale," I growled, "you're dead."

They all stood there like zombies, exchanging confused glances that translated to, *Who do we listen to?*

In any other situation, I wouldn't have played this hand. But as I observed the women standing protectively in front of the whale, I realized a good portion were Hawkins's women. In this fight, *we* were outnumbering Hawkins.

The tip of Hawkins's knife slowly turned on me. "Our deal is off, Brone, and you're fucking dead."

CHAPTER 11

"What deal?" Johnson asked.

"What was she talking about?" Hammer cut in, before throwing the entire weight of her body against the whale's side.

"Girl, that ain't gonna do shit," Coin said, sucking on her front teeth. "The thing prolly weighs tons."

"You're correct... Coin," Proxy said as if she'd been standing there the whole time waiting to give us another *Did you know...?* "In fact, it could weigh anywhere up to two hundred tons. Although... this one looks quite young. If I were to estimate, I would say that it weighs approximately six to eight tons."

Johnson rolled her eyes and replicated Hammer's body-throwing movement. "I think you're exaggerating, Lisa Simpson."

"Don't think she is," Rocket said, sliding a gentle hand across the whale's skin. She scooped water from the ocean into her hands and splashed it on the whale.

One by one, women around her started doing

the same.

Hammer threw herself at it again, but this time, grabbed her neck and made a sour face. Sliding down the side of the whale as if wearing an invisible neck brace, she said, "Ah, fuck. I think I pulled something."

Johnson burst out laughing so hard her voice carried over the crashing waves. She grabbed for her groin, squatted, and sat still as ocean water pooled around her waist.

"Are you seriously pissing beside us?" Coin asked.

Johnson's face was beet red and her eyes little moons. "I can't..." she said through broken laughter. Finally, she stood up, let out a relieved sigh, and threw her head back. When she caught everyone staring at her, she said, "My bladder isn't what it used to be, and that shit was funny!"

Rubbing and stretching her neck, Hammer walked long strides out of the water. "I need to go sit." As she walked by me, she grabbed my wrist. "I'll get it out of you sooner or later."

She was obviously referring to my deal with Hawkins, which I had no intention of telling her about. It was over, and it wasn't real, anyway. She wouldn't have gotten us off this island.

Right?

I shook my doubt away and helped Coin and several dozen women pull a net around the whale.

The thing was so massive that the women had tied numerous nets together to make a giant one. The whole thing had been Proxy's idea, so I hoped it would work.

At the other end of the Cove, Hawkins sat in her wooden chair, staring at us from a distance.

What was she planning?

Collins sat in the chair beside her, throwing her head back as one woman wrapped a bandage around her thigh.

Great.

Now two people at the Cove wanted me dead.

"Now!" Coin shouted as the tide came in, and all at once, women pulled the nets on either side of the whale. The whale moved a little as the tidewater went back into the ocean, and women bent forward, catching their breaths.

It was incredible to watch so many women come together to achieve something that appeared to be impossible. Was it even possible? Could we manage to help such a big animal?

I admired their tenacity, but I wasn't convinced that saving a beached whale with such limited resources was even possible.

"Now!" Coin shouted again, and the women pulled as hard as they could, while others pushed on the whale in the direction of the ocean.

Were they even moving it? It appeared to be in the exact same spot as before. It was like watching a thousand women attempt to move a brick wall.

"You just gonna stand there?" came Ellie's voice.

She jogged passed me while tying her hair up into a bun. I followed her and joined the women pushing the whale's body. Foam pooled around my ankles and then my knees. The sand around my toes was warm and creamy. I rested both hands against the whale's body, and a sense of calmness overcame me. Its skin was smooth and slippery like wet silicone, and the moment I touched it, all I wanted to do was save its life.

For the first time in my life, I was part of something bigger than myself. We, a group of so-called criminals, were fighting to save a life.

"Now!" Coin shouted, and pumped by the crowd's energy, I pushed as hard as I could, feeling my toes slip past underwater fungi.

It was moving! Or at least, I thought it was. Even if it had moved a centimeter, I thought, it was better than nothing. Or, was I the one moving? Were we simply slipping backward?

We continued this at least another dozen times, until finally, Coin shouted, "Big wave coming! Let's give it all we have!"

Everyone scattered away from the whale as the water came blasting toward us—the last thing we needed was for women to be crushed under its weight. Water came up above our knees, spilling out on the beach like a bucket of paint left unsupervised around a group of toddlers. The water, smooth and frothy, came back toward us, and as it did, everyone gave it their all.

We pushed, and pushed, and pushed while the women on either end tugged on the net's ropes as if holding on for their own survival.

And then, it happened.

Something shifted, and the whale's body slipped a bit deeper into the ocean floor—either the result of a natural dip in the sand or a sinkage caused by the weight of the whale. Women shouted in victory, fists blasting into the air, while others slapped hands over their mouths as if having witnessed a miracle.

Was it a miracle? It felt like it. It was difficult to imagine that we, such small human beings in comparison to this mighty creature, had come together to save its life.

The whale fought hard to make its way back into the depth of the ocean, though it was barely noticeable. It was so massive that every movement seemed to be in slow-motion.

But I knew it was trying. It wanted back into the depths of the ocean.

And then, like butter slipping across a hot pan, the whale turned away from us and sank deeper into the water. It slapped its giant tail atop the water and several women jumped out of the way.

But it had worked...

"Holy shit!" Coin shouted, slapping two hands over her fuzzy hair.

Women began cheering and throwing their arms around each other. What surprised me most of all was to see some of Hawkins's women grinning from ear to ear as if they'd won an international championship. Some of them even went as far as to hug some of my women. Then, I noticed the other groups were present, too—an interracial mix without hatred or intolerance.

Everyone was celebrating our astounding accomplishment.

We'd done it.

We had done it.

All of a sudden, the whale expelled a large amount of air through its blowhole, almost as if thanking us for saving its life. It slapped its tail one final time and methodically made its descent into the ocean's dark blue water. We all stood still, almost like wax figures, silent and in awe. I couldn't have been the only one who was feeling a high.

When was the last time I'd felt like *this*?

It was as if all the goodness in the world had been bottled and gifted to me. At that moment, all I could feel was love, contentment, and pride.

Nothing else mattered.

Not Hawkins, not Rainer, not the Northers.

"If we can push a fucking whale into the ocean,"

I shouted, and everyone's eyes rolled my way, "we can do so much more together! Don't you guys get it? We've been so caught up hating each other that our lives have been complete shit! Do you seriously want to keep fighting over pieces of jewelry? Over food? There's plenty of fish in the water, and I'm more than happy to teach any of you how to fish."

A handful of Hawkins's women scoffed and walked away, but everyone else listened attentively as if I were a world-renowned inspirational speaker. It wasn't even about me—it was the message I was delivering.

They knew I was right.

Nobody in their right mind *wants* conflict.

Only miserable people want conflict.

What if there was a way for us to work together at rebuilding what we once had under Murk's reign? Would that be possible? For sure, it would be difficult, but it wasn't impossible.

"The Northers took away everything we had—" I started, and some women looked away, no doubt devasted by the memory of that horrid day. "But they didn't break us. If you're standing here right now, it's because you're a survivor."

Women nodded as a gentle wave came slipping past their knees and ankles.

"You survived because you're strong," I continued. "We all did. Some of you"—I pointed to the women I recognized from the Norther city, the ones I'd rescued from imprisonment—"are experiencing freedom for the first time in your lives."

Then, something remarkable happened.

Hawkins's women, the ones wearing wooden plates and seaweed accessories, and with no hair on their heads, turned toward my people and expressed something I'd have never expected from them—empathy. Saddened grimaces and confused frowns scattered throughout the crowd.

Had they not been told about the prisoners? Or, had they chosen to ignore it?

"These women have been held captive by our enemies for weeks, months, and for some, even years," I said.

The prisoners, including Jack, bowed their heads and stared into the frothy water.

I let out a long sigh. "And they're still here, standing stronger together as a people despite the torture they've endured."

It was all sinking in—I could see it in their eyes. Women began embracing one another, shaking hands, and introducing themselves to those they didn't know. Like thick morning fog gradually lifting, all of the hatred that had once lingered over the Cove washed away.

"I'm sorry," some women said, while others nodded and offered shoulder pats.

Little by little, I turned sideways to catch a

glimpse of Hawkins at the other end of the Cove. She stood tall, knife in hand, and without any reaction at all, turned away into all that remained of her tent—a few sheets of soaked cloth drooping from soggy, cracked wood.

It didn't matter that she wanted me dead, or that she'd threatened to hurt Ellie.

Now, we outnumbered her.

All I could hope for was that this feeling wouldn't wear off—that women wouldn't return to their old ways after the *high* tapered off. I'd simply have to act fast and find ways to integrate our people.

"We have plenty of shelter," I said, pointing at the cave. "You're all welcome to sleep inside. Coin here"—I pointed at her—"is one hell of a Builder. She can make us all kinds of beds and equipment to make our lives easier."

A thin, scrawny-looking woman with large elbows, ball-like knees, and a shaved head stepped forward. "I used to be a Builder too. I can help."

"Me too."

"I can make clothing."

"I used to be in charge of the water station."

"Murk assigned me as a Battlewoman. I'm happy to train others."

One by one, more women began stepping forward, announcing the skills they'd developed under Murk's reign.

One older woman with salt and pepper hair and rounded shoulders, raised a trembling hand and everyone fell silent. "I used to make clothing," she said almost pleading, "but I've always wanted to cook."

She looked beaten and frightened as if voicing her opinion might get her banished from our society. The women around her, too, fell silent, their expectant gazes fixated on me.

This was it.

This was my moment to prove myself a worthy leader. I still couldn't wrap my head around the fact that I'd ended up in this position, but something within me told me I was on the right path.

I could make a real difference on this island.

Murk had seen something in me, and for the first time, I truly felt it.

"As long as we have equal coverage in all areas," I said, "I think you should do whatever makes you happiest."

Everyone's lips parted at the same time, without a doubt in disbelief that I would make such a rule. When Murk had been in charge, everyone had been assigned a specific task. Now, I was allowing women to choose their own work.

Didn't that make more sense? Why force someone to do something they didn't enjoy? The key to getting everyone working together was to have them be content with their daily lives.

Then, a short woman—short being an understatement—stepped forward, eyes darting from side to side. Her head reached Rocket's chest, and if it weren't for the wrinkles around her eyes, I'd have thought her to be a child.

"I-I can be a Battlewoman?" she asked.

Though her build wasn't ideal for a Battlewoman, it was what she wanted. How could I deny her what she wanted?

"Of course," I said.

She punched two fists into the air. "Yes!"

Had I been standing closer, she'd have probably thrown her arms around my waist.

As women grinned from ear to ear, their faces glistening from the ocean's mist, I couldn't help but wonder: was I making the right move? Was this what it felt like to be in charge? Was I going to keep doubting every decision I made?

Was this how all leaders felt? Uncertain?

Although I didn't enjoy feeling doubtful all the time, I'd gotten this far by making decisions based on what I felt was right. Had they been the right decisions? I'd never know, but they'd led me to where I was... alive.

That meant the best way to survive Kormace Island was to rely on my instincts.

And right then, my gut assured me that so long as I maintained a certain level of happiness among these women, not only could we work together to achieve anything—they would follow me into battle if necessary.

CHAPTER 12

Ellie stared at me, then focused her attention on the yellow, black-spotted gecko scurrying across the rocks in the sand.

If only my life were *that* simple, I thought, watching it slip in and out of small cracks.

Food.

Sleep.

Survival.

Without the Northers and without Hawkins, my life *would* have been that simple—well, for the most part.

"It'll be fine," I reassured her. "Jack already has a dozen women willing to watch over you."

Ellie scoffed and ran her hands up and down the skin of her unshaven legs. "I don't want bodyguards, Brone. I don't see why Hawkins would still come after me after losing that many women."

"Are you kidding?" I said. "She probably wants to even more now. She's crazy, Ellie, and I pissed her off. I don't care to be threatened... I'm used to it, and she knows it. But to have her threaten you? I won't stand for it."

I hadn't wanted to tell Ellie about Hawkins's threats, but it was necessary to warn her. It also seemed only reasonable to explain to her why Jack and a handful of women would be watching her for the next little while.

"All clear," came Jack's voice.

I smirked up at Jack, appreciative of her willingness to protect Ellie, even though she acted like an overachieving, straight A student. Ellie and I sat beneath the cave's rock shelter, while Hawkins had refused to come out of her broken tent.

We weren't in any danger, but Jack insisted on providing a status update roughly every half hour.

"Why didn't we run?" Ellie asked. "Isn't that what you said Fisher suggested?"

I nodded, gazing at the countless women splashing water at each other where the whale had been several hours ago. They were still celebrating.

Farther away from the crowd, Tegan sat in the water, froth pooling around her shoulders. Her matted brown hair resembled an abandoned broom head, and she observed the horizon as if patiently waiting for the sun to come down.

What was she doing?

"Brone?" Ellie asked.

I shook my head. "How were we supposed to run, Ellie? We have a few rafts to get around the Cove and back onto dry land. It wouldn't have been possible. At least not without Hawkins deciding to attack us. To be honest, I didn't plan for any of this. And Fisher and I talked before this whole thing happened with the whale." I rubbed my fingers through my hair but pulled them out when they got stuck in a bunch of knots. "I don't know what I'm doing."

Ellie rubbed my back as if trying to warm my skin through friction—small, rapid swirls against my shirt. "You always manage to do the right thing," she said. "Even when you don't know what you're doing. You'll figure this out."

At this, I smiled. It was a comforting thought to know that Ellie believed me to be a capable leader.

"I think we should drown Hawkins out," I said.

Ellie pulled her hand away, staring at me as if I were a serial killer.

"Drown her *out*," I repeated, laughing. "Not drown her."

"Oh," Ellie said, letting out a long sigh.

"If we can get more and more of her women to switch sides, she'll slowly become irrelevant."

"And you think she'll be okay with that?" Ellie asked. "You don't think she'll try to come after you?"

I smirked, even though nothing about the situation was funny. "She'll try. But we already outnumber her. What's she gonna do?"

Ellie didn't say anything. Instead, she pulled her

long brown hair over one shoulder, twirled it, and dipped its ends into the sand as if trying to paint a masterpiece. I couldn't believe how long it had grown. Elektra had asked her—while jumping up and down with a small blade—to cut it for her. Anyone who'd seen Elektra's work knew to refuse the offer, which was what Ellie had done—but in a sweet and loving kind of way.

When the silence grew heavy, I wrapped an arm around Ellie's shoulder and she rested her head on mine. I wasn't about to stress her out by revealing my long-term plan.

The truth was, she wasn't ready to hear it.

And despite my uncertainty about trivial decisions, one thing was certain—I still wanted Rainer and the Northers dead, and I wasn't about to let go of that plan.

But at that moment, all that mattered was the warmth of our bodies.

Plans could be made later.

I breathed in the scent of coconut and lavender, thankful that Tegan was back to her old soap-and-lotion-making ways. And as I sat there, holding Ellie close to me, I couldn't help but wonder what Tegan was thinking.

Why wasn't she moving? The sun was beginning to set, and a cool breeze swept across the shore. Most women had stepped out of the water and were gathering around a fast-growing fire. Rocket, Elektra, and the Hunters dropped a net of freshly caught fish into the sand, and women circled them within moments.

"Let's cook 'em up!" someone shouted.

Tegan, however, didn't even turn her head sideways to observe the celebration. Instead, she sat still like a clay statue, the setting sun casting a deep orange glow on her back.

I kissed Ellie on the forehead and gradually released my grip around her shoulder.

"Where're you going?" she asked.

"I'll be right back," I said. "Promise."

I walked across the shore, my toes kicking globs of wet sand into the air. Bit by bit, the Cove was returning to normal. It would, however, be a matter of days, maybe even weeks, before everything returned to the way it was before.

Coin had already begun rebuilding the shelters destroyed by the storm. As I walked toward Tegan, the clapping of her stone hammer echoed behind me. She'd been going at it for hours, and surely, she'd start again first thing in the morning.

"Hey," I said, reaching Tegan's side.

White foamy water swished past my ankles, then slipped up my calves and onto my knees as I made my way deeper into the water. Although crystal clear most of the time, it was now darkening to a teal blue.

When she didn't turn around or even glance

sideways at me, I reached a hand out. "You okay?"

She flinched, and then, as if coming to, looked up at me with wild, frightened eyes.

"Hey," I repeated, "it's okay. Everything's okay."

She searched the ocean, then turned sideways and stared at the women dancing around the fire. Biggie held a torch in her hand, and she pumped it up and down as if trying to punch the sky. Light speckles of sand stuck to her bare feet and ankles looking like white in contrast with her skin. Hammer, too, seemed to be enjoying herself—she twirled in circles with her mouth wide open. I couldn't tell whether or not she was signing; everyone was making so much noise as it was.

Then, Johnson came walking out of the rock shelter with a skull-shaped bowl in her hands. She carried it as if attempting to protect liquid gold, and still, droplets spilled on either side. What was it? Moonshine? Women on the island seemed to enjoy making their own alcohol.

Proxy was nowhere to be seen, no doubt steering away from the party crowd. Had there been a library on this island, she'd have been the type of person to stick her nose into a book and disappear from reality. And Rocket... Where was she? At once, I caught a glimpse of her tiny frame standing next to Elektra. She slouched forward and plucked a fish from the net and Elektra clapped. Then, Rocket handed her a knife and

Elektra, as if having done this countless times before, gutted the flapping fish in one slice.

I was about to turn my attention back to Tegan when I caught Fisher staring at me. She sat in her usual spot right by the rock shelter in the sand. A somber groove in the wall usually shaded her during the day. She rested her head back as she did every day and laid a hand over her bare, scarred leg that reminded me of Sumi's face.

Poor Fisher, I thought.

She'd lost everything.

Her sister, her lover... Then Trim, her best friend, and even Murk, the only leader she'd ever known.

I hoped she wouldn't do anything drastic. It wouldn't have been the first time a woman committed suicide on Kormace Island. In fact, as Rocket had once told me, suicide rates had increased so alarmingly fast at one point that Murk had assigned Night Watchers to scan the Village tents every night.

I couldn't lose Fisher. She needed a purpose... Something worth fighting for.

"It's so beautiful," Tegan said, breaking the silence.

I looked down to catch her gazing up at the stars.

Craning my neck back, I observed the thousands of stars floating in the indigo sky.

"You should get out of the water," I said, remembering everyone's warnings about being in the water early mornings and late evenings.

She sighed and tried to get up, but seemed to be having difficulty.

The whale, I thought.

"Tegan, are you hurt?"

She shook her head and extended an arm up at me as if to say, No, *just help me up.*

Grabbing her arm, I pulled her to her feet and quickly scanned her body for blood. There was no injury, but even if there had been, I wouldn't have seen it. Her clothes, typically thick and loose, were now wet and sticky. They clung to her skin like latex gloves around a hand, revealing every bulge and every protruding bone in her skeletal body.

I blinked once, twice, three times, wondering if maybe the darkness of the setting sun was causing me to hallucinate.

How was this possible?

It couldn't be.

She stretched her back and rested a hand on her protruding belly that stuck out like a basketball under a blanket.

"You're... pregnant," I breathed.

PART TWO

PROLOGUE

"Let me go!" I tried to shout, but with the piece of cloth shoved in my mouth, my voice didn't carry all that far.

What was going on? What were they doing?

"Shut the fuck up," came Collins's voice.

God, I hated her. Why was she here? Had Hawkins sent for me? And how was this even happening? I'd specifically assigned Night Watchers to guard the cave against Hawkins and her women. While I brushed past my guards, kicking and grunting, I realized they were as helpless as I; behind them, women with fierce scowls pointed blades at their throats and smiled at me as I passed.

My captors dragged me through the sand under the moonlight's glow. Despite my rough jerking to free myself, no one came to my rescue. Everyone was asleep, and the few who were awake to witness my kidnapping didn't dare stand up to Hawkins's women.

Ever since I'd stolen women out from under Hawkins's nose, the few who remained loyal to her trained for battle every single day. When they weren't fighting each other, they were busy carving blades and making arrows, while everyone else was afraid of them. It was as if they were preparing to kill those who'd betrayed Hawkins and come over to my side.

When we reached Hawkins's corner of the Cove at last, my captors threw me into the sand. With wrists tied behind my back, I fell flat on my face and winced when grains of sand scraped against my teeth. I blinked hard to clear my sight.

Was this it? Was I about to be killed?

Hawkins had threatened it, and she didn't seem like the type to make empty threats.

Collins tore the cloth out of my mouth at once and pulled me back up onto my feet. I coughed, and although I wanted to rub my eyes, I couldn't.

"Get in there," she growled, shoving me through a wood frame opening.

In the recent past, the shabby tent, which had hung on by barely a thread, had been reinforced with solid wooden beams. I hadn't seen who'd done the work, but it was obvious they knew what they were doing. The opening led inside a small shack that looked several years old—no doubt the result of the aged, cracking wood their Builder had used—and inside, small torches lit up the room so bright the wood of the walls looked orange.

Hawkins sat on a three-legged stool at the

center of the shack, her back rounded, legs spread apart, and elbows resting on her knees. What caught my attention, however, was the knife she was holding. She played with it, poking each one of her fingers on its tip, before looking up at me and grinning—a rotten grin I hoped would soon disappear.

"Brone, there you are!" she said.

Collins elbowed me in the back, and I fell to my knees.

"What the hell's going on?" I growled.

And why did Hawkins sound so cheerful? She was acting as if nothing had happened between us—as if I hadn't stolen some of her followers and begun my own society at the Cove.

She smirked and cocked an eyebrow at Collins, no doubt her way of saying, *Get out of here.* Collins did as she was told, ducked under a hanging piece of cloth, and disappeared from sight. Silence filled the air; the lone sound remaining was a persistent creak coming from Hawkins's stool every time she shifted her weight.

"I don't know what you're doing," I said, "but I can guarantee you you'll pay for whatever it is."

"Oh, hush, hush," Hawkins said, now gliding the tip of her knife along her bottom lip. "I'm not mad at you, Brone. I just wanna talk."

Not mad? She'd blatantly threatened to kill me. How did one go from wanting me dead to wanting to chat?

"Then what is this?" I asked.

She bent forward so far that her back resembled a ball.

"I had a plan, Brone," she said, now flicking the tip of her knife in my face as if scolding me. "The one problem is that plan included you... And, well, you fucked me big time."

I swallowed hard, prepared for her to snap any second. All I hoped was that she'd do it fast, whatever it was.

She gently traced the tip of her knife along my cheek, my jaw, and then up my ear to push my hair back. "Oh, Brone," she breathed. "I'm in a bit of a pickle, here."

My stare followed her knife.

"I can't trust you anymore," she said, "but I still need you... I need your women. And the only way to get them is through you."

What was she talking about? I had no intention of continuing her absurd idea of an attack plan—a Trojan horse. It was preposterous. I wasn't about to send my women back to where they'd spent countless years of their lives being tormented by the Northers.

"You're going to get me what I want, and in exchange, I'm going to save your life."

"What're you talk—" I tried, but she grabbed me by the collar and pulled me close to her.

"Hold still," she said, her rancid breath heating my face.

"What're you—"

"I said hold still." This time, it came out harsh and impatient.

Then, I felt the blade. She made it glide along my scalp, and piece by piece, my hair fell into the sand by my toes. I pulled away and stared at her wide-eyed, but all it did was aggravate her. She dug her nails into the back of my neck, and with a sadistic smile across her colorless lips, said, "What's wrong? Did I cut you?"

With my fingers, I touched the side of my temple, feeling prickly skin where hair had once been. Why was she doing this? I wanted to cry, or scream, I wasn't sure which. Part of me debated punching her in the face, but I was powerless—she was the one holding the knife. Why was she shaving my head?

"It's for your own good, Brone. You have to blend in with my women."

I didn't understand. What was she planning to do? Drag me along with her? It didn't make any sense.

All of a sudden, she laughed, the sound coming out like a failing car engine. "It's perfect... I mean, you actually did me a favor, Brone... By pulling what you pulled. I see now how devoted those women are to you. They'd never follow me. At least, not willingly. But they will follow you... They'd follow you anywhere, even if that means arming up and marching to battle to save your life."

Oh my God.

Was she going to use me as bait?

Hawkins continued on with her knife, whistling an unfamiliar tune in the process, and when she finished, I felt naked and humiliated. I ran my palms over my head, imagining what I looked like. What would Ellie say about this? Would she be repulsed by me?

"Beautiful," she said, staring wide-eyed at my head as if it were some famous artist's canvas. "Now, close your eyes."

"What, why?"

Instead of explaining anything to me, she made her eyelids go flat, which I knew was a translation for, *Don't question me.*

I did as she instructed, and she added, "Don't open them until I tell you."

My heart raced, but I figured if I went along with it, maybe she wouldn't kill me.

A sharp, debilitating pain suddenly seared from my eyebrow all the way down to my cheek. I let out a whimper and reached for my face, and the moment my fingers made contact, I wished they hadn't. Loose flesh hung open—a large gash—from my forehead down to the side of my jaw. It ran over my eyebrow, which was now split in half, and my palms became warm and wet with blood.

"Wh-what did you do?" I asked, my voice trembling.

"Collins," Hawkins announced, her voice authoritative. Footsteps entered the shack behind me. "Get Brone cleaned up."

I opened one eye—the one without blood pooling over it—and looked up at Hawkins pleadingly. What had she done?

She didn't smile at me this time. Instead, she wiped the blood from her knife onto her pant leg and stared down at me. "They won't recognize you now. You should thank me, Brone. I'm saving your life."

CHAPTER 1

"Oh, quit your whining," Hawkins hissed, sinking the raft's wooden paddle into the dark water below.

The water slipped through the raft's cracks, cool and silky against my skin, but it was so black. Aside from the moon's reflection casting white lines through its ripples, it was colorless and barely resembled water at all.

I bit down on the inside of my cheek as pain radiated across my face.

What had she done to me? What the fuck had she done? I must have looked like a monster.

She whistled that same tune again and pushed the raft forward. Collins stood on the other side, using the other paddle. At the center of the raft were seven of us, including me. The other six women, for the most part, all looked alike—shaved heads, scarred skin, and rags around their breasts and groin areas. Unlike Hawkins, they'd removed their wooden armor, which meant we weren't charging into battle.

Was Hawkins really going to do this? How

psychotic did someone have to be to want to be caught by the Northers?

I felt sick to my stomach.

This wasn't happening. Any moment now, I'd wake up with Ellie lying by my side, protected inside the Cove's rock cave.

This had to be a dream… I couldn't go back there.

Without warning, old bits of last night's trout came blasting out of my mouth and onto the raft.

"Yo, what the fuck!" shouted one of Hawkins's women.

She pulled away, causing the raft to teeter-totter.

With a quick swing of her arm, Hawkins's smacked the squeamish woman upside the head. "Pops, what the fuck did I say about sitting still?"

"Sorry, Hawk," said Pops, shoulders slouched, and a scowl directed at me.

"Rinse it off," Hawkins said, sticking her nose into the air as if having caught a whiff of feces.

I scooped water from the oil-black ocean and spilled it across the raft over and over again until my vomit disappeared. Pops sat at a distance from me, her dark narrowed eyes never leaving mine. But as I straightened my back to sit up, something hard gripped my neck and forced my head down into the water.

"That'll clean it off," I heard, a muffled voice

through the water in my ears.

The moment I was pulled back up, I swung a fist at my attacker but missed when Hawkins stepped back.

"Watch it, kid," she said. "Only looking out for your"—she wiggled a finger at her face, drawing a line over an invisible scar—"you know…"

How far would I get if I lunged at her right then? If I sank us both down into the water, would I have time to kill her? My heart, a ticking bomb in my chest, pounded hard against my rib cage. So hard that it became difficult to catch my breath.

I'd felt this before: powerlessness. Nothing enraged me more than being in a position of vulnerability and not being able to fight back. It reminded me of the Northers—of Zsasz and her goons. They'd beaten me, tortured me, and what had I done to get my revenge?

I ran… along with hundreds of women.

I suppose this was a form of revenge in itself. How would I get my revenge against Hawkins? She was leading me straight to the Northers, and there was nothing I could do about it.

"Infection's an ugly thing," Hawkins said through her whistled tune. The moment we reached the edge of the water, she dug her paddle into the sand and pulled us to shore. "Salt water's a godsend."

Maybe if I ignored her enough, she'd stop

talking to me.

"If ya don't clean it, you could be disfigured entirely," she added.

This time, I didn't miss. Without thinking about consequences, I swung a curved hook straight at her jaw, the cracking sound bringing me instant relief. "You already fucking disfigured me!"

My relief, however, was short-lived. The next thing I knew, Collins had me down in the sand, her fist beating down on my aching face. I wasn't sure how many hits she'd landed—four, five maybe— before Hawkins stopped her.

"Whoa, Colls, easy," Hawkins said. She knelt down beside me, threw her long blond hair over her shoulder so that it ran straight down her back, and examined my face by pinching my chin with her thumb and index finger. "Hmmm, gotta say, Collins. The bruising's a nice touch."

Collins smiled a set of half-missing teeth. It was the first time I'd ever seen her smile—it looked like she'd fallen face-first into a woodchipper. Her lips, too, were scarred and bubbly as if she'd eaten a grenade.

She was almost as ugly as Zsasz.

"Come on," Hawkins said, pulling me onto my feet and shoving me forward.

I followed her women through the narrow path alongside the Cove. It was dark and difficult to see. Frogs, insects, and night owls sang nearby, reminding me of where I was—a jungle. Warm humid air licked my throbbing face and I inhaled, my mouth filling with the taste of wet earth.

What was she planning? To walk North and hope to land on Norther territory? Or, was she expecting me to guide her? I'd only been taken there once; it wasn't like I'd memorized the damn path.

I bit my tongue as the pain in my face worsened and tried focus on other things, like Murk. Was she still alive? Was saving her still a possibility, or a delusional dream? And what about my face? Out of nowhere, a sharp pain radiated down into my lip like an electric shock. Oh God. How was I supposed to keep this wound clean once captured by the Northers?

They wouldn't help me, and if it got infected, Hawkins was right—I'd be disfigured or worse, dead.

"Keep movin'," Collins growled, punching me in the back.

I was already a prisoner, I thought.

Overhead, lines of white moonlight penetrated the heavy vegetation, illuminating bits and pieces of our messy path. Leaves rustled as we pressed on, and every step I took, I hoped I wouldn't trip on something, or worse, get bitten by a snake. My shoes, two slabs of wood with leather straps, made me feel naked and vulnerable. One bite was all it took for my life to be over.

My life…

Was it even a life? Was this even happening, or was I dreaming? The hot pain across my face reminded me that my reality was, without a doubt, *real*.

God, how I wished I'd been sentenced to an actual prison—a concrete building with armed guards, cold metal gates, and bulletproof glass. However unpleasant, it would have been a paradise compared to this goddamn place.

Slowly, the moonlight's cool glow and sparkling stars began to fade as the overhead sky turned a paradise purple. Within the next hour, the sun would rise and warm the jungle floor. My feet, now cold and wet, were another danger I had to think about.

What was Hawkins thinking, anyway? She had no idea how to trek through a jungle. She may have been a criminal mastermind in the real world, but out here, she was ill-prepared. Maybe if I got lucky, nature would take care of her.

By the time the sun rose, Hawkins's women complained about sore feet and aching legs. I fought the urge to smile, remembering how long it had taken me to adjust to long travels. No way would they adjust during this trip—by the time we were either caught or killed, their feet would be covered in bloody blisters.

This thought, as sadistic as it may have been, comforted me.

They deserved to be in pain.

Stretching my back, I caught a glimpse of Hawkins rubbing her left knee with a grimace on her face. A weakness, maybe? When she caught me looking, she jabbed her knife in the air and growled, "Keep it movin', Scarface!"

I glared at her, contemplating if one more punch would be worth another beating. But my right eye had already swollen over, making it difficult to see, and my lip, thick and cracked, tasted like rust. It wasn't worth it.

I was about to turn back around when I heard something—a static sound.

Then, with a malicious grin, Hawkins plucked from behind her belt the same communication device—the C-42 Transponder—she'd originally used to make a deal with me. It crackled several times before she reached it up to her lips, her glare still aimed at me.

"Ace, Hawk in the sky, over," she said.

The same man's voice I'd heard a few days ago blasted out of the transponder, "Ace in place, over. Location on the move. Eyes are in the sky."

CHAPTER 2

Tegan was pregnant, I suddenly remembered.

I'd been so caught up in my own nightmare that I'd forgotten. How was that even possible? From what she'd told me before—before turning into a speechless mess—she'd been on the island for over seven years.

No way had she been impregnated before arriving on the island.

It had happened here. But how?

* * *

"How'd this happen?"

"Why isn't she saying anything?"

"Tegan, can you talk to us?"

"Fuck off. Give her some space."

"Tegan," I said, my voice gentle, and everyone stopped talking. I moved in closer and sat next to her on the *main rock*—the largest and flattest rock at the Cove. Impatiently waving in front of my face, I urged everyone to back away. They were huddling around her like a bunch of seagulls around a picnic basket.

"It's okay, Tegan," I said. "You can talk to us."

But she wasn't talking. It didn't make sense—she'd made so much progress over the last few weeks that I was certain she'd gotten better. Now, she was back to being her silent self as she had been when imprisoned by the Northers.

What had they done to her?

And how had this happened? How the hell had a woman been impregnated on Kormace Island, an island full of female convicts?

So many thoughts rushed through my mind.

Had men somehow infiltrated the island? And if so, when would they have gotten to her? She'd been locked away like the rest of us.

"Tegan, please," I tried, but she sat there with pouted lips and eyes glazed over.

I pulled away and sighed.

"Still nothin'?" Coin asked, arms crossed over her muscular pecs.

Then, Arenas appeared beside me, short and mouthy as usual. She gripped her narrow waist, her bony elbows sticking out, and offered a cocky smile. "Ain't none of you heard the rumors when we were captured?"

"What rumors?" Coin asked.

Arenas scoffed. "Somethin' about Rainer trying to reproduce to build her army."

Rocket rolled her eyes. "Reproduce... Right. Because Rainer has a penis."

"Who are you to judge?" Hammer chimed in.

"Maybe she does."

"Man, this shit's getting way too weird," Coin said, staring toward the setting sun. "I'm goin' to bed."

* * *

Explosive laughter erupted behind me. I swung around, reaching for an arrow from my invisible quiver, but stopped when I realized I was unarmed.

"That's what I was thinking!" shouted one of Hawkins's women.

She was speaking so loudly—almost as if doing it on purpose—and swaying her arms over her head like one of those stretchy toys with elastic for arms. Was this Hawkins's plan at getting caught? Did she not realize that Northers weren't the only threat? That's when it hit me—she had no idea what Ogres were.

Hawkins had a one-track mind, which would lead to either her victory or her demise. The result would depend entirely on plain luck.

"Me too!" shouted another one of Hawkins's women.

Their eyes, wide glossy balls, darted from side to side as they spoke, reminding me of aspiring actors with zero talent. It was worse than watching a kid's school play.

And Hawkins relied on these women to protect her? What the hell was she thinking? She was going to get us killed.

The first one who'd spoken, a middle-aged woman with a bloody cloth for a top and brown fingernails, let out a choppy laugh and even went as far as to place a hand over her belly like Santa Claus.

At the same time, Hawkins slapped her upside the head. The woman flinched and reached for her matted salt-and-pepper hair but bit her tongue when she realized Hawkins had hit her.

It was evident Hawkins was as unimpressed as I was.

"Keep it moving," she growled.

Her smug walk and ugly smile didn't make an appearance. Clearly, she was getting tired and sore. How long had we been walking? Five, six hours?

For the most part, I was fine. Hungry, tired, and thirsty, but in no pain other than my face. Every so often, my eye began to water due to the searing pain, but I didn't reach for my face or make it obvious that I was hurting.

Besides, the last thing I wanted to do was touch the wound and risk infection.

"Brone!" Hawkins shouted, and my shoulders jerked forward. "Are we still headed in the right direction?"

Glaring into nothingness, I slowly turned around. Was she seriously expecting me to guide her to the Northers? How stupid did she think I was? I wanted Rainer dead and I wanted to save Murk, but at what cost? My life? We weren't prepared for this at all.

And that's when an idea hit me. What if, rather than guiding them to the Norther city, I led them elsewhere? How would Hawkins know? She'd never been on Norther territory. She didn't know that it sat at the center of the island. Besides, the island was huge. What were the chances we'd even find their territory? The safest way to get out of this mess was to let the jungle take care of Hawkins.

It was a risk.

Leading them to unknown territory may have been as stupid as leading them to Rainer, but it was a gamble I was willing to take.

"Yeah," I said grudgingly. "Keep moving North along the western coastline."

The Northers, I knew, didn't touch the western coastline. The closest beach they had—where the Russian orphanage plane had crashed—faced north.

At some point, maybe we'd get to that beach, but it would take a long time for Hawkins to figure it out—maybe long enough for us to be ambushed by someone, or something, else.

CHAPTER 3

Collins scratched the two rocks together as if her life depended on it. Now and then, a few sparks flashed, but not enough to start a fire. With nostrils flared and back as round as a basketball, she swore under her breath. Her arms, two sticks with small bulging muscles, shook vigorously.

She needed help.

Although my back was covered in goose bumps due to nightfall's cool and damp air, I wasn't too keen on offering any sort of help to Hawkins and her women. Besides, everything was damp. No way was anyone lighting a fire in these conditions.

"Brone," Hawkins said. She flicked a finger toward Collins, no doubt aware that as a Hunter, I'd acquired all sorts of survival skills.

I rolled my eyes and moved toward Collins. "First of all," I said, tearing the rocks out of her grasp, "you can't use this shit."

She glared up at me but didn't say anything, most likely taken aback by the anger in my voice.

"There's dirt all over this one, and it isn't a flint rock." I chucked both rocks into a pile of leaves.

"Plus, your notch is horrible."

In front of her crossed legs was a pile of damp leaves, three sticks, and two pieces of tree bark.

She crossed both arms over her chest like a fifth grader being given a fail mark on a spelling test. Turning around, I started searching near tree roots in hopes of finding sheltered leaves and branches. If something was hidden well enough, the rain might not have reached it.

That, however, didn't negate the fact that the humidity in the air was substantial.

"That's enough," Hawkins said as I moved farther away.

I threw both arms in the air. "You can't honestly expect me to build you a fire with anything around here. It rained for days. Nothing's dry. Or did you forget?"

She stared at me.

Hawkins was impulsive, rash, and thoughtless at times, but she wasn't stupid. Her eyes lingered on me, and I didn't look away. After a while, when she must have realized I was telling the truth, she nodded and said, "Then build us some beds or something."

Clenching my teeth, I made my way toward three large trees with countless hanging vines. Coin had taught me how to build temporary hammocks by intertwining vines and tying them around trees. Although it was time-consuming and not all that comfortable, it provided invaluable protection; Rocket had been the one to teach me how dangerous it was to sleep on the jungle floor.

Insects and critters crawled everywhere, waiting to take a bite out of human flesh.

As I thought about this, something poked me on my shoulder and I instinctively slapped my skin. When I looked down, a flat, crooked-legged mosquito the size of an American moth lay dead in its own pool of blood. That was something I'd never get used to.

At least when I'd been a Hunter, Trim always provided us with one of Tegan's concoctions—lemon eucalyptus oil. Apparently, lemon eucalyptus oil was known to repel mosquitos. When I'd asked Tegan about it, she'd told me that a long time ago, the mixture had been approved by the Centers for Disease Control and Prevention as an effective ingredient in mosquito repellents.

The part that had blown my mind, however, was when Tegan told me that a well-brewed mixture could provide 95% coverage for up to three hours. And she was right—every time we'd gone hunting, we'd return with little to no bites.

It was so effective that the women in the Village and Working Grounds started gathering lemons and eucalyptus leaves to give to Tegan, so that they too, could moisturize their skin with the oil.

I slapped my neck this time when another poke took me by surprise.

"Sucks, doesn't it?" said one of Hawkins's women.

She slapped her skin, the sound resonating around all of us.

"How long's this gonna take?" Hawkins asked.

I glanced back at her, noting the shadows spreading across her face. The cloudy evening sky, now bright cotton candy visible in bits and pieces, reminded me how of little time I had to work.

"It takes about ten minutes per hammock," I said, "and there're seven of us." I almost added, "You do the math, genius," but kept my mouth shut.

At that rate, and by the looks of the darkening sky, I'd have enough time to make three, maybe four, before it became too dark to see anything.

And without a fire, I'd be working blind.

"Collins, go help her," Hawkins ordered. "You too, BluJay."

Collins ran a hand over her poorly shaved head and rolled her eyes. It was obvious she wanted nothing to do with me, but if it meant having a place to sleep, she'd help.

BluJay, a young woman with blue eyes as bright as shallow Caribbean water, got up and stretched her back. Unlike the others, her blond hair wasn't shaved, but instead, short, unkempt, and uneven. I wondered if it had once been short and she'd allowed it to grow back.

Was that what I would look like once my hair grew back? Like a Barbie doll left in the hands of a two-year-old child? In an instant, all I felt was the air around the skin of my head. I couldn't believe I was bald, nor did I want to think about it. Thankfully, I couldn't see my own reflection. Besides, it would start to grow back soon enough.

Without a word, BluJay held her belly and waited for me to give her an order. She looked so docile. What was she doing with someone like Hawkins? Even her posture gave off the appearance of absolute submission—she stood with rounded shoulders and a bowed head as if she'd spent the last year being tortured by the Northers. Looking at her, I didn't see any hatred or anger, but instead, an overall sense of kindness and uncertainty.

"Do you have a knife?" I asked her.

She turned around, seeking Hawkins's permission, and when Hawkins nodded, BluJay pulled a short stone blade from her belt and gave it to me.

"How are you at tying knots?" I asked her.

She nodded.

Was that supposed to mean *yes*? Why wasn't she saying anything?

Hawkins must have sensed my confusion; she

leaned back, resting the back of her head in her palms. "BluJay doesn't talk," she said. "She's mute."

I hesitated. "But she can hear me?"

The moment the words came out, I felt like an idiot. Obviously, she could hear me.

Hawkins, along with all her women, laughed—the sort of laugh that made me feel like a moron.

"I said she's mute. I didn't say she's deaf, Brone," Hawkins said.

Then, another one of Hawkins's women—a tall, middle-aged woman with an egg-shaped head—stood up, withdrew her knife, and moved toward me.

"I'll help. Let's get this over with."

CHAPTER 4

The buzzing, croaking, and howling kept me up most of the night, and I was willing to bet I wasn't the only one who was getting up with aching muscles and a sour stomach.

By the time the morning birds started chirping, half of Hawkins's women were climbing out of their poorly constructed hammocks and grumbling under their breaths. Some of them had been forced to sleep together, which must have been uncomfortable.

"What's for breakfast?" asked one of the women, still lying in a hammock overtop someone.

The woman underneath her mumbled something and squirmed, no doubt trying to get out from underneath. At the same time, a branch snapped, and both women fell to the ground.

While most women started laughing, Hawkins jolted upright with a knife in her fist.

"It's Dufus and Dufusella," Collins joked.

Hawkins, clearly not impressed, climbed out of her bed and stretched her neck to the side until it cracked like a thick pretzel stick being split in half.

"Get up, all of you," she ordered. "The sooner we get there, the better."

What did she think this was? Some high school field trip? There was absolutely nothing to look forward to.

"Yo, what the fuck!" someone shouted.

I turned around to spot BluJay spinning in circles as if trying to catch an invisible tail. When she didn't find what the woman was shouting about, she shrugged.

"Right there!" that same loudmouth shouted again.

As BluJay twirled one more time, I spotted the blood before she noticed it. It was bright and blotchy and covered the back of her knee.

Hawkins took a step forward. "What happened?"

BluJay, not being able to see behind her own knee, ran her fingers down her legs and grimaced when her fingers slid over the blood.

"What happened?" Hawkins repeated, this time storming toward the shouting woman.

"I-I don't know, Hawks. She got up out of the hammock like that."

"A leech," I mumbled.

Hawkins swung around with so much force I was surprised her back didn't crack. "You got something you wanna share with the class, Brone?"

"I said it's probably a leech."

I almost added, "You'd know that if you knew anything about the jungle," but managed to keep it to myself.

Collins bent forward with the weight of her body on her knees and inspected BluJay's bloody leg. "Think Brone's right, Hawk."

"So, pull it off!" Hawkins snapped.

"No, don't!" someone said.

Slowly, Hawkins turned toward the woman, and if she'd been carrying a gun, she'd have shot her square in the face for speaking out like that.

The woman—Pops, I think her name was—elevated two trembling hands and bowed her head. "Um, respectfully, Hawk. Don't think you're supposed to pull off a leech. Well, I mean... That's what I've heard."

"Dude... Don't those things carry diseases?" someone else added, stepping away from BluJay.

Without moving her lower body, Hawkins rotated her chest to face me and arched an eyebrow.

I sighed. "No, it doesn't carry diseases. And you can pull it off, but there's a technique."

Hawkins didn't move, no doubt her way of saying, *Well, get to it, then.*

So, I moved toward BluJay with Rocket's voice in my head. "The goal," she'd said while hovering over Biggie's leg with slouched shoulders, "is to make sure you pull the mouth off along with the body. If you don't, it's like a tick... part of it stays inside." She looked up at me with furrowed eyebrows—a look of intense concentration that made her seem pissed off. "It might not carry diseases like a tick, but if the mouth gets stuck, it'll slow down the healing."

"Girl, hurry up!" Biggie had shouted.

Rocket then yanked the leech off and held it between her thumb and index finger as if showcasing some science project. "Look at that sucker."

Crouching down by BluJay's knee, I placed a sturdy hand around her calf. "Hold still."

Then, as Rocket had taught me, I slid my fingernail underneath the leech's sucker and at the same time, pulled it upward. Blood spat from its mouth and onto BluJay's knee, and it wiggled between my fingers. Not wanting to look at the ugly thing any longer, I threw it in the nearest bush.

"Might want to wrap that up," I said. "The bleeding can take a while to stop."

"Someone give her something," Hawkins ordered. "And let's keep moving."

The moment I turned around, something cold and clammy grabbed my forearm. I looked back to find BluJay staring at me with pleading eyes. Though she didn't say anything, I knew what she was conveying—*thank you.*

I smiled at her, forgetting at that moment that she was part of Hawkins's crew; for a split second, she was a girl... a young woman blindly following her leader. Why hadn't she joined my side after we'd saved that whale? Emotions had been running so high that countless women decided to follow me rather than succumb to Hawkins's abuse.

Maybe she was afraid.

"Any time," I said, and the corner of her lip twitched as if moving for the first time in years.

Hawkins hacked her way through a curtain of hanging leaves. "Let's move."

How long would she last today? Would her feet hurt after several hours? I hoped so—I wanted her to realize the mistake she'd made entering the jungle in search of Rainer.

For all she knew, Rainer would kill her the moment she saw her. Or, even more likely, she'd be killed by Zsasz on the outskirts of the city.

But it wasn't my place to get involved.

"Grab a bite," Hawkins said, pointing at a banana tree to her right.

I hadn't noticed it—the green bananas hung upside down and sat so close together it was hard to tell them apart. I'd seen banana trees before, and most of them held the fruit high up, making it difficult for us to cultivate them.

This tree, however, wasn't too tall, and with a good stretch of an arm, we could easily pluck the bananas away.

Hawkins's women lunged toward the banana bunches like starving monkeys. Collins even went as far as to elbow BluJay in the neck to be the first one to eat. I waited for them to stop grabbing fistfuls of fruit before making my way over.

They weren't yet ripe; pulling one off was tough, and it would likely taste like shit, but I was starving. I peeled it open, and it emitted a loud crack like a piece of wood snapping, and took a bite of the dry, chalky texture.

No one around me seemed to mind its bitter taste. As I swallowed hard, something caught my eye. Behind the tower of bananas was a small, frail-looking tree with a narrow trunk and bright green leaves. Attached to its branches were little green fruit—similar to limes but the size of lemons.

Guava, I knew.

I moved toward it, leaves cracking under my step, and reached for its leaves.

"What's she doing?"

"What'd you find?"

"Move!"

Before they had the time to circle me like a pack of wolves, I tore off a bunch of leaves from the guava plant, feeling insects rush off the tips of my fingers.

"What is that?" Collins asked, tearing one of the green fruits from its stems. "Guava?"

I nodded, and everyone came running with half-eaten bananas in their fists and mouths full of white mush.

"You eat the fruit, dumbass," Collins said, staring at my leaves.

Ignoring her, I turned around and pressed a few of them over the cut on my face. I'd learned about the benefits of guava leaves through Tegan when she'd been running the Potions tent, or as I knew it, *tent number four.*

Back then, everyone had called her *the pharmacist.*

Although she'd had an entire shelf devoted to herbs and plants, the one she spoke about the most was guava—something to do with how easy it was to find around the Village and how versatile it was. It hurt me to think of the old Tegan—tall, slender, and confident in the way she walked; she'd moved toward me like a cat, hips swaying from side to side. I remember thinking she was arrogant, but her long messily braided hair in conjunction with her plant-construction jewelry and plain hemp clothing told me there was more to her than I knew.

Soap.

That was the first thing she'd tried to sell me.

And now, she was pregnant and barely

speaking at all. What had the Northers done to her?

I'd gone to visit tent number four a few times after a long day of hunting and one hot, humid night—the night Hammer had threatened me at knifepoint—I entered the tent to catch her sleeping on a bed of leaves at the far back. The moment I'd entered, she'd jolted upright and laughed for having fallen asleep.

I remembered thinking she'd had too much to drink, but the truth, as I found out later, was that Tegan didn't drink despite being the person responsible for creating the Village's moonshine. She'd shared gallons of it with the entire Village that evening and hadn't touched a drop.

Outside, women shouted and sang, their feet stomping against the ground as they danced in drunken ecstasy around the fire.

I'd barely taken two steps inside her tent when she'd said, "Guava."

"What?" I'd asked.

"That cut on your neck," she'd said. "You want guava leaves."

She stepped toward a large wooden shelving unit standing on four legs and pulled from it two guava leaves. "On the house, doll. They're fresh from today. For your cut—" she wiggled a finger at her own neck to point out my wound. "Guava leaves have incredible healing properties. Cuts, abrasions, you name it. They're anti-inflammatory and antibacterial. I even use them to make tea... Helps with ear infections."

Stunned, I parted my lips to ask something along the lines of, "How do you know all of this?"

Surely, I wasn't the first person to act so surprised by the amount of knowledge she held in that brain of hers. She smirked and pulled her braid over her shoulder. "Spent three years in Neptune Correctional Facility before being shipped here. I've never been much of a social person, so I read. Like, a lot. My brother became a surgeon, while I got a six-year sentence. Reading up on medical books was the one thing that kept me from feeling like a total waste of skin. I figured when I got out, I'd go to med school. So, my brother kept bringing me medical books, including manuscripts on natural medicine. God, I wish they hadn't shut down Neptune Correctional Facility... I'd be in school right about now. And before you ask"—she waved a hand in front of her face, reminding me of a typical high school girl—"the only reason I'm here in the first place is that some son of a bitch broke into my house."

I stared at her. Was I missing something?

"I smashed his face in with a baseball bat. My big brother bought it for me when I got my first apartment." Shaking her bowed head, she rubbed her forehead. "To be honest, I should have listened to him... Moving into that ghetto neighborhood was a stupid idea."

She must have realized she'd been ranting; with a goofy smile on her face, she passed me the leaves. "I'm sorry... I don't talk to many people. Here. Apply that over your cut and it should take care of the infection."

CHAPTER 5

"Shut up," Collins hissed, but she retreated as soon as Hawkins gave her a narrow-eyed heinous look that translated to, *Learn your place or I'll teach it to ya.*

But the panic in Collins's voice, despite Hawkins's disapproval of the order, was enough to make everyone stop talking and stand still.

"What?" mouthed the woman beside her.

Hawkins, standing as stiff as a statue with her wooden armor plates and hand-carved sword, stepped toward the thick array of leaves and slid her fingers along the longest one. The sound of her steps, crackling jungle vegetation, were masked by overhead leaves shaking about—no doubt young curious monkeys hanging around to catch a glimpse of the human species.

"What is it—" one woman tried.

But Hawkins raised a tight fist and it was enough to cut the woman off. Slowly, she pulled on the leaf until a large gap appeared, revealing three women surrounding what appeared to be a carcass. They hunched over it like cavewomen, their backs round and their elbows sticking out.

What were they doing?

Their hair, matted messes atop their heads, resembled something out of a hamster's cage with pieces of wood, leaves, and dirt filling the empty spaces. The one nearest us was hunched so far forward that the spine of her back formed little spikes.

Ogres.

"Arki anool," one of them said, and the other two popped their heads up like terrified squirrels.

Hawkins released the leaf and pulled back. "What the fuck is that?"

Her question was directed at me.

"Ogres," I said.

She smirked, seemingly on the verge of laughing as if the term Ogre were the dumbest thing she'd ever heard, but instead shook her head and said, "Of course. Ogres. Right." Then, she focused her attention on all of her women and made her eyes go large. "Well? The fuck are you waiting for? Go kill them and take whatever they have."

Instinctively, I stepped forward, but Hawkins's knife poked me in the throat. "Don't try to be a hero, Brone."

Why was I trying to protect Ogres, anyways? They weren't worth saving. But, at the same time, it didn't feel right to attack someone from behind—

especially not people who weren't bothering anyone. They were eating. What was the point in killing them?

Out of nowhere, growling and shouting filled the air behind Hawkins, and she smiled at me. Although I couldn't see what was going on behind the leaves, the sound of stone penetrating flesh and blood splattering was enough to paint a vivid picture of it all.

As the rustling and hitting slowed, Hawkins jerked her head sideways as a way of saying, *All right, let's go.*

She pushed her way through the leaves, and I followed.

Collins, her fists balled on either side of her reddened face, was still smashing her foot down on one of them. The Ogre's head bounced up and down against the jungle floor, her eyes remaining open. It was clear she was dead, but Collins seemed to enjoy the beating.

When the Ogre's jaw unhinged with a loud snap and blood pooled out of her mouth, Collins laughed and struck down one last time.

What the fuck was wrong with her?

Clenching my teeth, I envisioned drawing an arrow and shooting her right through the throat.

"If looks could kill, Brone…" Hawkins said playfully, wiggling a finger in front of my face. "All right, Collins, that's enough. Anything good around here?" She walked around the bodies, crouching every few steps to loot them.

She raised what appeared to be a weapon similar to knuckle dusters but constructed of sharpened bone. She nodded slowly, an amused pout on her face. "Not bad, not bad..."

It slipped nicely over her fingers, and four sharp spikes protruded from it.

At the same time, Collins jumped up with a short, handheld spear. Its tip, dark stone with a gooey black substance, looked sharper than broken glass. A worn rope fastened the stone to a crooked wooden handle that appeared easy enough to grip. "Check this out!"

"Whoa, what's that?" someone asked.

Watching them made me sick to my stomach. They were acting like entitled brats tearing through gifts on Christmas morning.

"Give me that!" shouted the woman standing next to Collins.

"Fuck off, Stash! This one's mine!" Collins snapped.

"I had it first!" Stash said. "You fuckin' stole it from me!"

Stash—a heavyset woman with bumpy, acne-scarred skin and a poker game tattoo fading on her shoulder—grabbed for the weird Ogre stick, but Collins pulled away. At the same time, Stash let out a yelp and pulled her hand back.

"You cut me!" Stash said, blood now spilling out over her large breasts.

Hawkins, who was in the middle of tearing a necklace off one of the Ogre's necks, rolled her eyes and let out an exaggerated breath. "Would you two cut it out? God." She turned to me, and with a stupid, out-of-place smile on her face, added, "Are there any babysitters on this island?"

Was she trying to be funny? Without saying anything, I ignored her and looked at BluJay, who wasn't participating in any of the lootings. Instead, she fidgeted at a rapid pace, playing with the tips of her fingers.

I wanted to say something to her, but I didn't know what—maybe something along the lines of, *It's going to be okay*, or, *I'll get you out of this, promise*. But I couldn't bring myself to say anything.

"What's wrong with her?"

"What's going on?"

Hawkins jolted upright and rushed to Stash, whose face, now a deep purple, had swollen to twice its size. She clawed at her own neck, leaving red and white scratch lines. It was as if she were trying to pry apart her jaw to catch some air.

Hawkins reached for her wrist and opened her hand—Stash's palm was swollen and blistered as if it had been soaked in a bucket of boiling water. The stab wound, a gooey black line, sat right underneath her fingers. Perhaps she'd accidentally stabbed her palm right into the tip of Collins's Ogre stick.

"Put that thing down," Hawkins growled, glaring back at Collins.

Without arguing, Collins dropped the Ogre stick into the leaves and stepped away from it as if it were a grenade.

"It's poison," Hawkins said. "Shhh, it's okay." She rubbed Stash's face, which didn't even look like a face anymore, then gently brushed her bald head with her fingernails. "It's okay."

I'd never seen this side of Hawkins before—she was *actually* being nurturing. Did this mean she had feelings?

Stash started convulsing with froth foaming at her lips, and the entire time, Hawkins held her down, reassuring her that everything was going to be fine.

Finally, Stash kicked one last time before her eyes glazed over—a look I'd become all too familiar with. Sighing, Hawkins bowed her head, kissed Stash on the forehead, and with two fingers, closed her eyelids.

"Hawk, I didn't mean to... I... I had no idea—"

Little by little, Hawkins's cloudy gray eyes rolled up toward Collins. I swallowed hard for Collins's sake—any second now, Hawkins would lunge at her and slit her throat or snap her neck.

"Hawk... I swear, I didn't mean—"

Hawkins stood up, her clothing and wooden armor chafing against her thighs. Without a word, she stomped past Collins, raising her knees to waist level to get over a fallen tree branch.

No one moved. Instead, we all stood staring at each other like classroom children following a teacher's explosive outburst. It was awkward and uncomfortable.

Before disappearing too far, Hawkins turned around and shouted, "Collins, make yourself useful and find me that poison stick you threw at the ground. Then, wrap it up and give it to me."

CHAPTER 6

Although tempted to ask her what she needed the poison stick for, it wasn't my place to ask. So I bit my tongue and instead allowed my imagination to run wild.

The person Hawkins wanted dead more than anyone was Rainer. I stared at its handle—a crooked, finely carved branch no longer than two feet long, and it reminded me of a witch's broomstick you'd find in a Halloween picture book.

Its head, now hidden underneath three layers of banana leaf strips, hung upside down inside Hawkins' belt. What if she tripped? Would it pierce the leaves and penetrate her thigh? I could only hope. With Hawkins out of the way, maybe I could convince the other women that heading toward Norther territory was a suicide mission.

They had no idea—they were blindly following their glorified leader.

What if I snatched the weapon and stabbed her myself? When she turned around and caught me eyeing it, I looked away.

"How much longer, Hawk?" someone asked

after a while.

We'd been walking for several hours, and ever since Stash had been killed, no one had spoken a word. Hawkins, farther ahead of the line, didn't even turn around this time. Instead, she grunted and hacked her knife across two hanging vines. At first, it didn't cut through, so she swung again, her hair dancing wildly on her head. Her face, although hidden from view, had to be bright red.

"Fucking piece of shit!"

"Is it true?" someone whispered.

I turned to my side to find one of Hawkins's women—a black-eyed, pale-skinned blob with an AOP tattoo on her throat. On her left cheek was a crater, which I presumed was the result of some form of mouth cancer. She was exactly the kind of woman I'd have expected to find on Kormace Island before being sentenced here—a stereotypical low-life with nothing better to do than ruin the lives of others.

I was being judgmental, and I knew it. But I didn't care. Hawkins's women, in my eyes, were all low-life pieces of shit. Had I met her through different circumstances, I may not have thought so little of her.

"Well?" she asked, her sour breath making me wince.

As she walked, a putrid scent entered my nostrils—an overpowering combination of sweat brought on by poor nutrition and month-old water like that of an unwashed kitchen cloth. Did she even wash her clothes? Did she bathe? We'd been living on the Cove—there was no excuse for not bathing. Even something as simple as a dunk in the ocean's salt water was enough to cleanse off most smells. The sun, too, played its part in disinfecting our clothes.

I'd been smelling it for the last day but hadn't been able to determine where it was coming from.

Now, I knew.

And what the hell did she want, anyway? She was staring at me as if I had the answer to some privileged information.

"The girl," she went on, and the smell was so bad that I turned my head to the side.

"What girl?" I asked.

"The pregnant one!"

"Yeah," I said plainly.

All of a sudden, Hawkins's women grew excited. Some of them even started clapping and making their fingers click in the air.

"Oh, shit! There're men on the island!"

"Oh, come to Mama, Daddy!"

Rolling my eyes, I focused straight ahead. It was like being surrounded by lonely, middle-aged women at a Chippendales show.

"Would you shut up?" Hawkins snapped. "She's not pregnant because some sexy man made love to her, you fucking twits. She was abused. Have you not seen her? The woman doesn't even talk."

I was surprised to hear this coming from Hawkins. Every time she spoke, she came across as heartless. But every now and again, she said or did something that reminded me she was a human—a woman capable of caring for others if it aligned with her values.

What were her values, anyway? From where I was standing, the only thing Hawkins cared about was making her way to the top. Was it conceivable she could have any space in that black heart of hers to care for other women?

No one said anything after her outburst, but every so often, a few of Hawkins's women humped the air or made sexual gestures. It was immature and, to be honest, insensitive after what Hawkins had said.

Was it true? Had Tegan been raped? The thought made me sick to my stomach. I couldn't imagine how she must have felt. And how many times had it happened? Was it the reason she was so messed up?

We made our way across a narrow stream—something that looked familiar to me. Everything in this damn jungle looked familiar, with greens and browns decorated by vivid colors here and there. My favorite of all were the colorful birds overhead. Sometimes they cawed or cried; other times, they did nothing but hop from branch to branch, causing a few small leaves to flutter down onto my head. Some of them even went as far as to clean a certain area of the jungle floor. Rocket had been the one to tell me that certain breeds of birds danced for the purpose of attracting a mate.

"I've seen it happen once," she'd said, "but Biggie here's seen it a few times."

Biggie then clapped so loud I flinched. "Girl, if only all men were like that. You should see the fellas. They have a whole routine. Then the female gets all excited and shit, flappin' her little birdy wings. If she's happy with the dance, he gets to have his way with her. Think that's the most romantic thing I ever seen."

With Biggie's deep voice still in my head, I craned my neck to search the trees, blocking out the sound of Hawkins's women. Two yellow-tailed birds flew from one branch to the other, their wings moving so fast they disappeared, and for a moment, I almost smiled. Instead, I returned to reality and reminded myself that this little game I was playing wouldn't last forever.

Sooner or later, Hawkins would figure out that I was doing everything in my power to not guide her to the Northers.

I'd led her along the coastline, somewhere I'd never been before. When we'd been captured, we'd cut straight through the island. Had someone asked me for directions, I wouldn't have been able to give it to them. There weren't any road signs or landmarks to remember.

The moment I took a step over the flow of water, my heal jabbing into a sharp rock, someone behind me let out a loud yelp. I reached for my arrows but instead stood empty-handed staring at Pops, the squeamish one of the bunch. She ran in circles, her frail bony wrists waving over her head and her knees bouncing up as high as her flat tattooed chest. She wasn't even saying anything— she was just screaming.

At first, Hawkins stared with an arched brow— a look that said, *Will someone please figure out what's wrong with her?*

Pops twirled in circles, now resembling an amateur ballerina. "It—it—it's on me!"

Then, as if every woman around her were puppets held by strings, their heads dropped and their eyes searched the jungle floor.

"What touched you?"

"What is it?"

"Snake!"

Even Collins, who always went out of her way to look the toughest, skipped sideways and darted across the stream. The moment she landed, however, she missed her step and tumbled to her knees.

"Fucking idiots," Hawkins growled.

Stomping her way over the water and toward the group of frenzied women, she tore her knife out from her belt and grumbled something to herself. Squiggly veins appeared on her temples, which made her look like she was about to blow. As soon as she reached Pops's side, everyone scattered. Were they *that* afraid of her? She couldn't possibly be as bad as Rainer... She'd never killed one of her own, had she?

Pops recoiled like a frightened armadillo, dropping into the fetal position with her hands wrapped around her prickly shaved head.

Hawkins looked down at her as if she were dumber than a piece of turd. "The hell's wrong with you? Get up."

But Pops didn't budge.

"I said get up!"

Still, Pops shook with her face pressed into her chest and her elbows wiggling on either side of her body. Hawkins sighed, bent down, and grabbed Pops by the ankle. Pops let out a squeal—something you'd expect to hear from a pig—but didn't have much time to react.

With one clean cut, Hawkins sliced the vine wrapped around Pops's ankle. "Grow a pussy, you pussy."

Everyone looked at each other and then Collins cleared her throat. "Um, Hawk. Isn't the saying, *grow some balls?*"

"Don't you guys know anything about American history?" Hawkins said.

Collins shrugged, and everyone followed.

"Betty White?" Hawkins tried. When no one responded, she rubbed her forehead and rolled her eyes. "She's a historical figure from my grandma's time..." She waited, but still, no one said anything. "Balls are weak and vulnerable... Why grow a pair? It'll make you weak... Grow a vagina instead. That thing can take a pounding."

At first, no one reacted, but then all at once, everyone blew up into a fit of laughter. Collins clapped loudly and bent over, arms wrapped around her belly. Her smile stretched so wide that black gaps where teeth had once been became visible. "Oh, man... That's... That's perfect."

Although I wanted to smile, I couldn't bring myself to do it. Had the joke been delivered by Biggie or Rocket, I'd have no doubt pissed myself laughing. But Hawkins had been the one to say it, and the last thing I wanted to do was smile at her.

So instead, I stared angrily, wanting nothing more than to cut those curved lips right off her face.

Then, as if overtaken by a secondary personality, Hawkins's smile vanished, and she slapped the air in front of her face. "All right, that's enough. Let's keep moving."

CHAPTER 7

The fire barely flickered, reminding me of my best friend Melody's blue-and-orange lighter. She carried it around everywhere she went—something about getting to socialize with the smokers without being a smoker.

"Everyone always needs a light," she'd said.

If I stared long enough into the little fire, would I see her face? Would my mom make an appearance? Were they thinking of me?

"Some fire..." Collins mumbled.

I didn't have the energy to tell her off, so instead, I lay still, uncomfortable in my hammock. We'd dragged our hammocks along with us, but this particular one had been tied up all wrong and gave me almost no space at all.

Still, it was better than nothing, and it was sure as hell better than sleeping on the ground.

Turning onto my back, I stared through the overhead trees. I never made a habit of staring upward too long—the last thing I wanted was for something to fall into my eye. Flander had once told me about a new drop—a young girl full of life—

who'd spent hours stargazing every night until one night, a branch snapped and somehow managed to scratch her cornea. It was such a deep abrasion that by the time it healed, she'd lost most of her vision in that eye.

It's that easy, I thought, for your entire life to get turned upside down.

Collins jabbed a stick in the pathetic, flickering flame, and all that did was burn it out. She kicked a pile of leaves into the air and grumbled something.

I wanted to say, "What did you expect? We don't have enough dry material." But I kept my mouth shut. What was the point?

"All right, shut up, all of you," Hawkins said, sitting across from us in the darkness. "Get some rest."

Although I didn't want to, I closed my eyes and sucked in the jungle's moist, earthy air. I was getting used to running on fumes, but it was getting the best of me. Rubbing my legs, I felt my thigh muscles bulging out like smooth rocks. How much weight had I lost since landing on the island? Probably a lot.

Bit by bit, the jungle sounds blended together—a musical rhythm that drew me away from reality.

* * *

"Get up," she hissed, her breath slipping along my cheek and entering my ear.

I'd recognize that voice anywhere.

What did Hawkins want from me now? Without notice, she grabbed me by the arm and tore me out of my hammock. I tripped over a rock, but she caught me before I fell. It was still dark—dark enough that I couldn't see the grayness of her eyes.

Where was she taking me? Everyone else, as far as I knew, was out cold. And what time was it? Close to morning? The sky, a sheet of black with bright white speckles, sat still above us, only visible in bits and pieces.

When we were far enough from the others, she pushed me against a tree trunk, and my foot slid in something slimy. Mud? Mushrooms? A dead carcass? I'd never know.

"What're you doing?" I said, clenching both fists on either side of my waist.

If it was a fight she wanted, she'd get one. Maybe I'd win, maybe I'd lose—but I wouldn't go down without trying.

"Listen here, you little bitch."

Her silhouette moved, and although I couldn't confirm it, it looked like she was pointing a finger at me.

"I don't know what kind of game you're playing, but it ends now."

I tilted my head, trying to get a better glimpse of her. Why wasn't I afraid? Why wasn't I swallowing hard, or trembling at the knees? It was almost impossible for me to feel fear anymore, even when threatened.

Why? Did I not value my life anymore? Or, was it that everything about this fucking place seemed so surreal... so... impossible that now, everything felt like a game?

"I don't know what you're talking about," I said.

"Oh, you do," she growled, her breath warming my face.

How did she know, anyway? How did she know that I wasn't leading them toward the Northers? Well, at least not directly. We were still headed north. It was only a matter of time before we ended up on Norther territory. All I was hoping for was that nature would take its course before we got there. Or, that we'd end up on someone else's territory first.

So, theoretically, I wasn't doing anything wrong.

Exercise wouldn't kill you, I thought of saying, picturing her average-looking body. How old was Hawkins, anyways? Forty? Fifty? *Exercise has its benefits, especially at your age,* I said in my head, but I knew being a smartass was going to get me nowhere fast.

"How long until we get there?" she said.

Something sharp jabbed me in the throat, and she moved so close to me that her brows and cheekbones took shape—they were dark and without texture, but they were visible.

"If you don't get us there by tomorrow night, you're dead. You hear me?"

I heard her.

Loud and clear.

Fucking try me, I thought, my legs now trembling—not of out of fear, but out of anger; I was at once pulled back to when Hammer had held me at knifepoint in the darkness of the jungle's night hour. I'd promised myself I'd never allow anyone to bully me like that again.

Yet, here I was, standing face-to-face with an enemy who threatened to take my life.

Did she not know who I was?

Or, was I becoming arrogant? Whatever. It didn't matter. Nothing fucking mattered on this island.

Sighing, I pushed her knife away from my throat and stepped out of her hold as if to say, *Yeah, yeah, Hawkins, don't get your panties up in a bunch.*

But she didn't let it slide. In an instant, she pinned me hard against the tree, my head smashing against the hard surface as her fingers tightened around my jugular. The arrogance I'd felt seconds ago vanished. Although it must not have shown on the outside, I was panicking a bit on the inside.

I couldn't breathe.

It was like being held down by a man.

How was someone of such average weight and height this strong? It had come as a surprise.

Clawing at her wrist, I tried to inhale through my nose, releasing a loud snort.

Kick her.

Fucking kick her and take her out.

The only problem was, Hawkins had a knife, and I knew she wasn't afraid to use it. What did I have? Arrogance. Nothing more.

"Lose the attitude, you little shit."

I couldn't say anything, so I slapped her wrist—a submissive way of saying, *Okay, okay, you win.*

At last, she let go, and I fell to my knees, sucking in as much air as I could. It came in sounding like I was recovering from a bad case of laryngitis—a hoarse bark.

"Think you're so tough," she said, walking away. "The sooner you realize you're a sheep, and I'm a shepherd, the easier this'll all be for you."

CHAPTER 8

A sheep, I thought, glaring at the back of Hawkins's head.

Rubbing my neck, I side-glanced BluJay when I caught her staring at my throat. I didn't need a mirror to know it was red and likely bruised.

How was I going to get out of this one? I'd spent the last few days telling Hawkins to follow the coastline. And now, what? Was I supposed to tell her, "Hey, so, guess what? I've been making you take the long way there. If we cut this way, we should get there in no time"?

Even if we did cut back into the jungle, I didn't know where I was going.

Good job, Brone, I thought. *You tried to outsmart a con artist... a mastermind criminal... and now she's going to kill you.*

Again, I'd underestimated Hawkins.

I flinched when something touched my shoulder, but realized it was BluJay. She walked beside me with bony, rounded shoulders and thin strands of blond hair floating over her matching eyebrows. She tried to smile, perhaps in an attempt to comfort me, but her lips barely moved.

Why was she doing that? No one else seemed to care. Collins had been quick to blurt out something stupid, like, "Whoa, someone's into some kinky shit."

And the rest of the women? They'd cocked an eyebrow at me and kept on walking behind Hawkins.

They were sheep.

Not me.

I clenched my fists, tempted to kick up a pile of leaves, but the last thing I wanted to do was draw attention to myself.

"Better tell me if I'm makin' a turn, Brone," came Hawkins's voice at the front. She didn't even bother to look back. Instead, she waved an arm over her head from side to side. She was getting a kick out of this—reveling in the fact that I was at her mercy.

I glanced at BluJay, who obviously didn't say anything, though we shared a few unspoken words. It was obvious she wanted nothing to do with Hawkins, but she was too terrified to speak up. So why was she looking at me? Did she expect me to save her? Why hadn't she joined me the first time?

"Yo, check it out!" someone exclaimed.

BluJay's big blue eyes shot toward the sound. She was so mousey... Had Hawkins hurt her?

Physically? Or, was she an abuse victim?

"Holy shit!" someone else shouted.

Straight ahead, an opening in the trees brought in a blast of sunshine. As I moved closer, the yellow streaks warmed my legs, my chest, and then my neck. In the distance, seagulls screamed overhead and waves crashed.

We were approaching a beach.

What were they so excited about? Water? It wasn't like they hadn't seen a beach before.

But then, I saw it.

Halfway across the shore, rotting in the sand, was the remains of a massive passenger plane. Most of its metallic frame was missing, and one of its wings were snapped in half. Its windows, all black holes along the gray, contorted frame, made it look haunted.

The sun beamed down overtop the metal bars and support beams, forcing me to look away.

But it didn't matter.

I didn't have to look at it to know what it was, and who it belonged to.

"Sweet!" Collins shouted, running straight ahead of Hawkins.

Hawkins shouted something, but Collins was kicking through the sand, arms flailing as if trying to swim through the air. Pops and that other foul-smelling woman followed her, running straight toward it like a bunch of excited monkeys.

"Stop!" Hawkins shouted again, but no one listened.

I'd been about to shout the same thing, knowing that this area was protected by the Northers, but then a dark thought entered my mind. Why should I try to protect them? They weren't good people. Given the chance, they'd kill someone. They'd likely kill me. Besides, the less of them there were, the better my odds at taking Hawkins down.

Was I a monster?

I was knowingly allowing women to run straight into a trap.

In an instant, I saw Ellie's face—I saw my mother, my best friend Melody, and all of my Hunter friends.

I wasn't a monster; I was human, and I was a survivor.

Sticking my arm out across BluJay's chest, I stopped moving. Hawkins must have heard the sound of impact; in one rapid motion, she swung around.

"What're you doing?" she snapped. "Keep moving."

BluJay took a step forward, but I stiffened my arm to keep her from following Hawkins out on shore. "No," I said.

Hawkins's brows came so close together they looked like one oversized caterpillar. "No?"

At that exact moment, a familiar sound penetrated the air nearby—a high-pitched whistling approaching at an alarming speed, and Collins fell toward the plane, collapsing in the sand with an arrow protruding from her chest.

"Collins!" Hawkins shouted, charging forward.

Without hesitating, I grabbed her around the wrist. She swung back, her features demonically twisted.

"Brone, what the fuck—"

"That plane belongs to the Northers," I said.

Why the hell had I even helped her? BluJay shrank back, fingers curled up against her bottom lip, looking even more terrified than ever.

"Why didn't you—" Hawkins said, gazing out at her women.

Pops and the blob were left standing, scrambling around in the sand like ants around a disturbed nest. They tried to run behind the plane, but they didn't have time. Dozens more arrows came raining down, penetrating their limbs, their chests, and Pops's throat.

Hawkins winced and turned away.

Why hadn't I tried to stop them? As I stared at the panicked, dying women, I didn't see the panic—all I saw were my enemies being taken out for me. What was wrong with me? I thought of my mother—something I always did when fighting a moral battle—and for the first time, it did nothing.

I didn't feel guilty, nor did I feel like I was doing anything wrong. While my brain knew that death was wrong, no matter the reason, it didn't eat away at me from the inside like it would have when I first arrived here.

Collins clutched at her chest and screamed as a gooey glob of blood poured out of her mouth. The other two crawled desperately in the sand, their faces scraping against the grainy surface.

Maybe I'd seen so much death that I'd stopped understanding it at all.

If I ever got off this island, I thought, I'd never be normal. I'd probably be forced into a lifetime of therapy, and for what? To live a shitty, routine life full of...

In seconds, several heavily armed women emerged from the forest and a familiar rage tore through me. The tallest of them all, a woman covered in scars who wore a crusty half-skull mask over her jaw and had piercing eyes, with animal fur padded over her shoulders and metal armor plates fastened around her wrists, stomped through the sand and straight toward Hawkins's dying women.

Zsasz.

Hawkins tried to charge out into the open, but I pulled her back hard.

"You'll die," I said. "That's Zsasz."

Hawkins grumbled something under her breath, shoulders bouncing up and down as she breathed as if hyperventilating.

The rest of us stood still, watching in horror as Zsasz raised her leg and came down hard on Collins's face. There was a crack, followed by silence. Then, she pulled a knife from her belt and one by one, slit the other two women's throats, despite them begging her for mercy.

BluJay turned away, her head dug into my shoulder, and I wrapped an arm around her. She was so small, so fragile, that I felt an unusual need to protect her.

"It's okay," I whispered. "Come on, let's get out of here."

"We're not going anywhere!" Hawkins snapped. "I came here for Rainer—"

"Don't you see?" I snapped back. "You'll never get to Rainer. Zsasz is a killer! Sometimes she takes in prisoners, other times she kills them for fun. She's unpredictable! If we stay here, we have a fifty-fifty chance of ever making it to their city!"

Hawkins, now glaring at me as if I were the one responsible for the death of her women, clenched a fist by her face and bared her teeth. "I'll take those odds."

"What're you gonna do?" I said. "Walk out on shore? You can't possibly think—"

Something sharp jabbed me in the back, and the other two of Hawkins's surviving women let out a squeal.

What was going on?

"Zsasz!" came a loud, explosive voice from behind me. In the distance, Zsasz turned toward us, soulless eyes hovering above her deathly skull mask.

"Got some strays!" came that same voice.

Behind us were three Northers, one of which I recognized perfectly.

Rebel, one of Zsasz's goons.

When her eyes rolled toward me, I looked away and aimed my face at the ground. If she looked at me long enough, she'd see past my shaved head, my unsightly gash, and the dirt I'd rubbed over my face, neck, and shoulders during our trek in an attempt to mask my appearance. If she could identify me, I was dead.

She poked the tip of her spear into my back again and grumbled, "Get out there!"

CHAPTER 9

"Zsasz," Hawkins said cheerfully with two arms aimed at the sky.

She was acting as if she and Zsasz were long-lost friends, even though she'd only ever heard stories about Zsasz.

Zsasz cocked a hairless eyebrow and tilted her head, no doubt trying to figure out how Hawkins knew her name.

"I've heard all about you," Hawkins said, her voice calm. How wasn't she freaking out? Zsasz held a knife to her throat, and she stood there as if conversing over tea. "You're a big deal on this island," she went on. "Almost like a superstar, if you ask me." She grinned, and it looked so genuine that I found myself wondering if Hawkins was, in fact, admiring Zsasz or simply manipulating her.

Zsasz looked at her, confused. "Super... star?"

No way did she even know what the word superstar meant. How could she? Zsasz had grown up on this island. She didn't know anything about the outside world—about actors, singers, politics, none of that.

"Oh, never mind," Hawkins said playfully, making me sick to my stomach. How could she be so chipper? "I came here to find you."

"Is that so?" Zsasz said, pulling the knife away from Hawkins's throat. "And why would you want to do something like that?"

"Because," Hawkins said, "I heard about that little bitch who ran away from you. The one who took half of your people!"

I swallowed hard.

This seemed to intrigue Zsasz. With authority, she gripped her waist, and slowly, removed the mask from her face. It was even more scarred than I remembered, with fresh red scabs sitting at the corners of her lips. It was as if she'd tried to open her mouth so wide it had split the corners. Across her cheek was a brand-new cut; it was thin, long, and already starting to grow new skin. Her cheeks, lumpy pads of skin on either side of her face, slowly expanded as her lips stretched into her famous zebra-striped smile.

"What do you know of Brone?" she asked, and my stomach sank.

The sound of my name coming from her mouth was enough to make me want to hurl. My heartbeat sped up and I swallowed, my throat sticking together.

Zsasz had done something to me... broken me. How was it that I wasn't afraid of Hawkins, who'd only hours ago threatened to kill me, yet being several feet away from Zsasz terrified me? She was my nightmare—a constant reminder of what I'd been through, and the one person I knew wanted me dead more than anyone else.

"I know where to find your people," Hawkins said. "All of them. I can also get you Brone."

Clenching both fists, I instinctively took a step forward, the pad of my feet sinking into the warm sand.

What was she doing? This hadn't been her plan. She wouldn't sell us out, would she? She wanted Rainer taken out. What good would come of her killing my people?

"You're lying," Zsasz growled.

"Lying?" Hawkins said. "I know who you are. I know who Rainer is. I know who Brone is. I also know where all of your little prisoners are—" She wiggled a finger in Zsasz face, and in one quick motion, Zsasz snatched it and snapped it sideways.

Hawkins let out a scream so loud I didn't recognize her. She clutched her wrist and pulled her crooked finger up against her chest. "You broke my fucking finger!"

Without looking away, Zsasz smiled as Hawkins breathed loudly, her posture hunched and her cheeks a deep red.

Maybe now, she'd realize what kind of person she was dealing with; at last, she'd see that she was in way over her head thinking she could waltz onto Norther territory and start making demands.

"If you want your revenge," Hawkins said, staring hatefully up at Zsasz, "you'll take me to Rainer."

In a split second, Zsasz grabbed her by the throat, and with one arm, raised her into the air. Hawkins kicked her feet, her toes sprinkling sand toward Zsasz, and with her undamaged hand, she clawed at her throat.

"You don't get to make demands," Zsasz said. "You tell me where to find Brone, or I'll break every single bone in your body and let you burn in the sun."

CHAPTER 10

She was insane.

She had to be.

Hawkins sat in the sand with legs crossed, grasping onto her injured hand. But instead of crying, or begging for Zsasz's mercy, she laughed hysterically. Her throat, now red, blotchy, and resembling tomato sauce, expanded every time she threw her head back and chuckled. It didn't seem to bother her that Zsasz had threatened her.

In fact, she didn't look afraid at all.

"What's so funny?" Zsasz growled, towering over Hawkins.

"Don't think she takes you seriously," Rebel said.

For a moment, I glanced her way, wondering how someone that stupid was still alive. The rest of Zsasz's followers nodded their skull-masked faces and stepped toward Hawkins, prepared to teach her a lesson.

Zsasz raised a finger, assumedly her way of saying, No, *don't touch her... yet.*

"Think you're so tough," Hawkins said, still

laughing. "You might be tough on this island, but you wouldn't survive the real world."

Zsasz didn't say anything, and I couldn't help but wonder if she'd ever pondered the real world before. Surely, she wondered what was out there. All she'd ever known was this island. Was Hawkins getting somewhere?

"If you kill me," Hawkins said, "you're never getting off this island."

All at once, Zsasz's followers started bickering in Russian until Zsasz raised an arm and they went quiet.

"What're you saying?" Zsasz asked.

Although no longer laughing, Hawkins sat in the sand with an amused scowl on her face. "Take me to Rainer, and I'll get you off this island."

I bit down on the inside of my cheek. She was playing Zsasz same way she'd played me.

"She's lying, Zsasz," said one of the masked Northers, but then the woman standing next to her nudged her hard and growled something.

"It isn't possible," Zsasz said, staring down at Hawkins. "No one leaves this—"

Hawkins reached into a small, barely noticeable sachet around her waist and plucked out the C-42 Transponder. It beeped and let out a static sound. Zsasz, along with every other Norther circling her, tilted their heads like dogs trying to catch every word being spoken by their human master.

It was the strangest thing I'd ever seen—adults staring at a piece of technology as if it were some alien artifact.

"What is that?" Zsasz said, moving closer.

For the first time, I saw an orphan—a helpless girl robbed of her childhood and forced into a life of suffering and chaos. But I didn't want to understand her; I didn't want to feel sympathy for a cold-blooded killer, so I ground my teeth, reminding myself of a single image: Murk hanging beaten and bruised by her wrists.

Zsasz had done that. She was nothing more than a monster.

"It's a communication device," Hawkins said.

Again, all they did was stare. I glanced sideways at BluJay, who appeared as astonished as me. Moments ago, these heavily armed soldiers wrapped in animal fur and protected by metallic armor had been prepared to kill us. Now, they circled us with apparent curiosity, eyeballing a small piece of black metal sitting tightly in Hawkins's grip.

Zsasz reached for it, but Hawkins pressed something, and it made a high-pitched beep.

Like a wild animal, Zsasz retreated with bared teeth.

"It's best you don't touch it," Hawkins said. As she'd done several times in front of me before, she pulled the transponder close to her lips, pressed a button that emitted crackling static, and said, "Ace, Hawk in the sky, over."

The familiar man's voice came pouring out through the transponder's speaker. "Ace in place, over."

At once, everyone blew up into a cacophonous argument.

Zsasz shouted something in Russian, and Rebel pushed two women away from the transponder. Even Hawkins looked confused—obviously, she was expecting curiosity or excitement, not an outburst.

"Man!" Zsasz said at last, inching even closer to Hawkins.

And all at once, the Northers circled her like wasps around spilled soda.

"Easy, ladies!" Hawkins said, forcing her way onto her feet. She slipped the transponder back into her pouch and everyone's wild eyes followed it. "Yes, that was a man's voice. He's here to help us. To help you. Like I said... Take me to Rainer, and I'll make sure he gets you off this island."

Zsasz elevated her chin, staring at Hawkins as if trying to read her mind.

Finally, she cleared her throat. "Tie her up. Let's take her to Rainer."

CHAPTER 11

It was like traveling back in time, only with people I despised. Coin wasn't anywhere near me, nor was Hammer, Johnson, or Franklin. Right now, I'd have taken Franklin's big mouth over these women. I immediately felt bad for remembering the worst in Franklin—she was dead now, and it wasn't right to think ill of the dead.

"Ow," said the woman in front of me.

She stumbled and caught herself against Hawkins's back, pulling me along with her. I'd never get used to having bristly rope fastened around my wrists. The worst part was Rebel had been the one to tie us all up. She'd paused on me for a second, and even when I'd looked away, I felt her beady eyes searching me.

Was she figuring it out? Would she realize who I was? She'd hated me, no doubt as much as Zsasz did when I was held captive. Now that I'd escaped, there was a good chance she hated me that much more.

Did she spend her nights fantasizing about skinning me alive? If my cover was blown, they'd torture me until I begged them to be killed. My stomach sank at the thought of this. I'd partially accepted the high probability of my death on this island, but torture... That was a different story.

"Move it!" Rebel groaned, jabbing BluJay in the back with a dull stick.

BluJay let out a throaty sound that was neither a whimper nor a shout and I fought the urge to tell Rebel off. But the moment she heard my voice, I knew I'd be done for.

I'd have to either keep my mouth shut or learn to use a different voice. Something deeper, maybe.

"Get your ass moving!" came Rebel's loathsome voice again.

At the front of the line, Zsasz walked with her head bowed, inspecting Hawkins's C-42 Transponder. What was she planning to do with it? It wasn't like she knew how to use electronics.

With a press of a button, a loud static sound filled the humid air around us.

"Don't touch that—" Hawkins yelled, but one of the Northers knocked her in the back of the head with a long bone—a male hog's femur bone if I had to guess.

Fucking cavewomen.

In a moment, Hawkins reached for the back of her head. "Ow, you fuckin'—" and the Norther smacked her in the ribs this time.

Hawkins lunged straight for her, pulling us

along. At the same time, the two women tied on either side of her tripped and fell to their knees, the weight of their bodies stopping Hawkins in her tracks.

"Hey!" Zsasz snapped, turning only the upper half of her body sideways. She held the device in her large fist, eyes fixated on Hawkins.

Hawkins, now standing face-to-face with the Norther who'd hit her, raised her chin. "Keep beating me and see where that leads you."

The Norther stomped one foot down and tilted her head, the bone of her mask almost scratching Hawkins's forehead. "Is that a threat?"

"Vareek, back off," Zsasz ordered.

Vareek, the burly-looking Norther with a large bone for a weapon, squinted up at Zsasz, then at Hawkins.

"I said back off," Zsasz repeated. "This one's going straight to Rainer."

Vareek growled and stomped her way to the front of the line, arms sticking out as if trying to make herself look bigger. Hawkins, however, didn't seem to care that the Norther was twice her size. It was clear she knew what she was doing.

"If you break that thing," Hawkins said, her pompous voice aimed at Zsasz, "there's no repairing it."

Zsasz hesitated, no doubt contemplating whether the device was worth taking orders from a simpleton. She stood still for several seconds, averting her gaze between the transponder and Hawkins. It was as though she'd never been put in a situation like that before: forced to decide between power and an object.

Without a word, she raised her arm and the fur dangling over her shoulders shifted. Underneath the fur sat a small suede sachet. She twirled the transponder one last time in front of her face and slid it into the bag.

"We'll let Rainer decide what to do with it."

And once again, I was dragged by a rope around my wrists.

Someone at the front of the line moaned, probably rubbing the irritated skin around their wrists, and Zsasz swung a fist at the woman's face. When she passed out, Zsasz rolled her eyes and ordered the one behind her to drag the body. It took three of Hawkins's women to lift her up, while Hawkins stood there, huffing and puffing with her broken finger.

"Put your back into it," Hawkins growled.

Zsasz stared at her but didn't say anything. It was like she was trying to understand where someone as pompous as Hawkins had come from. This was possibly the first time anyone in Zsasz's presence didn't show any form of fear or hatred.

Not only was Hawkins strolling about carelessly, every now and then, she'd look at one of Zsasz's women and mumble something under her breath. Was her deranged confidence a result of her transponder? Did she feel untouchable?

When Rebel threw dirt in my face for looking at her, Hawkins spat at her and said, "Brainless primate."

I didn't care to look at Rebel's stupid, quickly inflating face—all I could think about was the burning on mine.

Fuck.

Bits of debris were probably stuck inside my wound, and it was burning worse than any injury I'd ever had before. A line of warm blood trickled down my chin, and I wondered how long it would be before the bleeding stopped again.

What was Rebel trying to prove? She was a survivor of this island—she of all people knew that wound cleanliness was crucial to one's survival.

So, was that her plan? Fill my wound with dirt so I'd die of an infection? If I didn't get this thing cleaned soon, the infection would spread.

"All right, let's get them inside," Zsasz spat, ordering two of her followers to tug harder on our rope.

The woman who'd been hit unconscious by Zsasz came to, but she stumbled aimlessly while the woman nearest to her helped her walk a straight path. "Where... where am I?"

Zsasz turned around, her stretched lips

resembling prison cell bars. "Your new home."

CHAPTER 12

"What the hell happened to her?"

"Shut up, Fran."

"Make me!"

The sound of bone hitting teeth spread through the cage, slipping out between the cracks in the bamboo prison bars.

Was this even real? Was I honestly sitting in the same pile of dirt I'd spent months sleeping on not too long ago? How long would they leave us here to rot this time? I glanced out through the bamboo bars at a city I didn't recognize.

The sun was beginning to set, filling the air with that same orange glow I'd come to think of as blood over this city.

Where there had once been hundreds of women, only dozens remained. The slaves of the city were now shackled around the ankles by metallic rings—some of these women's ankles were attached to ropes, while others walked about freely.

Was it a cycle? Or, was it based on trust? Would I be shackled?

Behind me, the shuffling stopped at last, and two women dropped into seated positions with bloody noses. Had they been fighting this entire time? I didn't care enough to look.

"Where you reckon they took Hawk?" asked one of Hawkins's women.

"Where do you think?" snapped another. She raised a fist in the air, but when her friend cowered, she lowered it. "To see Rainer, obviously."

"Who's Rainer?" came a frail voice.

"Fran, mind your business!"

Two women whom I didn't recognize sat at the far back of the cage, wiping the blood dripping from their nostrils.

"What?" asked Fran. "I keep hearin' the name tossed around. Sounds like she's important. Don't tell me you haven't wondered too, Pam."

Fran brushed her gray hair back, her sixty-some-year-old skin stretching along with it. How long had she been in here? Her arms looked like thin cheese strings—they were so thin that I could see veins everywhere. Her cheekbones stuck out as much as her nose, which was already too long and pointed. Her eyes, sunken and Dijon mustard-yellow, looked like they'd spent a lifetime beside cigarette smoke. Even her voice was rough and hoarse, which assumedly meant she'd once been a smoker who didn't give a rat's ass about maintaining her health. The woman looked like any minute now, she'd croak.

The woman beside her, Pam, shook her balloon-sized head. She was much plumper than Fran but didn't look all that much healthier. Her eyebrows were so thick, uncombed, and close together that it was all I could stare at. "Prolly the leader of this damn place." She scoffed and rolled her eyes toward me. "Served twenty-three years of my life sentence in the same old shabby prison, and what do they do? Throw me out to make room for the younger criminals. What kind of justice system is that? I'd have taken the damn electric chair over this."

"Um," said Fran, "they still do that?"

"Do what?" Pam snapped, the more impatient of the pair.

Fran sighed and slapped her forehead. "The electric chair, you twit!"

Pam shrugged. "Hell if I know, but I wish I'd gotten it!"

"You two new?" I asked, my voice croaky.

God, I needed water. Everyone turned to face me, including the meanest of Hawkins's women—Sammy, I believe her name was. But for the first time, she wasn't looking at me as if contemplating my murder. It was almost as if being separated from Hawkins had changed their opinions of me.

Or, were they so terrified that they looked to

me for guidance knowing I'd suffered here once before?

Fran and Pam shook their heads at the same time.

Fran wiped a bit of dry blood from her nose and stuck her thumb out at Pam. "Both from Saint Jerome Correctional Facility. Guess they decided to make some cuts, and instead of transferrin' us, they sent us to this shithole!"

Pam swung an open hand to slap Fran but missed. It was impossible to tell if they were friends, sisters, or enemies.

"We got caught a few weeks ago by these lunatics..." Pam said, gazing out through the prison bars.

I scoffed, though I hadn't meant to. "Two weeks is nothing. Get ready to be in here a few months."

"A few months?" Sammy shouted, puffing up twice her size.

She looked like the rest of Hawkins's women—a shaved head, pale skin, and hateful beady eyes that made me wonder if there was any intelligence floating in that hairless skull of hers. Out of all of us, she was the largest—both in weight and in height.

"How do you know?" Fran asked, leaning forward over her crossed legs.

"Well, this isn't the first time—" Sammy started.

"Not the first time I've heard about this place,"

I cut in, glaring at her.

I stared at her marble-like eyes, then at her throat, prepared to crush her trachea if necessary. I didn't care how big she was. If anyone found out about this being my second time around, I was done for.

Sammy crossed her dark-haired arms and dropped against the wall, the earth beneath us shaking as she landed in a seated position. I didn't yet know the other woman—the other one of Hawkins's followers—but she kept quiet and followed Sammy.

The other two old women sat on either side of her, while BluJay sat next to me, the growing peach fuzz on her head making her stand out from the rest of us. She turned to me, pointed at my face, and made a gesture I didn't recognize.

"She says you need to get that cleaned up," Pam said.

"You know sign language?" I asked her.

She sighed. "I may be a criminal, but I had a life before that little bitch—" She cut herself short, seeming to realize now wasn't the time to share how she ended up in prison. "I used to teach kids with disabilities. Learned a bit here and there."

Fran snorted, her cheekbones popping above her wide grin. "Can you believe it? This sweet ole lady used to help retarded kids—"

"Disabled, you skull-faced pillock!" Pam

snapped, throwing a fistful of dirt straight at Fran's face.

Fran reached for her eyes and grimaced. "Goddamn it, Pam!" She rubbed hard, then pulled the skin of her right eye down and picked at a few particles of dirt until she got it out. Glaring at her ex-prison mate, she continued. "One day she's pushing some kid's wheelchair, and the next she's shooting her husband's mistress!"

"She knew we were married!" Pam snapped, prepared to throw another fistful of dirt.

This time, Fran shielded herself with her arm, and Pam dropped the dirt before launching it.

"Did they send anyone else from that prison?" I asked.

Fran, with a rounded back and an arm still shielding her face, nodded at me. "Dozens of us were dropped off. I overhead the guards talkin' about a nationwide cleanse. Something to do with reducing costs."

Pam scoffed and threw her head back against the dirt wall. "Yeah, cutting costs all right. They're clearing out all us old timers. Anyone with a long sentence who's been sucking up taxpayer dollars. Smith turned seventy-four last month and they dropped her off along with us. Poor old bat didn't even make it to shore."

Shit.

It was getting worse.

How was this happening? Why weren't American citizens stepping up and fighting this? Or, maybe they were, only to be beaten down. I'd seen the riots in the United States—ever since President Seth had taken over, they'd become bloodbaths.

Every time a riot broke out, my school went on lockdown; there was no telling what kind of damage would occur.

* * *

"Public safety," said the clean-shaven news anchor. His hair was so slick I could almost smell the minty gel as I sat in front of my television. "This isn't about privacy, it's about nationwide safety, according to President Seth. This all seems a bit extreme, but then again, I'm not certain I should even be commenting given the government's new bill on hate speech. Can you tell us what's going on, Larson?"

The screen flipped over to a heavily armed man standing in front of the camera. Behind him, an explosion went off, sending a loose car tire flying across the city street. Larson flinched, almost dropping his microphone, but refastened his protective helmet and moved toward the camera. "Eighty-four casualties have been confirmed in what is being described as the deadliest riot in American history. The civil unrest started yesterday evening when Adam McClane was arrested in his own home after vocalizing fantasies about killing the president." He regripped his microphone and stared into the camera, almost as if seeing the news anchor at the other end. "Americans are furious, Stephen. They're calling this a complete breach of privacy and stating that their rights have been violated."

Stephen appeared on screen again, one neatly combed eyebrow high on his forehead. "But the government is stating that citizens knew this was coming—every electronic product we purchase comes with fine print suggesting that conversations can be recorded at any time without permission."

"That's true," Larson said, "but this is getting out of control."

All of a sudden, gunfire blasted through the streets, shattering car windows and puncturing the cement walls of government buildings. Larson scurried away from the camera, and the reporters followed him, the screen bouncing up and down. He bent forward, trying to catch his breath over the microphone—the sound coming across as static. Then, he stood up and slid his fingers under his helmet and over his ear. "I have a new report coming in, Stephen. There have been one hundred and twelve casualties confirmed, and many more are expected. Police have now arrested over five thousand rioters, the most arrests America has ever seen in a riot. We need to relocate, but I'll touch base as soon as we have more information. Back to you, Stephen."

* * *

Was this it? Were we going to be stuck here forever? Ellie had encouraged me to keep hoping that America would come to its senses—that the people would stand up against President Seth, and that a rescue team would come looking for us.

But that wasn't going to happen. At least, not anytime soon.

CHAPTER 13

"That's gonna leave a scar," Sammy said as if I didn't already know that.

It wasn't even worth responding to her. Maybe she was trying to be helpful, maybe she was unnecessarily cruel. Either way, I didn't care.

I didn't care about anything.

As the days went on, BluJay kept inspecting the cut on my face. Every time it rained, she'd pluck wet leaves through the cracks of the prison bars and use them as wet napkins over the wound. One woman in particular kept approaching our prison while looking over her shoulder. She'd been the one to bring me a leaf of aloe vera, which BluJay had used to apply its gel over my wound.

It was a long shot, but BluJay, although silent, looked confident. With hard features, she'd applied it using the leaf to avoid directly touching the wound. It was clear she knew what she was doing. When I said "Thank you," she tapped her chin and moved her hand away from her face while mouthing the words, *Thank you*, to teach me.

So I learned one word in sign language, and

every time she helped me, I used it. She'd then sign, *You're welcome*, which I learned, too.

How long had I been sitting in this same spot? My tailbone was hurting more than my face, and my bladder felt like it was going to explode. I hadn't urinated since yesterday due to dehydration, nor did I want to now. We'd made a rule that when someone had to go, everyone looked the other way.

It was the last bit of dignity we could give each other.

Goose bumps spread across my skin as the evening sky rolled in, bringing along with it cool, damp air. I'd worn the same clothes for eight sunsets now and my skin felt as dirty as our toilet corner.

I'd survived this before—I could do it again.

But what if I didn't want to? I was too tired. At least last time, I'd held onto the hope of escaping this place. But as I peered out into the city, I knew it would be impossible this time. By shackling women at the ankles, The Northers had taken every precaution to avoid having history repeat itself.

I'd come to realize that every evening, after the women had slaved away under the searing sun all day, a dozen Northers came by with their swords and spears, fastening a thick rope around the women's ankle shackles one by one. They were then led to the sleeping area, where they all slept side by side on wooden platforms.

How many women were there? Fifty, sixty? There had been several hundred before I encouraged them all to run. What had I done? The women who hadn't had the courage to run—the ones who'd remained most loyal to the Northers—were now being treated like cattle.

Bringing my knees up against my chest, I sighed and dropped my chin.

Maybe if I didn't eat for the next few days, I'd starve.

Starvation was better than a life of torturous slavery. I was so tired... so depleted, that all I wanted was death; I wanted to end this misery. I searched the ceiling, wondering if I might find a root hanging from one of the bamboo bars.

Would the women in here try to stop me if I hung myself?

Why was I even having suicidal thoughts? I'd never been suicidal before—at least not to this extent. But I had nothing left.

Nothing at all.

I wasn't going back home, ever.

And I was never getting out of this city.

I'd finally reached the end.

As I contemplated ways to kill myself, my eyelids became heavy and my head rocked forward until I fell asleep.

"Out of my way!" came Zsasz's venomous voice.

I cracked my eyes open, realizing I was still alive.

Oh God.

I was still here.

This was real... All of it. I swallowed hard, my throat sticking. BluJay paced back and forth, and I wanted to tell her to sit down—tell her that she didn't want to be the only woman standing if Zsasz came around—but I couldn't find the strength.

Even the idea of raising an arm to signal her felt impossible.

Was Zsasz coming here? I hadn't seen her since she'd captured us. She'd sent Rebel to our cage a few times to feed us, and all we'd received were bits and pieces of slimy, poorly cooked salmon.

And what about Hawkins? Where was she? She'd either succeeded in manipulating Rainer, or she'd been killed. She sure as hell hadn't killed Rainer; otherwise, we'd have heard about it by now.

As footsteps stomped through the city, I closed my eyes, waiting to feel the vibrations move closer.

Slowly, the dirt around my fingertips trembled, and Zsasz's voice moved nearer.

"Let's make this quick," she ordered. "Your mom said one each. No more, no less."

Mom? Whose mother was she talking about?

Oh my God... Were there children here? Children younger than Elektra? Fueled by a surge of curiosity, I pulled my head away from the wall and stared out through the prison bars.

Suddenly, Zsasz came into view, but she wasn't the one I was looking at. On either side of her were two men twice her size with large bare chests and skin as golden brown as Rainer's. They walked with their broad shoulders pulled back, their muscular arms swinging back and forth, and their dark eyes staring toward our cage beneath thick, black eyebrows.

A burst of adrenaline coursed through me and I swallowed hard.

How was this even possible? They looked exactly like Rainer—younger male replicas. Were they her sons?

And then it hit me.

Rainer had been pregnant when Murk cast her out of the Village.

"This is the litter," Zsasz said, moving toward our cage. She unlatched the lock, bent down, and lifted the gate wide open.

The two men searched the cage, their animallike eyes falling on me for a brief second.

Zsasz's gaze shifted between all of us until slowly, a nauseating smile crept on her face. She parted her dry, mangled lips and casually pointed a finger inside our prison. "That one. She looks fertile."

PART THREE

PROLOGUE

My belly hung over my thighs as if I'd swallowed a basketball.

Delicately, I brushed my fingertips across my skin and around my belly button. Around me, dozens of Northers stood tall with spears held in their hands, prepared to ward off any threat that might risk my child's life. How long ago had the Northers captured me for a second time around? A year?

I was losing track of everything.

Some days, I even forgot my own name—I'd grown so accustomed to being referred to as Brone that the name Lydia felt foreign to me.

At times like these, my mother's voice popped inside my head: "Lydia, my Little Lilac..."

I tilted my head back with eyes closed, and at the same time, a shadow cooled my face.

"For the baby," Zsasz said, forcing a smile.

She handed me a skull bowl chipped on one side and filled with a green liquid. It was grainy-looking with bits of dry leaves, or herbs, sprinkled across the white froth in the middle.

"What is it?" I asked.

"For the baby," Zsasz repeated.

Holding my breath, I took a sip; to my surprise, it didn't make me want to puke my brains out. Instead, it tasted like chocolate milk.

How was that even possible?

"For the baby," came her voice again as if set on a repeat cycle.

I arched an eyebrow and chugged the rest of the chocolate-flavored goo. "Yeah, I get it. For the baby."

At once, Zsasz dropped into a crouching position with her favorite bone knife, its serrated tip pressed firmly into the groove of my throat. Her face was so close to mine she looked inhuman with her bloodshot eyes and overly scarred nostrils.

Her breath, a rancid mixture of rot and sweetness, warmed the side of my face before slipping into my mouth. "If that baby dies," she said, "you die."

CHAPTER 1

I woke up with a jolt, my sweat-soaked shirt sticking to my back. Instinctively, I slapped a hand over my belly, feeling nothing more than a flat surface with bony ribs on either side.

"Thank God," I breathed.

"Shut up," someone hissed, their face invisible within the darkness.

What had happened? Where was I?

BluJay, I now remembered.

Oh God... They'd taken her. Why? Because she was prettier than everyone else in this cage? Is that what they did? Pick the woman they thought would procreate beautiful babies?

And what did they do? Take turns with her? Zsasz had told Rainer's sons to each to take a woman, yet they'd only taken BluJay.

I swallowed hard, sick to my stomach. I couldn't even imagine what BluJay was going through... The worst part was that she couldn't speak; she couldn't vocalize her thoughts or express pain through words.

It all made sense now. Tegan. That was

precisely why she'd turned out the way she did. She'd stopped talking, and in a sense, had lost her mind. Oh, poor Tegan. How much torture had she endured? How much abuse?

The idea of rape infuriated me more than Zsasz's violence.

As I sat shivering in the darkness, I thought of only one thing—freeing BluJay and any other women forced into reproducing children. But how could I? They were being kept behind that massive wooden gate. For all I knew, they were housed within the mountain under Rainer's protection.

Why hadn't we heard from Hawkins? Had she failed in her attempt to kill Rainer? That was her plan, wasn't it? Then again, Hawkins was a liar—stating she wanted to kill Rainer didn't necessarily mean it was true. Maybe she had bigger plans in mind.

But she'd brought me here as an escape plan. Why? She'd been so sure that my women would come fighting for me, which in turn guaranteed her freedom. What game was she playing at?

By the time the sun came up, my shirt was still damp, and the smell of old water and fast-spreading bacteria spread through the cage, making me wish I'd lost my sense of smell when Franklin punched me in the face.

Sammy, the one with the brow piercing and the meaner-looking of the two remaining skinheads, groaned as she stretched her flabby arms and sat upright. Within a few weeks, she had shed some extra pounds, losing that huge bulldog look that amplified what she was no doubt trying to achieve—meanness. The dozens of blue frog and flower tattoos that covered her arms were already stretched out on her sagging skin, making her look several years older.

"They could come back for any one of us," she said, casting her eyes toward the ground.

I glared up at her. "They took BluJay."

It wasn't Sammy's fault this had happened, but I needed someone to blame. And with the way she'd looked at me in the past—full of contempt and hatred—it was easy to direct my anger at her.

Her eyes narrowed into slits. "You think I don't know that? I was here."

Obviously, BluJay meant more to her than I'd initially thought.

Rubbing her shaved head that now looked sprinkled with pepper, she sighed. "Man... We shouldn't have followed Hawkins... We shoulda switched to Brone's side."

I was a bit taken aback by this. Sammy reminded me of Collins—a complete bitch who only cared about herself and who foolishly followed Hawkins no matter how dangerous it was.

But as she stared at the dirt over her slanting eyebrows, it was obvious that she regretted ever obeying Hawkins.

"Watch it," came a familiar voice.

Hugging my knees closer to my chest, I glanced out through the prison bars. Across the morning dew came a figure marching straight toward us, a limp in her walk.

"Time to start working," she said, her voice monotone.

I craned my neck to catch a glimpse of her face, but at the same time, she turned sideways and unlocked the gate's latch. It was only when she lifted the bars up above the cage that I saw her.

Alice Number Two.

Her cheeks, once covered in bright little freckles, now looked like filth on her face. It was as if the freckles had either merged together or she hadn't cleaned her face in months. As the morning sun shone down across the city, her hair didn't light up a fiery orange the way it used to—it was dull, matted, and it hung over her eyes like sixty-year-old drapes.

In her right hand, she held a tall, crooked staff and leaned the weight of her body against it. It wasn't hard to understand why she required the support; her right leg was mangled, as was her right arm and part of her face. Even her clothes were mauled—or at least, what remained of them. The beige suede was torn at her sides, at her shoulder, and so badly around her hip that part of her butt cheek was showing. The suede itself had darkened to a rusty brown, obviously the result of blood loss. What had happened? Something had no doubt attacked her. By the looks of the deep scratch marks and the large puncture wounds, I could only assume it was a wildcat. But when had this happened?

It was highly unlikely that a wildcat had entered the city.

As her tired, sunken eyes rolled our way, I couldn't help but wonder: had she tried to escape with us the evening we made it out? Had she tried, and... failed? Suddenly, I remembered the rumbly growl of a wildcat and how it had attacked one of the Northers guarding the city's perimeter.

Could it have also caught Alice Number Two?

"Come on, get up," she said, a finger lazily tickling the air in front of her.

When we were held captive in the past, Alice Number Two had done everything in her power to make sure we understood that we were nothing more than slaves. But the way she acted now reminded me of a call center operator working a night shift after twenty-five years of service.

She had zero interest in being here, but she'd been forced to continue her part.

"I said get up," she repeated, her voice barely rising.

Clearing my throat, I grabbed the wall behind

me for support and rose to my feet. Everyone followed, including Fran and Pam, who moaned in pain as they stood.

Alice Number Two stared at me with flat eyelids, obviously realizing that everyone in the cage seemed to view me as some sort of leader. This meant that I'd have to be the first one to step outside of the cage.

The moment I did, I closed my eyes and sucked in a lungful of fresh air—something I hadn't breathed in a while. No more urine, no more feces, no bacteria-infested earth.

Just as I was enjoying the cleansing breath of air, something cold touched my ankle and I flinched, pulling it away.

"Hold still," growled Alice Number Two.

I wasn't sure why I still thought of her as Alice Number Two—the other Alice who'd died in that same cage with us had died a long time ago now. And Arenas wasn't anywhere nearby to roll her eyes and correct us every time we referred to Alice Number Two simply as Alice.

Crouched by my ankles, Alice Number Two struggled not to tip over by leaning on her staff. What was she trying to do? Shackle me? In her left hand, she held what looked like thick, oversized handcuffs fit for an Ogre. They were choppily cut and constructed of unpolished metal.

Who the hell had made those? I turned around,

remembering Smith, the fat blob who sat in that same tent every day, working with metal and forging weapons for the Northers.

To my surprise, she was still there, slaving away with sweat dripping down her bare back. I'd do my best to avoid traveling to the front of the tent, not wanting to watch her sagging breasts sway from side to side every time she hammered metal.

"It isn't meant to be comfortable," said Alice Number Two, finally clasping the restraints in place. "But they want these on you."

They? Why was she referring to the Northers as a separate people? She'd never done this in the past. Obviously, she wanted nothing to do with them.

Leaning her weight against her staff, she stood up. "Evenings, you get in line and someone'll tie you up... attach you and all the other prisoners together."

"What for?" I asked, though I was taking a risk by playing stupid.

She turned to me, eyed the unsightly cut on my face, and grimaced. "You need to get that re-opened up and cleaned out."

I reached for my face and she slapped my hand away.

"The infection's stuck under the scab." She turned her attention toward my cage mates. "Didn't anyone tell you how red—" But she cut herself short, no doubt realizing that no one could have possibly seen the redness inside of that cage—the sun didn't reach us. "Go see Mashi over there. She'll give you something to disinfect it. But you'll have to ask someone to peel off the scab and clean it all out for you."

Mashi... I knew that name. I followed Alice Number Two's eyes to a little Asian lady with a small black helmet for hair. She was frail-looking, though I remembered Sumi telling me how healthy she was for a sixty-something-year-old. I also remembered Sumi basically saying that Mashi was the drug dealer in the city; she'd pick up all kinds of drugs during her cultivation runs out around the city's perimeter.

Sighing, I jerked my head sideways, signaling everyone to step out of the cage. When Alice Number Two bent down to try to fasten the ankle shackle around Sammy's thick ankles, I took it from her hands and did it for her.

"What the hell are you doing?" Alice Number Two asked, but she was too weak to stop me.

"Helping."

"By shackling your own friends?" she asked.

I glanced up at Sammy, then at the rest of them. "They aren't my friends."

Alice Number Two didn't say anything. Instead, she let me fasten the shackles around the rest of them, all the while leaning on her staff and breathing hard to catch her breath. Did she visit Mashi often? Sumi had made it quite clear that any drug could be obtained through Mashi. Although I didn't believe in drugs, I hoped that Alice Number Two was taking something to ease her pain.

Finally, I shackled the last shackle around Fran's veiny, almost translucent leg, and she jumped when it clicked into place.

"How do these come off?" she asked, staring down at what now looked like giant doughnuts sitting over her feet.

Fran took a step forward and nearly fell. "They're heavy as shit. Can you believe this, Pam? Treatin' us like goddamn animals."

"They don't," said Alice Number Two.

Fran looked up at her, her wrinkled brows slanting so much it was a wonder they stayed attached to her face. "Don't what?" she said.

"They don't come off," said Alice Number Two. "Well, unless you die. Then Smith over there cuts it off your leg. Well, cuts off your leg."

Everyone's eyes bulged out. Was this some sort of sick joke?

Alice Number Two rolled her eyes. "You seriously think Smith has the intelligence to create some fancy locking mechanism and design a key? Even if she did… she doesn't have time for that. She makes them lock into place and we deal with the mess after."

I stared down at my shackles, the skin of my ankles already turning pink. They were cold, uncomfortable, and heavy. How was anyone supposed to get used to these?

"And don't go doing anything crazy, either," said Alice Number Two. "No jogging, no running... One woman kept jogging despite my warning and it chafed into her so bad that it led to an infection, and well, she's dead now."

I swallowed hard, feeling like more of a prisoner now than I ever had since arriving on Kormace Island.

CHAPTER 2

"It's pretty simple," said Alice Number Two. "You take this, you cut off some flesh"—she pointed at the dead elephant lying in the sand—"and you bring it to Bear over there. She does all the curing."

Pam, the more explosive of the two old ladies, let out a scoff. "What's she curin'? Cancer?"

Sammy rolled her eyes. "They're curing the meat... as in preserving it, dipshit."

Fran clenched two bony little fists no larger than the size of tennis balls. "Who you callin' dipshit?"

I waited for Alice Number Two to step in and warn everyone that if they took a swing, they were ending up in a death match. But she didn't say anything. Why wasn't she interfering?

Fran raised her clenched fist, two trembling balls of skin and bone, and Sammy laughed so hard that her brow ring wiggled on her face. If she wasn't careful, someone would rip that thing right out.

"Bring it on, you old hag." Sammy grinned smugly.

Fran shook her fists and took a step forward, nearly tripping over her shackles.

"All right, you two," said Alice Number Two. "You're wasting my time. And you're wasting precious meat-cutting time."

"How long's it been dead?" I asked, staring at the massive creature's bloody rib cage.

"Fifteen minutes," said Alice Number Two. "Rainer wants all the meat stripped from the body as soon as possible so it can be cured and stored before the meat goes bad."

Although I felt awful for the elephant, Rainer obviously knew what she was doing. Cured meat, as far as I knew, could easily last years if cured and stored correctly. I'd never done it myself, but I'd seen women go through the curing process with tons of sea salt.

I glanced toward Bear, a woman whose name suited her. She sat in the middle of a pile of bloody meat, her thick arms—a combination of fat and muscle—swaying in every direction as she grabbed salt, tied meat up on a wooden rack, and moved about as if she had eight arms attached to her body.

It was easy to understand why she'd chosen the name Bear. Although not as thick as a man's, a short, fuzzy beard covered her lower jaw and blended into her long, shaggy brown hair. Every time she moved, she grunted as if incapable of speaking English. Blood stained every inch of her skin, but she didn't seem to mind; she kept on working, wiping her sweaty forehead every few minutes and spreading streaks of blood onto her hairline.

She grabbed a thick slab of meat with two hands, puffed out her cheeks, and raised it into the air with a loud grunt. As she did that, two large patches of shaggy black hair made an appearance underneath her armpits.

"Here," said Alice Number Two, handing us serrated knives. "Don't be smug... Don't go cutting off pieces too big to carry. Bear doesn't need to struggle any more than she already does. Stupid women trying to prove their strength. Don't be that woman. Don't be an idiot. Also, don't go cutting each other with those. I don't give a shit how much you hate someone. If you kill them, you get stoned."

Stoned? That was new.

"What if the person doesn't die?" I asked.

It wasn't like I had any intention of stabbing someone—I simply wanted to hear Alice Number Two talk about the death match. But she didn't. Instead, she regripped her walking staff, hopped into a more comfortable position, and said, "Then count yourself lucky, I guess."

So they'd stopped that rule... Why? Was it because of their low population? It made sense, after all. Before we'd run away, there were so many people here it didn't matter if one or two died every other day. The Northers kept capturing new prisoners.

"Well?" said Alice Number Two, popping her lifeless eyes out at us. "Get your asses moving."

For the first time, I recognized her. Did she not recognize me? Although it was a good thing she didn't, I couldn't help but want to tell her it was me. I'd never do it... but part of me wanted to reassure her that she wasn't alone.

"This is disgusting," Sammy said, marching straight toward the elephant. "Why are we the ones doing this?"

"Because it's dirty work," said Alice Number Two from behind us. "And newbies get to handle the dirty work."

Another handful of women were slicing away at the elephant's flesh. It broke my heart to look at the poor creature. It lay so still with its legs crossed over top one another that it almost looked like it had been slain during a nap.

Obviously, that wasn't the case. Dozens of stab wounds penetrated its thick, wrinkled gray skin over its chest. They'd probably caused it so much unnecessary suffering.

Pam and Fran stood there looking like two old ladies waiting in line to play bingo. They didn't do much at all and instead watched everyone else.

"No way I'm touching that thing..." Fran said, pointing a bony finger toward the elephant.

"Me neither," Pam said.

Sighing, I marched past them with my knife held firmly in my hand. I'd skinned and gutted animals before—admittedly, I hadn't wanted to do it the first time, or the tenth time. But after a dozen or so kills, I'd gotten used to it. I didn't enjoy it, but it was about survival.

And I knew exactly how this place operated; if we didn't do as we were told, we'd become dispensable. Turning around, I jerked my head sideways at Fran and Pam and said, "Come here, I'll show you how," but they weren't having it. Instead, they both gave me a full up and down as if to say, *Who the hell do you think you are?*

Who was I kidding? They weren't two frightened little ladies. They were both hard-ass criminals who'd probably spent the last twenty years of their lives operating some illegal drug trafficking scheme inside prison walls.

"Your funeral," I said.

Pam breathed out so hard through her nostrils that something clicked. "What'd you say, little girl? I may be old, but I ain't—"

"What?" Sammy asked, smirking. "Deaf? Is that what you were gonna say, you old hag? You must be if you're askin' Brone here to repeat herself." She then grabbed one of the elephant's ribs and started hacking away the meat attached to it.

"You snot-faced little bitch. I could have you killed—" Pam started, but Sammy rolled her eyes and started singing some tune I'd never heard before. She then reached for a piece of meat with both hands and tore it off the bone. The loud tearing noise was like tape being pulled off a piece of plastic.

A proud grin stretched across her face as her first cut dangled in her hands.

"Done this before?" I asked.

She shook her head. "Nah, but I don't mind getting my hands dirty. Never did. My pops used to get me to put the worms on the hooks and I didn't mind it." She shrugged. "I liked it."

Did you also like burning ants with a magnifying glass, you psycho? I didn't voice my thoughts, and instead, stared at her as she hacked away. Sammy was the kind of woman who didn't give a crap about anything or anyone. Nothing seemed to bother her, not even the time we'd spent starving inside of that cage.

Why hadn't they left us there to rot like last time? The population, I thought. Why let us rot when we can be put to work with shackles around our ankles?

Unexpectedly, a familiar voice came from behind me.

"You may be old, but that's no excuse to stand

there like a bunch of idiots. You have arms and legs. Use them. Contribute. Otherwise, you're a waste of skin."

Before I could even turn around, I imagined Fran and Pam fuming with veiny fists held at their sides.

Who was brave enough to talk to them like this?

I knew who it was... I knew exactly who it was even before I caught a glimpse of her face.

I stood straight and turned around to find her standing with her chest puffed out, blood splattered across her thick neck and muscular arms, and short snow-white hair spiked upward and held together by rust-colored blood.

"Murk," I breathed.

CHAPTER 3

Her glassy blue eyes rolled toward me a bit longer than necessary, and I couldn't help but wonder if she recognized me. How was she even alive? The last time I'd seen her, she was strapped up by her wrists and forced to dangle in place while Zsasz beat her senseless.

I'd wanted nothing more than for her to be alive, but the truth was, a part of me assumed they'd killed her.

Why had they let her go?

With a long bone-constructed knife, Murk walked right in between Fran and Pam without blinking. Their hateful gazes followed her intently until Fran finally said, "Thinks she's so tough—"

And in one rapid, half-second motion, Murk swung her elbow upward and sideways, knocking Fran right in the mouth. Her head whiplashed, and she stumbled backward with both hands over her mouth.

Pam, too stunned to react, shifted her gaze between Murk, who expressed no emotion whatsoever, and Fran, who now had blood spilling out from in between her fingers.

"She—she knocked out my fucking toof!" Fran shouted.

When her hands came down, a black gap sat right in the center of her mouth where one of her front teeth had once been.

"Where'd it go?" Pam asked, searching the sand as if she'd lost a lover's ring.

"I swallowed it!" Fran said, her mouth now filling with blood. She spat out a glob and without warning, charged straight for Murk.

But Fran stopped running the moment Murk turned around and pointed her knife into Fran's throat. Fran copied Murk and raised her knife to Murk's throat. So they both stood there, challenging each other.

Unlike Fran, whose hands were trembling and face was turning a deep shade of red, Murk stood calm, staring straight into Fran's eyes without any fear whatsoever.

"You have no idea who the fuck you just messed with," Fran said.

I wasn't trying to be ageist, but watching a woman aged for retirement threaten someone at knifepoint was a bit unusual. It was easy and quite honestly delusional of me to assume that all old people were frail, uncoordinated, and for the most part, kind.

Fran was probably someone's grandmother,

yet here she was, prepared to slit Murk's throat.

I supposed Murk, too, was old enough to be a grandmother. Would that be me in forty years? Did a person truly change on the inside as they aged? It wasn't like I could discuss these things with my mom anymore.

"Let me be perfectly frank with you," Murk said. "You may have been some scum lord back in the real world... Hell, you may have even taken more lives than I can count. But out here, lady, you're nothing." She gave Fran a full up and down, the corner of her lip pulling upward. "You're new. I can smell it. I may not be able to kill you where you stand, but I can sure as hell break every frail, calcium-deprived bone in your body. I also have countless ways to make your death look like an accident."

Fran swallowed hard, forcing the tip of Murk's knife to bounce off her throat. She then grimaced and pulled away with a stomp in her step.

I stared at Murk as she moved toward the elephant. As she walked away, one thought crossed my mind: what if I could get Murk out of here? It would solve everything, wouldn't it? She could become a leader again and rebuild the Village. I sighed. Obviously, I was getting way ahead of myself.

We hacked away at the elephant for hours until the sun began to set. Every time Murk walked past me, I stared at her intently, hoping she'd look up at me. But she never did. She'd stare at the ground and ignore everyone around her.

It was like watching a workaholic on the job—she didn't care about anything other than getting the work done.

Finally, when Alice Number Two came by to tell us to go grab a bite to eat, I slowly made my way to Murk near the elephant's head. With no one around to hear me, now was my chance.

"Murk," I whispered.

Her eyes shot up at me, but the moment they met mine, she looked away.

"Murk, it's me," I said again.

She didn't answer.

Instead, she picked up her last slab of meat and started dragging it through the sand and toward Bear.

"Murk," I hissed. "It's Brone."

She dropped the meat and swung around so quickly that I flinched.

With her knife pointed at my face, she said, "I don't know you, kid. Don't ever talk to me again."

She picked up her meat and kept on walking.

Oh my God.

What had they done to her? She'd assigned me the title of Archer. I'd become one of her best Hunters... How could she not know who I was?

I watched as she walked away, the evening sun

casting a deep orange glow across her suede-covered back. It made today's fresh bloodstains on her shirt look brown and her hair yellow.

Murk, I pleaded in my head.

CHAPTER 4

We walked toward the sleeping area with full bellies and aching muscles. At least, I assumed everyone's muscles were hurting, especially if mine were.

"So this is our life?" Fran said, her words coming out with an awkward lisp.

I still couldn't believe Murk had knocked out her tooth with her elbow.

Pam shrugged. "I'll be dead soon."

"Do you two ever stop talking?" Sammy said. "You've been bickering all damn day."

"Only because of her," Fran growled, casting a hateful glare in Murk's direction.

"Well, get over it," Sammy said. "If you knew anything that didn't involve you, you'd know that Murk's Rainer's sworn enemy and she was the leader of an entire village."

Pam's eyelids went flat. "And we're supposed to care about that because...?"

"I'm just saying," Sammy said, "the bitch has been through hell and back. Two chicks were even talkin' about how Murk was tortured for months...

Like, really bad." She lowered her voice. "I'm just sayin'… she isn't someone you wanna mess with."

I was surprised to hear this coming from Sammy, who always acted like she wasn't scared of anyone. She played with her eyebrow ring and stood still when two Northers came toward us, their heavy equipment making chafing sounds as they walked.

One by one, they started tying us up at the ankles.

"What if I have to pee?" Fran whispered, now tied to another dozen women.

"Or take a shit," Pam added, looking pale.

"You shut your mouth and hold it in," came Alice Number Two's voice.

Fran grumbled something. "That's not always poss—"

"Then you piss yourself," said Alice Number Two. "But not on the bed. The wood will soak it up. And Kasey doesn't have time to make more platforms right now. She's busy enough as it is. You have enough slack to roll over and do your business in the dirt. Besides, most people don't shit at night. If you do, I feel bad for you."

Bile rose in my throat. How was anyone supposed to live like this?

No one said anything, no doubt thinking precisely what I was thinking—that being killed was more merciful than being forced to live a life of slavery here.

With dry lips and a parched mouth, I lay down on one of the poorly constructed platforms. Who was this Kasey person? Their builder? If so, she sucked. It was as if she'd taken rotten wood from the jungle, sanded away the roughest spots, and tied them together with crisp vines. Every time I repositioned myself, the logs underneath the large leaves moved.

Not only that, but every time someone moved too much, someone else would shout at them to stop, likely because the rope was yanking at their ankles.

So I lay there awake all night, staring into the darkness overhead, wondering how frightened Ellie must have been to learn I was captured and taken away from the Cove.

* * *

By the time the sun came up, I felt like I hadn't slept in a week. I shivered, wanting nothing more than to pull my legs up to my chest to preserve some of my body heat, but I knew if I did that, the rope would pull someone's shackles and I'd be yelled at.

The last thing I wanted was to make enemies, so instead, I froze all night.

"Let's go!" came an authoritative voice.

It was a Norther's voice—the voice of someone who believed themselves to be superior to all living creatures on this island. "Now!" she growled, her voice carrying through the forest's trees.

Everyone slowly sat upright on their platforms. If I'd had to guess how many women we were all together, I'd have estimated sixty or seventy. Although it looked like a big crowd, especially given that we were all tied together, it wasn't all that much compared to how many women used to be here.

One by one, we formed a line, and the Norther slipped the long rope that connected all of us out from our shackles. Both ends had been tied to a tree, and before bed, all of our knives were collected and counted.

"If you don't return this knife to me at the end of the day, you're dead," Alice Number Two had warned us yesterday. "Literally," she'd emphasized. "The Beasts will tie you up at the front of the city for everyone to watch and cut your limbs off one by one with one of these knives." She smacked one of the serrated bone knives in the palm of her hand. "It isn't a clean cut, either. You'll understand when you start trying to cut through the elephant's skin with one of these."

It hadn't looked like she was joking, and I'd swallowed hard at the thought of it.

Psycho Northers was all I could think.

While handing me the knife, she didn't let go before adding, "It's happened twice already, and no matter how much of a monster you think I am, believe me when I say it isn't fun to watch. Don't become a statistic."

"You, newbies," came Alice Number Two's voice. "To the elephant, now."

And we were back at it again as if stuck in some alternate reality—the kind in which every day repeats itself over and over again. Legs quivering, I made my way to the elephant's carcass and started hacking away.

One meal per day, I thought. How was that enough to get us through these days? I was starving and sick to my stomach, yet I'd have to wait until the evening to finally get food in my stomach. How long would we be at this? Surely, not long—the meat was probably close to spoiling out in this heat.

By the time the afternoon sun started heating our backs to an uncomfortable temperature, the cut on my face started throbbing again. When Alice Number Two walked by, I called out to her.

"Alice Numb—" but I cut myself short, realizing how stupid I'd been.

She turned around so quickly her reddish-brown hair swept through the air. "What did you just say?"

Shit.

"Numb. My face. It feels numb."

It didn't feel numb at all—quite the opposite, actually. But I had to convince her that something was wrong with my face if I wanted Mashi to help me get rid of the infection."

Her glare slowly disappeared. "Oh… Right. Yeah, go." She threw her thumb out in Mashi's direction, and I nodded before jogging away.

As I did, the shackles bounced up and down, hitting hard against my ankle bone. So I stopped, grimacing. I understood now why Alice Number Two had warned us against running.

When I reached Mashi, she sat in the dirt with a basket of vegetables and funny-looking leaves in front of her. Her dark, narrow slits for eyes rolled up inside puffy bags.

"Yessss?" she asked, her voice nasal.

Her eyes were so narrow it was impossible to tell if she was even looking at me or if they were closed.

"I was told you could help me," I said, pointing at my face.

Without a word, she raised a finger and nodded slowly, reminding me of some wise, ancient sage. She reached into another small basket behind her, her movements slower than pouring molasses, and extracted a small round bone filled with a dark green powder.

What was that? A knuckle bone? A piece of spine? It was the size of a golf ball… Maybe a rodent's skull.

She held it in the air, waiting for me to grab it.

"What is this?" I asked.

"You cut scab," she said. "Add water. Put. Put on face. Turn to paste. On wound." She pointed at my face, her finger dancing in the air as if she'd drunk ten cups of coffee.

"Right over the scab?" I asked.

She shook her head, her black helmet hair barely moving at all.

"Take off. You treat under. You treat infection. Then. Only then scab come back."

I fought the urge to touch my face. I was afraid to know how bad the cut was. And now that it had become infected, there was no doubt in my mind that I'd be stuck with some unsightly scar.

So instead, I ran my hand over my shaved head, feeling little prickles poke my fingers. It was already growing back—a soft fuzz on my head.

Once the scar had healed and my hair grew back out, would everyone recognize me? Was this infection saving me?

"*Privyet*," someone said. It came out sounding like *Pree-vyet*.

With the small golf ball-sized bone held in my hand, I turned toward the voice.

Seated across from Mashi was another person I'd completely forgotten about—Olga. In both hands, she held a hand-carved wooden bowl filled with seeds. My eye was immediately drawn to her wrinkled wrist where that Russian tattoo was printed: numerical digits, which I'd learned meant she was imprinted at a Russian orphanage.

She'd been the one to care for the Northers—the Orphans—who'd crashed in that plane after being cast away on this island as kids.

She made a come-hither motion with her index finger, though it looked more like she was scratching the air with those long, curling fingernails of hers. I took a few steps forward, hesitating. Her shaggy, salt-and-pepper hair hung on both sides of her face, covering most of her fruit-stained shirt. What did she do with that thing? Take it off and use it as a strainer? It was filthy.

"You need clean," she said, her accent as thick as it was the last time she spoke to me. She pointed at my face, and I became self-conscious about my wound.

"Vat happened to you, child?" she said, patting the dirt beside her. "Come. Olga take care of dat ugly cut on face."

CHAPTER 5

"What the hell happened to you?" Sammy asked, staring at me as if I'd shoved my entire head up the dead elephant's ass.

What did she care? And why was she even talking to me? We weren't friends. If anything, we were still enemies. She'd helped Hawkins drag me to this awful place.

I hope you're proud of yourself, I wanted to say. *For following Hawkins into a life of slavery. She's probably dead now, by the way. Either that, or they're torturing her back there*—and then I'd point toward the back of the mountain where Murk had been strapped by her arms and tortured.

But I kept my mouth shut. What was the point?

Fran and Pam turned their old, ostrich heads my way, too. Olga had warned me that there might be some swelling, especially after Mashi's paste was applied. She'd also warned me about the redness. Maybe it was a good thing that I looked like a freak—sure, people might look at me funny, but at least no one would recognize me.

What mattered was that she'd assured me the

infection was cleaned out. She said if I hadn't taken care of it, it might have spread farther on my face and gotten into my eye. She'd gone off for almost half an hour about how one of her orphan girls had nearly lost an eye because of an infection.

It was only when Alice Number Two came swearing at me that Olga hurried what she was doing and sent me on my way.

"I don't like this any more than you do," said Alice Number Two, now standing in front of all of us. "I don't want to be chasing after you guys all day. This is my job, okay? You think I like this?"

She ran two hands through her dull, orange hair, and when her fingers got stuck, she pulled them out so aggressively I was surprised no strands fell out.

"I'm not even supposed to be here..." she continued. Was she talking to me? Or all of us? Even Sammy stopped cutting into the elephant's hind leg to listen to Alice Number Two. "I mean... I was so close. I shouldn't be here. Everyone was running... They were all following that Brone girl. She ignited something in all of us. It's like she gave us the courage to do something about this shitty nightmare." She let out a broken laugh, but it was obvious she was doing it to keep from crying. "I was so... close." She reached a hand out and clasped the air in front of her as if catching an invisible insect. "But then that fucking leopard turned on me... On me! Out of all people. I wasn't even trying to protect that stupid Beast. It turned on me for no reason."

She swallowed hard, a bulge rolling down her throat, and shook her head at the sky. "Why am I even talking to you? You have no idea what the hell I'm talking about. You're all a bunch of newbies." She threw one hand in the air, stabbed her walking stick into the sand, and turned around. "Waste of time... Total waste of time."

When she disappeared behind Smith's tool tent, Sammy hacked her knife against the elephant's femur bone and looked at me. "Sounds like this Brone chick did everyone a favor."

Why hadn't she said anything? She knew who I was. Why was she protecting me?

"Do they want to use the bone for anything?" she then asked.

Murk pushed her way through, her arms soaked in blood and her hair flattened with sweat atop her head. "Just leave the bone. Alice said they'll get someone else to come clean it up after."

It was the first time Murk had said anything since yesterday.

When she caught me staring at her again, she looked away.

Did she honestly not remember me? Or, was she only trying to protect me?

Either way, I hated the feeling.

She sawed away, elbow coming in and out at her side, until a piece large enough was ready to be torn away from the bone. A ripping sound filled the air as veins and tendons snapped, and Murk pulled off a piece large enough to cover her entire torso.

She walked straight toward Bear, and several women moved out of her way.

"Big piece for such a weak woman," someone blurted out.

I turned around to see a face I'd have recognized anywhere—it was black and full of white speckles across the cheeks, forehead, and chin, almost as if a snowball had exploded in her face.

Snow Face.

The woman who, along with her clan, had bullied me and my friends—the one who'd threatened us all at knifepoint, warning us not to cause any problems inside the city. And what had I done? I'd caused the biggest problem of all. I'd worsened this place for the slaves who'd stayed behind.

"Leader of scum," said Snow Face.

She hacked and spat a glob of mucus on Murk's bare foot.

Murk ignored her and dropped her slab of elephant meat on a pile by Bear, who nodded and grunted.

What had she meant by that, anyway?

Were all of Murk's people now considered bad for everything that had happened? Was that why they'd released Murk into the general population? So that others would constantly harass her?

"You think you are so strong, but you are nothing," Snow Face continued, her thick accent making her sound native to this island.

Either that or she was shipped here from another country—maybe even a third world country.

When Murk didn't say anything or even bother to look up at Snow Face, two tall women as black as Snow Face threw their arms out in front of Murk like a bunch of preteens bullying a geek in high school.

"Get your arms out of my face," Murk said.

Snow Face's two guard dogs were so tall they made Murk look like a child.

Murk let out an irritated sigh. "Are we really going to keep doing this every day?"

"You were her leader. You did this. You are responsible," Snow Face continued, her black, soulless eyes narrowing on Murk.

"I don't know what you're talking about," Murk said calmly, more at the tall bodyguards than at Snow Face. "Now move."

Without saying anything, Snow Face took one step toward Murk and backhanded her across the face, sending Murk down onto one knee. Snow

Face then raised her overly long leg and kicked Murk right in the face, a loud click resonating around us.

"Hey!" I shouted, charging toward Murk's bullies.

With a bowed head and a twinkle in her eye, Snow Face smiled up at me. "What do we have here? Another one of your people?" She stepped over Murk and stood face-to-face with me, her bony black shoulders looking brown underneath the afternoon sun.

Her lips, thick and pale, stuck out so much it looked like she was pouting.

I wanted to say, *Back off, polka dot*, but then I realized something—I wasn't Brone. I couldn't be. Right now, I had to be someone else... someone who didn't have the courage to stand up to someone like Snow Face.

So I bit down hard on my tongue, the pain making me wince.

Don't say anything, don't say anything, don't say anything.

"Brave girl," Snow Face said. "You look familiar."

"Yo, fuck off, you stupid splatter face!" snapped Sammy. She came toward us like a girl pulled right out of a rough neighborhood—arms flailing over her head and fingers pointing at Snow Face as if firing invisible bullets out of her fingertips. She came up to Snow Face, craning her neck back to look her in the eyes, little skin rolls forming at the back of her neck. Their height difference didn't seem to bother her in the least. "You wanna start shit? 'Cause I'm ready. Right now."

Her nostrils flared so wide it was a wonder she didn't fly away with them. I'd never seen Sammy this angry before. It was like watching a steam cooker tragically explode.

At the same time, Hawkins's other two women—Scorch and Dibs, I'd learned were their names—came up beside Sammy with arms crossed over their chests as if to say, *You mess with Sammy, you mess with us.* They weren't as thickset as Sammy, but with their shaved heads, tattooed skin, and fearless scowls, it was enough to make anyone think twice.

Snow Face, along with her two guard dogs, smiled at us before walking away.

"What the hell was that about?" Dibs asked.

She then offered Murk a hand, but Murk ignored it and forced herself up with a pained wince. She rubbed at her reddening jaw and angrily tore her knife out of the sand. "You didn't have to do that."

"Yeah, we did," Sammy said, fists still clenched. "You may have been a pain in the ass as our leader, Murk, but you were still the best leader we ever had."

CHAPTER 6

The sound of wood cracking carried across the city before Zsasz's obnoxious voice came within earshot. One by now, heavily armed Northers wearing fur, metallic shoulder plates, some even chest plates, came marching out with swords fastened to their sides.

What was going on?

"Out of the way!" Zsasz shouted.

"Out of the way!" Rebel repeated, reminding me of some dumb Chihuahua trying to be a Doberman.

The massive gates continued to open until out came several women wearing typical suede clothing. Unlike the rest of us, they looked clean and well-fed. Some of them even smiled as they stepped out into the city, hands held up over their brows to block the early afternoon sun.

But what caught my attention most of all were their bellies—most of them stuck out past their breasts. Some were large and round, others small and hard-looking. A few women barely had a bump at all yet still walked with a hand held gently over their stomachs.

"What's going on?" Dibs asked, leaning into Sammy.

Sammy did the same thing to Murk, who was in the middle of chewing a piece of poorly cooked plantain. She didn't say anything and instead stared at the ground through loud chews. She hadn't spoken a word to us since Sammy had essentially announced to Murk that she was one of us.

"Serenity Day," someone said.

I turned around to find a girl likely close to my age chomping down on some braided leaf. The tip of her crooked nose was covered in dirt as if she'd tried to locate food underground.

Then, without a care in the world, she shrugged and added, "Pregnant ladies pretty much get a spa day. Guess to keep them happy, or, whatever. You know. For the babies."

Sammy scoffed. "A *spa day*?"

The brown-nosed girl shrugged again. "Yeah. The Beasts basically give them free rein every five sleeps. They even take 'em to the beach to go swimming. Not like they'd ever let us do that."

I watched as the dozen or so pregnant women crossed through the city, accompanied by Northers on either side of them. They weren't shackled at the ankles, nor were they tied to each other.

"In other words, they get sex and treated like royalty?" Dibs asked. "Why the hell didn't one of those men take me?"

"'Cause you're ugly," Scorch said.

She must have been projecting; Scorch was the one with the burn marks across her face. They reminded me of Sumi's burns—bubbly pink flesh that resembled melted rubber. The burns ran along the right side of her face, slanting her brow down into an abnormal position. It looked fairly fresh, which meant the burns had no doubt happened during the attack on our Village.

Dibs retaliated by pinching her arm and Scorch swatted back at her.

"Stop it," Sammy growled, and the two smaller skinheads stopped their childish bickering.

"One of our women was taken by those goddamn bastards," she said. "You honestly think they're taking BluJay for a joy ride? This isn't some sick fantasy. Those brutes are having their way with her and probably abusing the hell out of her."

Everyone cast their eyes to the ground until Dibs reached across Scorch's shoulder and grabbed a green banana from underneath the food tent. Today, they hadn't given us any meat, but we'd received lunch—nuts, fruit, and vegetables. It didn't make sense to me given the amount of elephant meat we'd gathered. What were they hoping to do? Cure all of it? Why couldn't they share a bit with us? Every now and then, some of the Northers came to Bear's corner to grab fresh meat and pile it up on a wooden plank fastened by ropes. They'd then open the gates and drag it inside.

So that's why the pregnant women looked so healthy—they were fed a balanced diet. The Northers were no doubt also feeding all of this meat to their growing army. I'd seen it for myself... They'd captured tons of women and brainwashed them into becoming their perfect little soldiers. They'd done such a good job at it that I could no longer tell the brainwashed soldiers from the Orphans unless I caught a glimpse of an orphan tattoo on a wrist.

They were all Northers to me; they were all Beasts.

And as for the Originals, well, I hadn't seen them since I'd come back to this god-awful place. I'd learned to tell them apart from the Orphans by the wrinkles on their faces—they were much older than the Russian Orphans being that they'd escaped with Rainer decades ago.

Where were they now? Relishing in their lavish life of luxury? Eating grapes off grapevines and sleeping in feather-constructed beds? That was the whole point of our slavery, wasn't it? So that they could enjoy their life on this island?

"Where's BluJay?" I asked, eyeing the lineup of

pregnant women.

They disappeared into the thick greenery, excited chatter bouncing off the trees.

Sammy shrugged. "Maybe they haven't managed to impregnate her yet."

I felt sick to my stomach.

"Maybe she was useless to them and they killed her," Fran said as if describing the weather.

Out of nowhere, Sammy grabbed Fran by the throat. "What'd you say, grandma?"

Without hesitation, Pam came to her friend's rescue. With a plump red face and a fist clenched so tight her knuckles looked like glass shards, she punched Sammy in the side of her shaved head, right on her ear.

Surprisingly, the impact was pretty hard—as hard as a punch delivered by someone far younger. It made a loud clapping sound, and Sammy's head shook as she stumbled back, reaching for her ear.

"Yo, what the hell—" she started, looking disoriented.

As she tripped over her own feet, her elbow jabbed Snow Face in the back of the ribs.

Slowly, Snow Face turned sideways to spot the person stupid enough to touch her. Where had she come from? I hadn't even noticed her standing there.

She didn't have to say anything. Her eyes, hateful slits with webbed wrinkles on either side, shifted between Sammy and all of us.

"What da hell are you lookin' at?" Fran said, her missing upper tooth still causing her speech problems.

Snow Face's stare lingered on Fran for a few seconds, but she didn't say anything. What was she thinking? Was she planning something?

When she didn't look away, Sammy puffed up with fists clenched at her sides and her chest sticking out farther than her face. "What's your problem, coke face? Piss off!"

Snow Face, along without her regular crew, simply smirked at Sammy. It was impossible to read Snow Face, which made her that much more unpredictable. Did she have it in her to attack someone? Or, was she all talk?

Finally, her deep, monotone voice carried over our heads. "You are foolish to make enemies here."

Sammy scoffed. "You're the one who's *foolish*."

Her last word came off in a mocking tone as if no one had used it in over a century.

Again, Snow Face smiled at her but didn't say anything. Instead, she turned away and made her way through the crowd and toward the city's center tents.

"Dumb bitch," Sammy muttered.

"I wouldn't go trying to make enemies with her," I said.

Sammy looked at me like I was as stupid as

Snow Face.

"Brone, if you let people walk all over you, that's exactly what they'll do."

"Brone?" Pam said, her thin, overplucked eyebrow rising past her brow bone. "You're Brone? That girl everyone keeps talking about?"

My stomach sank.

CHAPTER 7

"Whoa, easy tiger," Pam said, a raspy chuckle coming out of her rotten mouth.

How was any of this amusing? This was my life we were talking about. I refastened my grip around the collar of her shirt and pushed her even harder into the tree's coarse bark.

"I'm not threatening you," she said. "All I ask is for a fair exchange."

I turned my head sideways and glared at Sammy, who seemed a bit embarrassed that she was the reason this was happening.

Obviously, Pam wasn't willing to let go of this new information... Not without getting something out of it. And beating her wouldn't solve any of my problems. The more she hated me, the more likely she was to tell everyone who I was to get revenge.

I shoved myself off of her and the back of her head hit the tree.

Rubbing it, she said, "No need to get aggressive, *Brone*."

I raised a fist, prepared to bash in what remained of her rotting teeth, when she elevated two submissive hands and let out a short laugh. "Okay, okay... Relax. I won't say it again."

"Why not?" Fran said. "Those big ladies are looking for her, aren't dey? Maybe this new info will buy us a ticket inside those gates. Maybe we can get some action." She then slapped both sides of her hips and with them, made a swaying motion in the air.

I grimaced.

"What?" Fran said. "Don't judge me. I haven't been laid in over terty years. A woman'll take what she can get."

Fighting the urge to roll my eyes at her, I shook my head. "This isn't going to buy you a ticket anywhere, trust me. Those Northers don't give a shit about you." She seemed offended by this, so I added, "They don't care about anyone but themselves. All you'll be doing is sentencing me to death. That's it."

Fran's eyes glazed over, and for a moment, I didn't see an older woman—I saw someone capable of slitting a person's throat without any remorse whatsoever. "And how's that our problem?"

"Because it is!" I snapped. But then, I took in a long, deep breath to recenter myself. "Look. It's my problem, not yours. But the truth is, you need me."

Pam and Fran both scoffed at the same time.

"Girl has a point," Sammy cut in.

"How the hell—" Pam started.

"This girl saved hundreds of lives," Sammy said, jabbing a finger toward me. "She did the impossible. She got women out of this shithole. Don't you realize where you are? Hasn't it hit you yet?"

"Who cares?" Pam said. "I only have a year left of my sentence—"

Sammy slapped a hand over her forehead, the clapping sound loud enough to make Pam blink. "You dumb old hag. You don't know, do you?"

"Know what?" Pam sneered.

"Sammy—" I tried.

Was it worth telling them the truth about this island? They were new here, and up till now, they'd somehow managed to remain in good spirits despite their circumstances.

"No!" Sammy snapped, her finger finding its way to Pam's face. She jabbed it so hard Pam flinched and pulled her head back. "She needs to know. They both need to know."

For the first time, Pam and Fran looked a bit worried. They withdrew into themselves, staring at Sammy's quickly swelling face.

"You ain't getting off this island, grandmas!" Sammy said.

Somehow, I wished she was a bit more poetic about it.

"Is that a threat?" Pam said, lips curling over her front teeth.

Sammy threw her head back and laughed. "It's not a threat. It's the truth. Man, how dumb are you? You think some helicopter's gonna come down here and pluck you out? You think that would even be possible?" She then twirled her finger above her head to imitate helicopter blades and started stomping the dirt with her bare feet, her eyes focused on the ground as if flying above Kormace Island. Then, with a nasal voice, she continued, "Rescue mission here. We've reached Kormace Island. Oh, look, I see Fran, right there. Oh, and that's Pam. Yeah, that's got to be them. I see their little gray heads. Looks like the pictures to me." She pointed at her toes. "Yep, that's definitely them. Let's throw a rope down there and hope those other bitches don't grab on."

"Sammy—" I tried again.

"What's that, George?" she continued. "Oh... Those are rotting bushes and not heads of hair? Damn it."

"What the hell are you saying?" Pam shouted, her age-spotted skin darkening to a deep purple.

"You're not getting out of this fuckin' place alive!" Sammy shouted back, the veins in her neck bulging out so far it was a wonder they didn't split through the skin. She was so angry with her giant eyes and her finger jabbing the air over and over again that I thought she might pass out. "You hear me? You're stuck here! Forever!"

CHAPTER 8

After Sammy had calmed down, I'd agreed to take Fran's dull meat-cutting blade.

That was it.

That was all they'd asked for after Sammy's explosive outburst. It was a good deal, come to think of it. The dullest of the blades no doubt made cutting the elephant meat twice as hard, resulting in a lower production rate and a faster burnout rate, but I could handle it—probably much better than someone Fran's age.

Fran had been stuck with that same knife the evening before and had spent all morning rubbing her arms, legs, and wrists.

When Fran handed me her blade—I knew it was the dull one because the tip of it was chipped off as if someone had abused it—I took it without saying a word.

With eyes cast at the ground, she nodded and walked toward the elephant.

Poor Fran and Pam.

Ever since Sammy had shouted in their faces, they hadn't spoken a word.

I wanted to talk to them—let them know that with time, things would get easier—but I didn't have the energy. And besides, I'd gone through this, too. What they needed was time. It had taken me quite a while to finally accept my new reality. The only thing that had helped me, however, was my delusional dream of one day getting off this island.

But these two? They were likely in their late sixties, which meant they'd already lived half their lives. Soon, their salt-and-pepper hair would turn white, and their bodies would begin to morph into weak, slouched shapes.

How could anyone survive this place at that point? Would the Northers abuse seventy- or eighty-year-olds? I had yet to see anyone that old on this island; no doubt, they had died of disease, infection, or injury.

Every few hours, the two of them looked at each other knowingly—it was a look that said, I *guess this is our life now.*

Sammy didn't seem to care that she'd basically broken them. In fact, she looked happy about it, whistling to some old tune and hacking away at the bit of remaining elephant meat. After dropping off bits and pieces of hard-to-reach meat, she came to the back of the elephant, where half of its spine was visible, and leaned into me. "Ladies think they're invincible when they don't have much time to serve. Well, on this island. Ain't like that in prison. If you don't have much time left, you keep your damn mouth shut."

When I didn't respond, she cleared her throat and jabbed her knife against one of the elephant's vertebrae. "They needed to know. Otherwise, they mighta gotten themselves killed."

I stopped cutting and glared at her.

"What the hell do you know?" I said. She released her knife, letting it sit halfway in a thick piece of muscle, and stared at me. "If you hadn't called me by my name, none of this would've happened. How can I trust you not to do that again? You do realize that if you do that in front of the wrong person, I'm looking at torture. Disgusting, inhumane torture. If they're willing to cut women's limbs off for not returning a damn knife, what the hell do you think they'll do to me?"

I was breathing so hard my shoulders were moving back and forth.

"Look, I'm sorry..." she said, averting her gaze to the ground.

I was surprised to see Sammy like this. With everyone else, she was fearless, bold, and downright arrogant. But ever since Hawkins was taken out of the equation, it was as if she'd turned to me to be her leader, which was saying a lot when Murk was always right next to us.

"You got a nickname or something?" she asked.

"If I can call you something else, this won't happen again."

I didn't have any nicknames, at least none that I was aware of, and the idea of being called Lydia didn't feel right to me. If anything, it drew me into my past, making me feel weak and vulnerable. I wasn't that person anymore, and I didn't want anyone calling me by my old name.

"Any passions? Favorite places?"

I stared into the webbed design of the elephant's skin. It looked like wrinkled clay, full of bumps and uneven lines. Did I have any passions? I couldn't remember. And what did she mean by favorite places? In the old world? It felt so distant to me. Some days, I wondered if I'd spent my whole life on Kormace Island and somehow fabricated this idea of land known as America.

I was losing my mind.

So no, I didn't have any favorites. When would I have had time to think of something I like? Every day was spent trying to survive.

"What's your favorite animal?" she asked.

I stared at her. Did I even have a favorite animal? Not really. Not since I was a kid. I hesitated, trying to remember what it was. It may have been a koala until someone told me they were incredibly vicious.

Grinding my teeth, I shook my head.

"Hey, I get it," she said. "It's hard to remember

these things… That's why I've been repeating mine ever since I landed here. It reminds me that outside of this place, I'm a person. I have *favorites*, you know? It might sound stupid, but it helps." She smiled, her rounded cheeks lifting up to form hills under her eyes. "Wanna hear mine?"

I wasn't sure I did, but she went ahead anyway. "Red zebras eating at Louisiana Steak House."

It was impossible not to smirk.

"Red zebras?" I asked.

She smiled proudly. "I love the color red. I love zebras. And I looooove"—she wiped a line of drool from the corner of her mouth—"Louisiana Steak House."

Then, something strange happened. For a split second, I felt a warm, fuzziness inside. Favorites, I thought. I'd always loved the color purple. I'd also loved green, but I'd spent the last two years surrounded by nothing but green. Purple, however, was a rare find in this jungle. Then, I thought of sloths and how they were the strangest yet cutest-looking creatures I could think of. Ever since my mom had taken me to a museum where they'd had a special baby sloth exhibition when I was nine years old, I'd fallen in love. The memory hadn't surfaced until now. I was grumpy that day because my best friend at the time had fallen ill and couldn't make it.

So I was stuck with my mom.

On this island, looking back, I'd have done about anything to go back and enjoy that day with my mom. I wouldn't complain or think about how my best friend wasn't with me. I'd be grateful to be with the one person I loved most in the world.

Why had I been such a stupid child?

"You okay?" Sammy asked.

I nodded slowly. "Purple sloths eating mom's homemade spaghetti."

She smiled. "Sloths, huh? I'm gonna call you Sloan. You know. Sloth and Brone."

Shrugging, I said, "Yeah, it's weird, but I find them adorable."

"You know we have some here."

I made my eyes go big. "What do you mean?"

"On the island," Sammy said. "I've seen one. It was chillin' out in a tree, chewing on a leaf near the Village."

And then, my face did something it hadn't done in a long time. It stretched, forming a cheesy grin. My face muscles felt foreign, like they weren't meant to move that way.

"You know they have zebras, too," I said.

Sammy punched me in the shoulder and I scowled at her, but she was so excited it was impossible to keep scowling. "Shut the front freakin' door!"

CHAPTER 9

"What're you two smiling about?" Dibs asked as Sammy and I made our way around the elephant.

Sammy flicked her wrist in the air as if to say, *Don't worry about it.*

Purple sloths, I kept repeating in my mind, and I smiled to myself, envisioning purple sloths. But then, something loud snapped behind me and I swung around, fist held up by my face.

"Relax, kid," Murk said, staring intently at me. "It was a piece of wood someone dropped."

She pointed under her foot, where a broken slab of wood lay in the sand.

Wood, I thought.

While I knew everything was fine, my heart couldn't slow down. An unusual rage built inside me and all I wanted to do was punch Murk in the face.

"Whoa, Sloan, you okay?" Sammy asked, eyes narrowing on me.

Sloan? Who the hell was Sloan? But then I remembered. Why was she asking me if I was okay?

"You're all red and shit," she said, wiggling a

finger in my face. "Here, too." Her finger came closer to my chest and I slapped her hand away.

"Don't fu—don't touch me," I said.

Raising two hands on either side of her face, she took a step back. "Hey, no disrespect. It's all good."

I wiped my clammy hands against my suede bottoms and inhaled a deep breath. A loud high-pitched frequency rang in my ears, and I fought to maintain my balance.

"What's wrong with her?" Dibs whispered. "She's actin' like my brother used to after the war in North Korea."

"That's called PTSD, you dipshit," Sammy said.

"Well, maybe that's what she has."

"You mean like everyone else on this goddamn island?"

Out of the blue, I felt like I was back in the darkness of the jungle with a fire-lit stick in my hands and with Proxy following close behind.

"It doesn't only affect veterans," Proxy had said. "A single traumatic event can trigger PTSD. Most women on the island suffer from it. In America, seventy percent of people experience or witness a traumatic event at least once in their life, and out of that seventy percent—"

I'd cut her off and asked her to keep moving because I didn't want to receive a lecture.

Now, as Dibs and Sammy bickered back and

forth about my mental health, all I wanted to do was jab one of them in the eye with my knife. Why wouldn't they shut the hell up?

"Maybe she has it worse," Dibs whispered, her voice sounding like glass shards in my ears.

"I don't have fucking PTSD!" I snapped, and everyone around me went quiet, including Bear, who stared at me from underneath bushy eyebrows, a slab of meat hanging in both hands.

Inhaling a deep breath, I regripped my knife's greasy handle and made my way around the back of the elephant. "Get back to work."

Everyone went back to work, but from the other side, sharp whispers were exchanged. Every time I looked up through the elephant's now hollow body, they turned away. I knew they were likely talking about what a head case I was, but I didn't care; I didn't care what anyone thought. I was on edge... So what? Wouldn't anyone be in my position?

But suddenly, as if turning on a television in the dark, flashes of violent images knocked me sideways, and I tripped into the elephant's carcass. I tried to catch myself against its skin but instead landed into its bloody rib cage, the warm smell of flesh filling my nostrils.

"Br—Sloan!" Sammy said, reaching in to help me.

I pulled away and my hand slipped on squishy

flesh. When I pulled my hand back, tendons and veins wrapped around my fingers. It only pissed me off more, so I swung my upper body as hard as I could and rolled out of the carcass, my clothes now stained in a rusty brown.

Why the hell were we still pulling meat off this thing? How long had it been dead now? Fifteen hours? How was that even safe?

"What's going on here?" came Alice Number Two's voice.

Through the elephant's hollow rib cage and organless body, I saw her standing next to Sammy with two arms crossed over her chest. I should have kept quiet and shut my mouth, but there was so much rage inside me that it had to come out one way or another. Feeling like I'd lost all control of my body—like I was nothing more than a spectator—I stormed around the dead animal and threw my knife by Alice Number Two's feet.

Her bright, orange-speckled eyes rolled up at me—a mixture of shock, anger, and confusion.

"This isn't safe anymore," I said. "There are fucking flies flying around the damn thing. I get that Rainer wants to preserve as much food as possible, but she's going to end up killing everyone!"

"Calm your little ballerina shoes," said Alice Number Two. "Do you think Rainer's an idiot? She knows what she's doing. She had everyone disinfect their weapons before killing the thing, and she even made sure the intestines weren't punctured to avoid having bacteria spread fast from the inside. Rainer's been on this island for over twenty years. I'd be willing to bet your mom was still wiping your ass. If you'd given me a second to talk, you'd know that I came here to tell you to finish up because we've reached the time limit. We're going to start harvesting the bones."

Feeling stupid, I bent down and tore my knife out of the sand.

Who was I to argue with someone like Rainer? I may have been a Hunter, but I knew nothing about the whole meat curing or storing process. All I did was kill the animal and help tie it up to bring it home—that's it. Although tempted to apologize for blowing a fuse, I didn't.

Maybe it was pride, or maybe it was my unwillingness to further embarrass myself.

So instead, I avoided eye contact.

"There are some good bones over here, Sloan," Sammy said, obviously trying to break the awkward silence. "Why don't you help me out?"

Alice Number Two stared at me until I turned away. As I did, my feet sliding in blood-soaked dirt, a loud shriek filled the air around me, kicking my adrenaline into overdrive again. With bulging eyes, I followed the sound to find Zsasz dragging a woman in the sand by the wrist.

But it wasn't any woman—it was an older woman with long curly white hair, loose veiny skin, and arms so thin I feared they might snap in Zsasz's grip. Behind them, another older woman with gray hair ran with two balled fists swaying over her head.

"Stop it! You stop it!"

Without warning, Zsasz swung around so fast that a disturbing snap echoed, and the woman she was dragging cried out in pain. "My arm!"

Without letting go, Zsasz said, "Oh, shut your trap, you old *ved'ma*."

The woman chasing Zsasz finally caught up to her and blasted her fists against her chest. It was like watching a four-year-old try to fight off an abusive father—she didn't stand a chance. Zsasz stood there, staring down at the frail-looking woman as if amused by her attempt.

"She has osteoporosis!" the woman shouted, fists still banging against Zsasz's armor.

"Osto—what?" Zsasz said, her head bowed at a 90-degree angle to look at the woman.

The injured woman in the sand yelped, trying to pull her broken arm out of Zsasz's tight grip.

"Jazz! Iron Tits!" Pam shouted, lunging forward.

At the same time, Alice Number Two threw her arm out, knocking Pam right in the mouth and into the bloody sand.

"Hey!" Fran said, coming to Pam's defense.

"You go out there, you're dead," said Alice Number Two. "You hear me? I don't care who those women are to you. Don't get involved if you want to live."

Pam rubbed her bloody lip and glared up at Alice Number Two.

"That's Iron Tits out there." She pointed at the woman standing up to Zsasz, and it was easy to understand where she'd received the nickname. Although frail-looking, her wrinkled chest was three times the size of her head. Obviously, she'd gotten implants at some point in her life. Pam then pointed at the woman in the sand. "And Jazz. They're like sisters to us. We already lost Smith. We can't just—"

"You can, and you will," said Alice Number Two.

Zsasz pushed Iron Tits away from her, and she tumbled backward and fell into the dirt. Without warning, Zsasz turned around, raised her boot, and smashed it into Jazz's face. The cracking sound was so loud, so disturbing, that there was no doubt in my mind she was dead.

"Jazz!" Iron Tits shouted. She rose to her knees, and with her fingers wrapped in her hair, screamed as loud as she could. "Why—why would you do that? Oh my God... Why? Why would you—"

"We don't keep people with disabilities," Zsasz said plainly. "They're useless and they eat our food."

Iron Tits glared up at Zsasz as if prepared to rip out her eyes with her bare hands. "You fucking idiot! She had osteoporosis! She wasn't disabled, you dumb stump! What kind of idiot—"

In one swift motion, Zsasz drew out a long, metal sword from a holster on her hip and sliced it straight through Iron Tits's neck. Her head made a thumping sound as it landed on the sand, and slowly, her body fell to the side.

All of a sudden, time seemed to slow.

I glanced sideways to see Fran's reaction—eyes so bulged they seemed to stick out farther than her cheekbones, and a wide-open mouth with white froth forming at the corners.

Any second, sound would come out.

Quickly, I grabbed her as hard as I could, bringing her down into the dirt with me, and flattened a hand over her mouth to keep her from crying. At the same time, Sammy jumped on top of Pam, forcing both her hands over her face.

We wrestled in the dirt for several minutes, the sound of Pam and Fran's muffled shouts and feet kicking in the sand echoing around us. As we struggled to keep them quiet, Alice Number Two, Dibs, Scorch, and even Murk stood in front of us, blocking us from Zsasz's view.

CHAPTER 10

The city continued to vibrate as it did every evening—women were scattered around the food tent chatting and eating as shackles clanged against shackles, and shouts were exchanged as arguments broke out. For the most part, everyone spoke about Jazz and Iron Tits, reenacting the whole event with invisible swords and the word osteoporosis being brutally butchered.

"Ostee-oh-prosees!"

"It's osteoporosis, you dumb twit!"

"What's that?"

One woman then slapped the one next to her upside the head. "What'd they teach you in school?"

A woman resembling a porcupine, with hair so erect it could surely be used as a weapon, made a slicing motion in the air and laughed when someone threw a watermelon in the dirt and it rolled a few inches.

What the hell was wrong with them?

At the same time, a dark-sandaled foot came blasting down on the watermelon, pulverizing it into slimy red mush.

"Hey!" shouted the porcupine woman.

"Have some respect," growled Snow Face.

Although she didn't look our way, I was certain she'd seen Fran and Pam huddled close together, their eyes pink and puffy and their faces glistening with tears. They refused to eat supper, and instead, stared at the pink sand where Iron Tits's head had been only minutes ago.

One of the Northers had come to clean up the mess.

"Oh, relax," said the porcupine woman, neck craned back so she could look Snow Face in the eyes. "We just havin' a bit o' fun here. Ain't that right, ladies?"

The women around her, a group I'd have imagined to find in an insane asylum, nodded their heads like a bunch of bobbleheads.

"This is not fun," Snow Face said, pointing a finger millimeters away from Porcupine's right eyeball. "Two women lost their lives today." Finally, her eyes rolled our way. "Some women are grieving."

Porcupine glanced toward us, shamefully bowing her head.

"Go!" Snow Face shouted, and the bobblehead crew scattered in opposite directions. When they were out of sight, Snow Face slowly turned toward us, placed a fist over her heart, and tipped her head forward. She didn't have to speak—it was obvious what she was saying: *I'm sorry for your loss.*

Taken aback by her gesture, I acknowledged her wordless condolences with a quick nod. Why had she defended Fran and Pam? Why had she taken our side? The other day, she wanted us dead.

"There's a bit of food left," came Alice Number Two's voice.

No one looked up at her but me.

"I have extra," she continued, raising a wooden bowl filled with fruit. "You sure you guys don't want any?"

I wanted to thank her for what she'd done—thank her for caring about us. But I was too angry about what had happened for my words to match my thoughts. "What're you doing here?"

She tilted her head and scratched it.

"Why're you helping us, Alice? You aren't one of us. You're one of them. You aren't shackled. You get to walk around all fucking day making sure everyone else is working. So why'd you do it? Why'd you help us? What are you hiding? You trying to get some information out of us? Information you can take back to those monsters?"

Why was I lashing out at her? She'd done nothing but try to protect us. Yet, here I was, directing my anger at the only person who could make our lives somewhat tolerable in this hellhole.

She parted her lips to say something but closed

her mouth, shook her head, and scoffed. "You know what? I don't know why I'm helping. If anything, it's going to get me killed. I don't need this." She threw the bowl of fruit into the dirt and a handful of blackberries rolled out.

Sammy bent forward, plucked them off the ground, and threw some into her mouth. "Thanks," she said, her mouth full. When Alice Number Two stormed off, she threw a blackberry at my face.

I flinched when it hit my lip and slapped the air in front of me, no doubt looking like a total loser.

"Why the hell'd you do that?" Sammy said. "She didn't do anything wrong."

Scorch and Dibs didn't seem too impressed with me, either. Fortunately, Murk wasn't anywhere around. I was happy about that; the last thing I wanted was her bright, judgmental gaze fixated on me.

"That was stupid," Scorch said.

I was surprised to hear her talk. Her voice, a bit raspy yet still feminine, suited her small-featured face and thin figure. "Alice is the one who tells us what to do all day. She's probably gonna have us doing all the crappy work from now on."

I wanted to apologize—I honestly did. But the words weren't coming out. Inside, I was fuming. How could so many women, including myself, stand around as lives were being taken? Was it shock? Fear of reprisal? Fear of death? Or, was it intelligence? Was it knowing that we were outnumbered?

"Let's hope she doesn't take it out on us," Sammy said.

I shoved the rest of my coconut into my mouth and walked away. Behind me, the whispering continued, but I didn't care. Maybe later, I'd care... But right now, all I wanted to do was go to sleep and never wake up.

As I kicked through the dirt, the image of Iron Tits's head rolling like a bowling ball flashed in my mind. What kind of higher power, or God, would allow anyone to end up in this miserable place twice in their lifetime? Better yet, what kind of God allowed a monster like Zsasz to exist on this planet?

There was no God.

There was no afterlife.

There was nothing.

I went to sleep that evening without saying a word to anyone. Everything around me felt like a distant, obscure realm. Women whispered, others shouted, but it all sounded the same to me.

Closing my eyes, I inhaled the jungle's moist, earthy air and prayed to a God I didn't believe in.

Don't let me wake up. Don't let me wake up. Don't let me wake up.

CHAPTER 11

"Wake up, you worthless swine!"

A woman next to me grunted when a boot came blasting into her rib cage.

"I said, get up!"

I jolted upright to avoid being the next one to get the boot. One by one, everyone started rising from their poorly constructed beds. I stretched sideways, then backward, until my lower back cracked loudly. Had I even slept? My eyelids, flat and heavy, barely moved as I looked around.

At one end, a Norther wearing a weapons belt with a long, metallic sword bent down, untangled the rope, and let it drop into the dirt. At the other end, a third Norther pulled on the rope, making it slither between our ankles until we were all freed.

The usual gang found their way to me—I wasn't sure why after the way I'd behaved the day before. Somehow, they still seemed to think I was their leader.

"What're we working on today?" Sammy asked. "Elephant bones?"

I was about to shrug when a loud, explosive

voice made my earlobes vibrate.

"There they are!"

Zsasz.

I swallowed hard, feeling a tight knot in the pit of my stomach. Her heavy boots stomped through the jungle's moist earth as she made her way over to us. Beside her, Rebel followed, her narrowed eyes darting in every direction as if trying to shoot lasers at the prisoners, her arms swaying too far away from her body.

"What's going on?" said Alice Number Two, practically jogging to keep up with Zsasz's long strides. Her eyes shot my way, and for a moment, she looked afraid.

"Who are you looking for?" she repeated.

At once, I felt awful for having lashed out at her. It was clear she wasn't on their side; she looked afraid of who Zsasz might harm.

"Zsasz, what's going on?" she continued.

"Those four," Zsasz said, pointing a scarred finger at me, Sammy, Scorch, and Dibs.

Oh God... Someone had ratted me out. Now, Zsasz wanted my followers and me. I swung around to find Fran and Pam, but when I did, they were standing next to each other with overly slouched postures and terrified looks on their faces.

It couldn't have been them.

After what had happened to their friends, no

way would they have wished that upon anyone. Unless they were upset about how we'd stopped them from going after Zsasz. Was that it?

I didn't have time to figure out what was going on. With a grip stronger than I'd remembered, Zsasz grabbed me by the back of the neck with one hand, and Sammy with the other. Rebel did the same to Scorch and Dibs, who both winced and raised their hands on either side of their faces.

"What'd we do?" Scorch said.

"What's going on?" Sammy asked.

Zsasz shook her hard. "Keep your mouths shut."

As we walked past Alice Number Two, she bit her bottom lip and shook her head—a look that said, *I'm so sorry... I have no idea what's going on.*

Zsasz's grip tightened as we moved toward Rainer's large wooden gates. As we drew nearer, two women on either side waved their arms and the massive doors slowly swung open.

Fuck.

Were we about to be used as reproductive cattle? So many thoughts rushed through my mind, including the idea of turning around, snatching Zsasz's holstered knife, and stabbing her in the neck. I'd likely die trying, and I'd definitely die if I succeeded, but no way would I ever allow anyone to use me for reproductive purposes... I would have preferred death.

"What's going on?" I asked, my morning voice husky.

Instead of responding, Zsasz dug her fingers so hard on either side of my neck that a searing pain shot up into my skull. It didn't take a genius to know that meant, *Shut the hell up.*

The moment we entered the gates, it was like traversing into another realm. The grass, covered in morning dew, was so vividly green it looked edible. The wooden cabins that were once lined up in front of the mountain remained intact, looking even more sturdy than before. One by one, pregnant women emerged from the cabins at the far back, and from the others came the Originals. I knew it was the Originals by their tired and aching postures.

Out from the other side of the mountain came a few armed Northers carrying bows, spears, battle sticks, and axes. Rubbing their eyes, they made their way toward the same training grounds that were there when I'd last passed through here.

What did they do? Train all day? Most likely.

Zsasz grumbled something and pushed us when we slowed down to look at everyone. "Keep it moving."

When I tried to look at Sammy, Zsasz's boot caught me in the ankle, right under my shackle, and I let out an involuntary whimper.

What I would give to kill her... to rid this world

of such a monster.

Instead of fantasizing about the gruesome, inhumane ways of killing her, I inhaled a long breath and focused on moving one step at a time. I hated this feeling so much. It was worse than having a knife held to my throat. At least during such a circumstance, only two options existed—life or death. Now, however, things were uncertain. It was the unknown that scared me most of all... more than pain, more than violence, more than anything.

We were led up small wooden steps and into a hole in the mountain. The tunnel itself was much smaller than Murk's quarter under the waterfall, and it smelled of salt, dirt, and damp stone. Ahead of us, two Northers led the way with torches in the air. They were both so tall that they had to slouch to keep moving.

No one dared to speak a word as our feet crushed the cavern stone beneath us. Instead, we continued deeper and deeper, making me want to projectile vomit the remains of my previous night's supper.

I knew precisely where we were headed—Rainer's lair.

CHAPTER 12

She was as frighteningly beautiful as I remembered—long black hair tied up high and held atop her head by a metal clasp, piercing emerald eyes outlined with black ashy powder, and a fur scarf wrapped around her neck and shoulders. As we entered, she stood up, a sly smirk making her look even more stunning.

It was easy to imagine how women followed her mindlessly—she stood with shoulders drawn back, chest heaved pridefully, and chin elevated so high she exuded absolute dominance.

"This is them?" she said, her voice calm and calculated.

Zsasz fastened two hands behind her back and nodded like a soldier.

"Thank you, lovely," she said, sweeping past Zsasz and rubbing a heavily ringed finger along her scarred jaw.

Zsasz cast her eyes to the ground like a timid dog being praised for good behavior.

A deep grumble resonated from behind her, and only then did I notice the two men sitting on either side of Rainer's chair. Their dark eyes lingered on me as I watched them. Their chests, completely bare and smooth, resembled Rainer's complexion—a silky, tan olive. For bottoms, they wore skirtlike wraps made of stringy fabric that hung on either side of their thick, muscular legs.

How old were they? Nineteen? Twenty? They appeared to be my age.

Their light eyes were traced with the same charcoal powder as their mother's—that, combined with their attire and fearless gazes, made them look like ancient Egyptian gods. Short dark hair sat atop their heads and blended with the hair on their faces; their beards ran down their jawlines and hung from their chins, something I hadn't seen in a long time.

Out of nowhere, Rainer appeared in front of me, her penetrating gaze inspecting every inch of my scar. She then moved along to Scorch, Dibs, and Sammy, eyeing them from head to toe. What did she want with us? With my gaze still fixated on the two young men at the back, I swallowed hard.

At that moment, I was more afraid of them than I was of Rainer.

"I see you watching my sons," Rainer said, her metallic plates clinging together as she turned to face me again. "Are you interested?"

Interested? What the hell was that supposed to mean? Did she honestly think we were such animals? That we, as females, became weak and filled with desire in the presence of males? I glanced sideways at Sammy, who didn't make eye contact. She appeared as uncomfortable as I was.

Dibs, on the other hand, smirked, revealing a silver tooth where her canine one had once been.

How was any of this okay? A psychopath was standing in front of us, wielding a sword forged from a plane's remains and basically asking us if we wanted to mate with her sons. What the hell did Dibs have to smile about?

Had it been that long for her?

Rainer arched an eyebrow at Dibs, who was now licking her lips. "Sorry... Too short."

Dibs's smirk evaporated in the blink of an eye. She scowled at Rainer, seemingly offended by the comment.

"I require a certain... body type," she said, gliding her fingers down Dibs's neck. Then, with her index finger, she pushed Dibs's lip up to reveal her rotting teeth. "Your teeth indicate you have weak dental genes..."

"You mean like everyone else on this island?" Dibs said, Rainer's finger still in her mouth.

Rainer pulled her hand away and turned around. "I haven't brought you here for reproductive purposes. I already have women carrying children."

I wanted to say, *Then why the hell are we here?*

but decided it best to keep my mouth shut. I also made a point to keep my head bowed as low as possible. If Rainer recognized me, she'd pull that sword out of its holster and slice my head right off. Our last encounter was less than desirable and even though she'd allowed me to live, she'd only done so to protect her image as a merciful leader to her people.

I was willing to bet she didn't give a damn about being merciful anymore—not after what had happened. Not after I'd taken more than half her city away from her.

Rainer turned to Zsasz and the others who'd brought us here and nodded as a way of saying, *You're dismissed.*

Obviously, Rainer didn't need much protection—she could take care of herself.

"Isaac," she said, turning to the man sitting on the right.

He sat up straight, his pectoral muscles large and round, and waited to receive an order.

Without saying anything, she flicked her finger toward the corner of the room. Whatever it meant, Isaac understood it. Clasping both hands around his wooden chair's armrests, he pulled himself up.

All of a sudden, I felt small.

His torso was long and perfectly defined with over a dozen abdominal muscles bulging out. His skin was so smooth-looking it glistened underneath the fire's glow. He took a step forward, and I felt the vibrations of his weight under the pads of my feet.

As he turned around, I was taken aback by all the muscles bulging through the skin of his back. Were those even muscles, or deformations? I'd never seen so much of it in my life. What was she doing to these men? Having them train every hour of every day?

Slouching forward, he plucked a torch from one of the sconces and disappeared through a narrow passageway in the wall, the orange glow diminishing as he moved.

Everyone stood silent, waiting.

Finally, the orange glow returned and out came Isaac with a small woman at his side. When he stepped out, I realized he had her by the arm—it was like watching a father drag his disobedient daughter out of a birthday party. She hung there, barely responsive, her matted blond hair masking half her bloody face.

It was only when they broke out into the light of the room that I recognized her disfigured face.

Hawkins.

"Hawk—" Sammy started, but I nudged her in the ribs.

I wasn't sure what Rainer was up to, but I was willing to bet she was going to use Hawkins against us, which meant it was important we didn't react.

Rainer walked across the room with one hand behind her back and the other holding a round stone. At the same time, Isaac tied Hawkins's hands behind her back and pushed her to the ground.

"Does this woman look familiar to you?" Rainer asked, bending forward and pulling Hawkins's head up by the hair.

Hawkins coughed a glob of blood through two missing front teeth. Her nose, which was once average in size and only slightly crooked at the bridge, was now twice its size. It sat so crookedly it was as if someone had taken vise grips and pulled it sideways.

Sammy parted her lips to speak but must have sensed my preparedness to launch another elbow in her ribs. So we stood there silently, staring at Hawkins.

"I'm going to ask you one more time," Rainer said, her voice frighteningly calm. "Do you know this woman?"

When we didn't answer, Rainer's grip tightened around the stone and her knuckle cracked. Why was she so angry? Was it cooperation she was after? And why ask us if we knew her? She knew we knew—why else bring us in here?

Just as she raised the stone above her head, prepared to smash it into Hawkins's face, I said, "Yes, we do."

CHAPTER 13

A loud snap carried throughout Rainer's lair, and Hawkins bellowed in pain. Her head then fell forward and hung there as she sobbed, her finger bent sideways. She tried to reach for it, but Isaac kicked her arm away.

Smiling, Rainer turned to us. "This doesn't have to be complicated."

She raised the C-42 Transponder and shook it gently in the air. "One of you knows what this is, and you're going to tell me."

Hawkins's pleading eyes rolled toward me. Dozens of cuts ran across her forehead, her cheeks, and her chin. Beneath both her eyes were swollen black circles, no doubt the result of her broken nose. If Rainer had brought us in here to learn about the transponder, obviously, Hawkins wasn't spilling.

Rainer arched both eyebrows and turned to Isaac. Without any facial expression, he took a step forward, prepared to break another one of Hawkins's fingers.

"Wait!" Scorch said, and Hawkins's hateful eyes

rolled toward her.

Slowly, Rainer turned, observing Scorch from her peripheral as if waiting to determine whether her information would be enough to stop her from ordering another break.

"It—it's a communication device."

Isaac stared at Rainer, waiting for her command. Then, without warning, she nodded, and Isaac moved in on Hawkins.

"No!" Hawkins shouted.

"What are you doing?" Sammy yelled. "Scorch just told you what it is!"

Rainer swung around so fast her long ponytail swept through the air. "I know it's a fucking communication device, you idiots. You don't think I already pulled that out of her? I received that information after I pulled out the second tooth." Her lips curved upward, a sadistic glimmer in her eyes. Under Hawkins's upper lip, two dark holes sat where her teeth had once been. Along the gumline was a white, pasty texture, likely infection spreading. "I want to know how it works," Rainer continued. "Every time I press this damn button, nothing happens."

She went ahead and pressed the button she was referring to. "Who is this?" she asked, lips touching the transponder's speaker. Holding the transponder in her palm, she stared at the cavern's orange ceiling, waiting.

Nothing happened.

How come? Was the man at the other end ordered to take commands only from Hawkins? Why wasn't he speaking back? Was he no longer there? Had the communication been altered? Or, was it because we were standing inside a mountain? At this point, did that matter? We were miles and miles away from the outside world. It was highly unlikely that a bit of stone would get in the way of such an advanced piece of equipment.

Rainer growled and held the communication device above her head as if prepared to smash Hawkins in the face with it. But, likely realizing she didn't want to break it, she inhaled a long breath with eyes closed. Soon, as if turning on a different personality, she smiled and started pacing across the room.

"Your beloved leader used this piece of equipment to get close to me." She shook it gently in the air. "She thought that if I were intrigued enough, I'd drop my guard. What was it you promised me, Hawkins? More women? Unlimited resources? Advanced weaponry?"

I stared at Hawkins in disbelief. She was nothing but a liar. She'd promised me freedom, and now, she was promising Rainer precisely what she wanted. All that woman did was play on people's desires. Would it have been so bad to let Rainer beat her to death? Despite my hatred for Hawkins,

I hated Rainer more. And even though I despised Hawkins, I would have never wished for her to be tortured.

No one deserved that... Not even Rainer, who I considered my worst enemy. Death, maybe... But torture was unnecessary. It was cruel and barbaric.

Rainer scoffed and continued pacing across the room. "What was it you said? That you had a way to communicate with a man on the outside? Someone capable of providing supply drops? And then what did you do, Hawkins?"

Hawkins didn't say anything. Instead, her eyes rolled toward us, almost as if pleading with us to keep our mouths shut. Did her women know the truth? What was the truth, anyway? Did she actually have the ability to control the man at the other end? Were perhaps supply drops truly a possibility?

I clenched my teeth.

No way.

Hawkins was a manipulative con artist. Something was up.

"Cat got your tongue, Hawk? Tell your women what you tried to do."

Again, Hawkins kept quiet.

Suddenly, Rainer swung an open hand across Hawkins's face and then plucked a small, handheld stick from the side of her thick weapon belt and brought it close to Hawkins's right eye. The tip of the stone was covered in a black, gooey substance, and the stone was fastened to the crooked handle by frayed rope.

The Ogre stick... The same Ogre stick Collins had accidentally sliced into Stash, the poison killing her instantly.

Although tempted to glare at Hawkins, I didn't react. How could she have missed her mark? The whole reason we'd come here—the whole reason she'd dragged me along—was to carry out her plan to kill Rainer.

But she'd failed.

And now... what? We were left to deal with her mess? What did she expect from us? To protect her? To get her out of this?

"One of you knows how to operate this thing..." Rainer said, her piercing eyes rolling our way. She stiffened her back and rested her hand on the handle of her long, metallic sword hanging at her side. "And you're going to tell me exactly how it works."

CHAPTER 14

Dibs stared at the transponder in her palms as if looking at a dying mouse. She shook the gadget from side to side and attempted to pass it along to someone else. "I—I don't know," she said. "I know there's a guy Hawk talks to. That's all I know."

"That's all you know?" Rainer said, leaning so close into Dibs that Dibs took a step back. Rainer wasn't overly tall, but the way she stared was enough to make anyone feel half her size.

Dibs nodded quickly, and Rainer pinched the bridge of her nose. In one unpredictable move, Rainer tore her sword out, and with both hands, and stabbed it upward through Dibs's torso, right between her rib cage.

Scorch shouted and bolted toward Rainer, but Sammy threw an arm out to block her.

Dibs fell to her knees, dark blood pouring out from her mouth. When Rainer pulled the sword out, a disturbing ripping sound bounced off the cavern walls.

Dibs fell flat on her face, the cartilage of her nose crunching against the stone ground.

Rainer pulled her boot away in time to avoid Dib's pooling blood from touching her and nodded at Isaac, ordering him to break another one of Hawkins's fingers. The snap made me grimace, but it was Hawkins's high-pitched scream that made my stomach sink.

"I'm not in the mood to play games," Rainer said. She walked around Dibs's body, picked up the transponder, and threw it into Scorch's hand. She caught it as if she'd caught a ball of fire, allowing it to bounce in her palms a few times.

"You're up," Rainer said.

Scorch swallowed hard, a bulge rolling down her throat. "I—I don't know what you want from me. We already told you what we know."

When Hawkins's eyes narrowed into dark slits, Scorch raised a trembling hand by her face.

"He... he probably only responds to her voice," Scorch said.

She leaned her head forward to inspect the gadget, the burned side of her face a bright pink underneath the flickering flames around us.

Rainer twirled the handle of her sword, its sharp tip scraping the stone floor by her feet. She paused, sealed her lips tight, and eyed the transponder. Was she allowing Scorch's information to sink in? Was it making sense to her?

Without warning, she raised her sword and Scorch shrieked, raising her arms over the ugly grimace on her face.

At the same time, I did something without thinking.

I lunged in front of Scorch and shouted, "Wait!"

With her sword held up by both hands, Rainer froze midair. "What?" she hissed.

"She's telling you everything she knows," I said. "Hawkins didn't give us any details. I swear. We know as much as you do. Can I look at it? I'm the youngest one here, which means I might be more familiar with this kind of technology."

Slowly, Rainer lowered her sword and elevated her chin. Without a word, she jerked her head sideways, signaling Scorch to hand me the device. With shaky hands, Scorch gave it to me, the sweat of her palm soaking the device's metal shell.

What the hell was I doing? I knew what I was doing… trying to buy more time. But at what cost? My life? Rainer would have killed Scorch, and afterward, it would be my turn to give her information that I didn't have.

This way, I'd saved Scorch.

Then, as if reading my mind, Rainer pointed her sword at Scorch. "Figure it out, or she dies."

Her voice became distant and muffled as if she were speaking with a cloth over her mouth. At that moment, all I cared about was figuring out how the transponder worked. I slid my index finger over its buttons, along the small-holed speaker, and up across the thick, rubber antenna.

"Well?" Rainer spat.

I didn't respond. Instead, I flipped the transponder around and stared at the engraving at the bottom.

In perfect font, between two small silver screws, was the word *Malvric*. Whatever, or whoever Malvric was, the name had been imprinted during production. The company name? The brand? I recognized the name. Where did I recognize it from? Was it military? And then, I noticed something else. The back plate of the device was a different color than its body. They were both black, but the shading was different. Why?

I popped my head up to look at Rainer. "Do you have a small knife?"

She smirked, almost as if amused by my boldness.

"Why would I give you a weapon?" she asked, still smiling.

With flat eyelids, I pointed at her sword. "Do you actually think I'm going to try to kill you when you have that thing pointed at us? Unless you have a screwdriver, I need a knife. The sharpest one you have."

"Wh-what're you... doing?" Hawkins growled.

Without being ordered to do so, Isaac stepped forward and kicked Hawkins to the ground. She let out a whimper when her jaw smashed against the floor.

Rainer didn't bother turning around. "Keep your mouth shut, Hawkins."

She reached behind her back, extracted a small curved knife no larger than a butter knife, and handed it to me. Using its tip, I twirled the screws out of place and slowly lowered myself to the ground. Carefully, I flipped the transponder over to allow the screws to fall out and caught them before they rolled away.

The only reason I knew what I was doing was that I'd taken apart my microcomputer when my cat knocked it into the kitchen sink full of dishes and water. I hadn't paid the extra money to waterproof it, so in a panic, I took it apart to dry off the interior components.

I had no idea what I'd find inside this transponder, but the difference in plate colors made me wonder if something was hidden inside. It almost looked as if someone had replaced the back plate.

Carefully, I pried the device apart to reveal microchips, small wires, and little metallic components inside. My heart racing, I raised the open device to eye level and inspected every bit. The last thing I wanted to do was damage it—if that happened, I was done for.

Surprisingly, no one spoke, not even Rainer. It

was as if everyone in the room was holding their breath, afraid that one wrong move would destroy the transponder completely.

And then, I saw it. Underneath one of the flat blue chips was another set of engraved words. They were so tiny that I had to bring my eye right up to the device.

Silverback Tech Inc.

Toys in America

900154999564

Oregon, USA

Silverback Tech—I knew who they were. They weren't some secret military organization. Hell, they weren't even military. They were a new electronics company that had come out in 2082 when I was a preteen and that had launched the very first VC Ring (short for Voice Command). I'd saved up for months to order my very first command ring—a small, silver ring with voice recognition technology that controlled intelligent software. My mom didn't have enough money to buy all of the advanced AI machinery, which included pretty much anything and everything such as lights, television, appliances, doors, recliner sofas, thermostats, and even vehicles. The only decent thing I had was the light in my room. My mom had bought it for my birthday, so every night when I went to sleep, I'd say, "Turn off the lights," and my room would go dark.

Apparently, the command ring was the next best thing to some of the most popular competition out there. It was small, portable, and incredibly advanced. For people who had a lot of money, they were able to control their gadgets anywhere they went—their vehicles, their garage doors, their exterior lights. They could even control items inside their home if they were away. In one memorable advertisement, a man wearing a fancy suit and of course his VC Ring was seen driving some expensive car down a newly paved highway. The sun setting behind him filled his car with a purple glow, and he kept tightening his knuckles around his steering wheel, obviously in a rush to get home.

"Lights on," he'd said, and his car's headlights turned on. "Make ravioli for supper," he said, and the camera's view switched to the interior of his home. There, his stove light lit up, as did his fridge, and his appliances went on to make supper.

At the end of the video, his wife and children came home to a fresh-cooked meal, and cheerful music started playing. I'd never be able to afford appliances like that, I thought at the time, but it was fun to dream about.

So as I stared at the small text imprinted inside the transponder's interior, specifically at the Toys in America line, which was Silverback Tech's toy production line, it all made sense to me.

On the inside, where the buttons sank into the device, were small icons beside each one. Three of them specifically jumped out at me.

Play.

Pause.

Record.

On the outside, the buttons had no labels or logos—they were plain black, which made it impossible to know what you were pressing.

This thing wasn't some advanced transponder or communication device capable of communicating with the outside world—in fact, it wasn't even a transponder at all. It was a children's recording device reshaped to look like some military gadget.

Hawkins was playing us all.

PART FOUR

PROLOGUE

The classroom smelled of cheap perfume and spring-scented laundry detergent. In front of me was a bright white screen with a title that read, *Employment Assessment*.

The whole point of this assessment was to gather information about each student to help them figure out where their skills would be best suited. It started with a quiz on your passions, pastimes, preferences, likes, and dislikes, then moved onto a personality questionnaire.

In a few months, I'd be graduating high school, and only now were they distributing some questionnaire designed to guide us in the right direction, like, *Here, tell me about yourself, and I'll tell you what you should do for the rest of your life.*

We were asked to remain silent throughout this important hour dedicated to our future, but all I could focus on was the fly buzzing around the classroom window. It twirled in circles over and over again before flying right into the glass, a soft *tick* resonating throughout the room.

Sighing, I reached for my pencil, dropped my

head into my palm, and stared at the questions. It was the kind of quiz that made you select from a scale, with 1 being the lowest score and 5 being the highest score.

Where did I see myself in five years after graduation? I'd never given it much thought. I always figured that things would fall into place—that whatever I was meant to do, that's precisely what I'd end up doing. I scribbled away at the answers, wanting to get it over with, and during the entire quiz, the same question kept popping into my head.

What the hell am I going to be?

By the time I finished the quiz, I was still mulling the question over in my mind.

"Name here," said Mrs. Tyson, pointing a dark, heavily ringed finger at the bottom of my screen.

I leaned forward with my Tech Pen and scribbled my name at the top of the exam. She then placed her small UpPod at the corner of my screen—a tool designed to upload documentation within seconds—and continued on to the next desk.

Melody, my best friend, turned to me, her thick black-rimmed glasses almost falling off her face. "How'd you do?"

Smiling at her, I shrugged. "I don't know. Don't really care. I have my whole life to figure out what I want to do."

Unexpectedly, a loud smacking sound exploded throughout the classroom and I flinched so hard I threw my Tech Pen off my desk.

Jackson, one of the jocks in my class, held an old-school paperback flat against the window. When he pulled it away, a flat fly sat crippled with its guts spread across the glass. Jackson gave everyone his goofy grin—the kind that said, *What? I did what had to be done.*

Then, another loud smack filled the air around me. This time, it was followed by a loud scream.

"Well?" Rainer snapped, turning toward me. "Are you going to tell me how to use the transponder?"

The transponder... The toy.

I stared at Hawkins, who now lay flat on the floor with blood spilling from her split lip. Her eyes, a lifeless gray, remained fixated on me as if she were trying to communicate telepathically.

She knew that I knew the truth... The transponder was a fake. If Rainer found out, Hawkins had no leverage over her.

Hawkins let out a pleading moan, and at the same time, Isaac smashed a foot down on her calf. She yelped in pain again, her eyes disappearing behind small black lines.

I knew what Hawkins was thinking.

Don't tell Rainer the truth.

Before Rainer could order her son to hurt

Hawkins again, I snapped the back panel of the fake transponder back into place and started dropping the miniature screws into their holes.

"I know what this thing is," I said, sensing Hawkins's penetrating gaze.

Without saying anything, Rainer took a step toward me and waited, a tight grip fastened around her sword.

"It's a C-42 Transponder," I said, matter-of-factly. "I've seen this before when I was in the scouts."

I'd never been in scouts, and I hadn't the faintest idea what I was doing. But I did know one thing—Rainer wanted answers, and if I didn't give her any, she'd kill me. It was better to give her false information to buy us some more time than to tell her this thing was nothing more than a toy; if I did that, she'd likely kill us all in a fit of rage.

"It's being used to communicate with one specific man," I continued. "The reason he isn't responding to you is probably because Hawkins uses code language."

Rainer tilted her head like a predator preparing to attack its prey, and I swallowed hard.

"I can get him to talk," I added. "Maybe even get him to drop the supply boxes."

Hawkins closed her swollen eyelids and let out a long, relieved breath.

CHAPTER 1

Rainer turned around, fingers resting against her chin in a pensive manner. "So, you're telling me if you speak a certain way, this... man, whoever he is, will listen to you?"

Glancing at Hawkins, I nodded. "I can show you."

Rainer threw her chin out at me as a way of saying, *Go ahead.*

Pulling the fake transponder up to my lips, I allowed my index finger to cover the same button Hawkins had pressed when showing me the device for the first time. Now that I'd seen the inside of the device, I knew this button was one of the play buttons. There appeared to be several different recordings, but I hoped to God the button I was about to press was the basic message I'd heard more than once.

This was a huge risk... I was going in blind based on assumptions. But what choice did I have?

I pressed and held the communication button—the one that did nothing but crackle—and said, "Ace, Hawk in the sky, over."

Then, with my index finger, I pressed the play button and held it down—the holding it down part was a total gamble, but I assumed that if Rainer hadn't been able to produce any sound out of it, Hawkins had ensured some sort of protective mechanism to avoid having the wrong hands press all its buttons. Then, as I held the button, that familiar man's voice came blasting out through the transponder's black speaker. "Ace in place, over."

Rainer lunged straight for the transponder and tore it out of my grasp. She brought it up to her lips, her wild eyes darting from side to side, but then stopped herself as if realizing that another unfamiliar voice might interfere with her ability to obtain supply drops.

With a stiff finger trembling at the transponder, she said, "Tell him... Tell him to bring us more supplies. Tell him I want weapons. I want grenades. I want seeds."

Behind her, both her sons stood tall with balled fists on either side of their waists. With slouched postures, bearded faces, and a fiery curiosity in their gazes, they reminded me of primates. That's when I realized they'd never seen any form of technology before. The idea of sound being emitted from a piece of metal must have been far beyond their understanding. It would have been equivalent to pulling a man from Ancient Egypt through a time machine and into modern civilization.

Their minds couldn't comprehend it.

Zsasz and the other Northers had had similar reactions, no doubt the result of being raised on this island. Rainer, however, had grown up in the real world before being sent to the island pregnant.

"I'm happy to help," I lied, "but this is going to take time. I don't know anything about this man."

Rainer, now blowing air out through her flared nostrils, slid her sword back into its leather sheath. "You have one day. Tomorrow, I expect to have additional resources landing on this island."

I nodded, though what I truly wanted to say was *Are you insane?*

Even if the fake transponder had been some military-grade piece of equipment, and even if a man had been waiting at the other end... No way would any request be met within twenty-four hours. What about travel time? Resource preparation?

Regardless, it was never going to happen because the communication device was a fake.

And Rainer was a lunatic.

Without warning, Isaac marched across the room and grabbed me by the arm as if I weighed as much as a pigeon's feather. I fought to catch my feet but ended up hanging by the arm, the tips of my toes dragging across the cold floor.

"Make her comfortable," Rainer said, flicking a finger in the air. "If I don't have those supply drops by sunset tomorrow, you, Hawkins, and your friends here are all dead."

CHAPTER 2

I stared at Isaac's dark bulging back as he left the room and closed the small wooden door behind him, leaving me alone with Hawkins's toy and twenty-four hours left to live.

Surprisingly, the space wasn't what I'd expected. The bed was a perfect rectangle with cotton sheets—a luxury I hadn't seen in as long as I could remember—and right above it was a small circular hole in the wall, no larger than a basketball, to allow for natural light to enter. I was thankful for this seeing as Isaac hadn't left me with any torches; assumedly, they didn't want to give me any tools that could help destroy Rainer's lair.

Whether this window had naturally formed or had been carved out by the Northers, I didn't know. But either way, I appreciated the white light and the scent of fresh leaves sweeping through the hole. I stopped myself from sticking my entire face against the hole when I noticed large dead insects lying still throughout the tunnel, their stick legs wiggling as the gentle gust of fresh air came through.

Would this be the last of outside I would get to see? The last earth-scented air I'd pull into my lungs?

Twenty-four hours wasn't much time, and as exhausted as I was, I couldn't allow myself to be tempted by the small wooden bed in the corner of the room.

I wasn't here to sleep.

I was here to figure out how I was going to save myself and my people from Rainer's blade. Squeezing the fake transponder in my fist, I stared at the room's wooden door. It appeared to be held together by metallic screws, which had no doubt been taken from the plane wreckage. Its handle wasn't a typical handle—it was a groove in the wood, and on the other side was a locking mechanism with a latch that slipped in and out.

The moment Isaac had left, I'd heard the click, which meant I was locked in here until Rainer came to get me. They'd left a small loaf of bread on a three-legged stool at the foot of the bed. It wasn't much, and the edges appeared dry and hard, but I'd eat it.

Would it be my last meal?

Sighing, I sat down on the bed, promising myself I wouldn't lie down.

How am I getting out of this one? There's no way out.

Staring at the gadget, I pressed the play button

again. "Ace in place, over."

Had she used this to gather new followers? Had she also promised them freedom? I thought of Sammy, who'd been dragged away by Rainer's other son, and wondered if she too had fallen into Hawkins's trap. I'd hated her at first as I'd hated Collins... But was it their fault for following such a monster?

I, too, had chased after Hawkins's empty promise—and because of this chase, I was now sitting in isolation, away from the people I loved.

There was no way out of this one. I'd hit a wall. Dropping the radio onto the bed's cotton sheets, I grabbed the loaf of bread and made my way to the hole in the wall. If I was going to die, I wanted to at least enjoy the bit of time I had left.

The crust was hard and stale, but once pulled apart, the interior was soft and spongy. It was room temperature and had a sour taste to it, but it felt good going down into my empty stomach. At the same time, I inhaled a breath of moist air and closed my eyes, appreciating all of my senses—the sweet and sour taste spreading across my tongue, the faint howling caused by the air traveling through the tunnel, the smell of home-cooked bread rising up into my nostrils, and the crust's smooth texture against the tips of my fingers.

For a moment, everything was perfect—in my mind, I wasn't captured, nor was I less than twenty-four hours away from being sentenced to death.

No... in my mind, I was simply me. I was alive, breathing, feeling.

Was this the calm before the storm? Was this my euphoria before death?

When I cracked my eyes open again, a small bird sat at the end of the window in the stone wall. Its feathers were of a gorgeous azure—almost turquoise—blue, and under its chin was a plum-colored patch that ran down to its neck.

A plum-throated cotinga, as Proxy had taught me. She'd also taught me that the males were blue, while the females were typically brown.

I stared at its vivid blue plumage, mesmerized by its beauty. Its chirp, a high-pitched squeal, reminded me more of a monkey than a bird. When it turned its head sideways, the bird focused its small yellow eye on me as if realizing I was watching it.

"Hey, buddy..." I whispered.

It expanded its wings for a second before pulling them back against its body.

A hello?

I smiled.

"You're gorgeous," I whispered, oddly comforted by the small creature.

It stood there for a while, turning its head from side to side as an array of sounds escaped the jungle's forestry.

But something startled it, and it flew away so fast I didn't have the time to say goodbye.

A shout? Screaming? What was that?

Turning my head sideways, I brought my ear up to the window, held my breath, and listened.

In the distance, women shouted at the tops of their lungs. It wasn't the kind of screaming that erupted from the city when a fight broke out. This was something else... something far worse.

CHAPTER 3

Through the wooden door, heavy footsteps marched down the mountain's cavern.

What was going on? I ran to it, pressed my ear against the grainy wood, and listened.

"What do you mean, an attack?" Rainer growled, her voice growing distant.

Where was she going? Was she leaving her lair?

Zsasz's deep commanding voice followed close behind. I could tell it was Zsasz, but I couldn't make out anything she was saying. She was talking faster than usual, which meant something was up. Zsasz was always a slow talker—so slow it was as if she enjoyed hearing herself speak.

Through the window, the shouting continued to louden until I found myself pulling at the door in a panic, the wood rattling against the stone frame.

What the hell was going on? Why weren't they letting me out? Was the city on fire? Oh God… Would it enter Rainer's lair? If so, would they leave me here to burn to death? Out of nowhere, a familiar whistling sound entered the tunnel window and bounced off every wall in the room.

Arrows.

Why were arrows being fired?

I blasted my fists at the door. "Let me out!"

The wooden door's planks wiggled as I hit it, but the construction was too sturdy to break apart.

"What's going on?" I shouted, pounding my fists against the door again.

Something clicked and I instinctively stepped away from the door.

Shit.

Did I piss someone off? Was Isaac coming in here to shut me up?

The door flung open and smashed against the inside of the damp, stone room.

Sammy.

She stood with her lips parted and shoulders bouncing up and down with every rapid breath.

"What's going on?" I said, my heart now racing.

She frowned. "The city's under attack."

I darted for the doorway and stuck my head out. Where was everyone? Zsasz? Rainer? Isaac and his brother whose name I still didn't know?

"They're all out there," Sammy said as if reading my mind. With the back of her wrist, she wiped her sweaty forehead, causing her eyebrow piercing to wiggle. Around her wrist was frayed rope wrapped several times.

"How'd you get out?" I stared at her wrists,

which had assumedly only been tied minutes ago.

She looked as surprised as I felt. "Eliot let us go."

"Who's Eliot?" I asked.

"Rainer's son," she said.

The other brother.

Why had he helped them?

"Rainer told him to watch us and she took Isaac with her," Sammy said. "You should've seen the armor she put on him, Brone. Something messed up is going on. The guy looked like a fuckin' gladiator. Rainer, too. She put on a bunch of metal gear. A chest plate, shoulder plates, and even leg plates."

"So what's going on out there?" I asked.

Sammy shook her blond, fuzzy-haired head. "I have no idea. But whatever it is, people are dying. We have to go before Rainer comes back. Eliot showed me where Rainer keeps her weapons. Come on."

She swung around and darted toward Rainer's main room, where Hawkins had been left to lie in her own pool of blood. Before we reached it, I grabbed her by the rope around her wrist.

"Why'd he help us?" I asked.

She shrugged. "Honestly, I don't know. He isn't like his mom or brother. There's something good in him, Brone, and I think he wants all of the slavery to end. So do me a favor... when you get yourself a bow, don't kill him, okay?"

I nodded and followed her back to Rainer's room, where Scorch and Dibs stood in front of a pile of weapons. Even Hawkins, who held her broken fingers in the air, stared hatefully at the pile as if trying to decide which one would slide through Rainer's heart the easiest.

But what caught my attention more than the weapons was Rainer's son who stood behind his mother's throne, shamefully averting his gaze toward the ground.

At that moment, I didn't see a man... I saw a boy. A frightened boy who never asked to be born into a life like this.

I walked toward him and he took a step back.

"Eliot?" I asked.

His eyes, large and black as the night sky, darted between me and the women behind me. It was like cornering a frightened animal.

I wanted to hate him... I truly did. I knew precisely what he'd been doing to helpless women... holding them down and raping them to bring new life into this world. But as I stared at his terrified eyes, I realized something: he, too, was a victim in this.

His mother was basically forcing him to have intercourse because *she* wanted an army.

Was that why he looked so ashamed? Did he know what he was doing was wrong?

"I'm Brone," I said, resting a flat palm over my chest.

He nodded quickly but didn't say anything. Did he even speak English? Had Rainer held her sons captive, away from society, up until they were old enough to begin reproducing? Had he been held prisoner as well?

"I wanted to say thank you," I said.

He nodded again, his dark beard brushing against his bare chest, and grunted. He then gripped the back of his mother's throne, and that's when I saw them—scars, hundreds of them. They ran across his fingers, over his wrists, up his forearms, and all over his chest.

They were small and white, and it made me wonder if he'd been disobedient as a child—if Rainer had used violence to mold him into the man she needed him to be.

I wanted to know more... to question him and understand what had happened, but there was no time. Behind me, the sound of metal scraping against metal filled the room as Scorch raised a massive battle-ax into the air. It was so heavy it didn't stay up for more than two seconds before coming down hard, clanging against the stone floor.

"Watch it!" Sammy said.

Scorch winced and bared all of her surprisingly white teeth as if to say, *Sorry!*

"Do we even know who's attacking out there?" Dibs said. "What if it's some psycho tribe. Who should we be going after? The Northers, or the ones attacking?"

When Sammy reached down to pull a long spear from the pile, everything shifted, and a wooden bow appeared at the very bottom. But it wasn't any bow...

All sound seemed to disappear around me as I slid my thumb along the smooth cherrywood and along its curves. The string, a forest green, was constructed out of some plant. I ran my finger over the engraved E in the wood.

"Eagle," I breathed.

"What?" Dibs said. "What's going on? Why aren't any of you answering me?"

This was Eagle's bow—the one she'd used to fight off the Northers during their attack on our Village. She'd died using this bow, and Flander had given it to me. When Zsasz and her goons had captured us, my bow had been kicked aside.

I thought it to be gone forever... One of the Northers must have collected all of our weapons that day.

The skin of my palm was fiery hot against the bow's perfectly shaped grip and a sense of invincibility overcame me.

"How many arrows are there?" I asked, searching the pile.

"Um, two here," Sammy said.

"Four here," Scorch said.

Dibs held up a fistful of arrows. "There's, like... a bunch here."

Hawkins bent down and with her uninjured hand, grabbed two metal-head arrows that lay against the tips of her toes. She gave them to me, an unspoken exchange lingering between us.

It was as if she was sorry for what she'd done to me... as if, at this moment only, we were on the same team. I supposed we were since we had a common enemy. She stepped toward me, her swollen bloody face inches from mine. The split in her lip was wide enough for a coin to slip through.

I threw my old quiver over my shoulder, took the arrows, and threw them in.

Hawkins bent down again and aggressively tore a curved, black-handled sword from the pile. "Let's take this bitch down."

"Who?" Dibs asked. "Rainer? You guys still haven't told me what the hell we're doing."

She was trembling like a small breed dog, her entire figure shaking from side to side. It was obvious she was terrified to fight, and it was even more obvious she wanted answers before charging headfirst into a bloodbath. "Whose side are we on? What if we're being attacked by people worse than Rainer?"

I plucked at the string of my bow, the snapping

sound relieving me instantly, and smiled up at Dibs. "We aren't being attacked... We're the ones attacking."

CHAPTER 4

To the death.

I was ready.

Dying in battle was far better than being slaughtered like an animal at the hands of my nemesis.

It was a huge risk but one I was willing to take. The women behind me marched down Rainer's narrow cavern, which resembled a rectangular hall cut out of the mountain. Their heavy weaponry clanged behind me and their footsteps clapped against the solid ground.

We were all petrified, but with the way they walked—heads held up proudly and unblinking gazes aimed at the mountain's opening—they were as ready as I was to give this all they had.

Besides, what choice was there? We couldn't sit around and wait for the battle to be over. What if the Northers won? What if Rainer returned to her lair to execute us all? At least this way, we stood a chance and we would be providing strength to our people from the inside.

It was our people, right?

For a split second, I questioned myself. But I knew Hawkins had planned for this precisely. She'd dragged me along, knowing all too well that my people would come looking for their leader.

It had to be them.

The moment I stepped out, my foot catching the wooden stairs, an arrow came spiraling down so fast I jumped back. It snapped against the mountain wall, inches away from my thigh. The arrowhead was constructed of stone and held to the shaft by a seaweed-like string.

The craftsmanship was all too familiar with its bright red feathers for fletching and the way the string was wrapped around over a dozen times.

This was Hammer's work.

With my bow held firmly against my chest, I watched as another dozen arrows came raining from the sky. Women with shackles ran under the tents, while the armed Northers charged straight toward the city's edges with swords held high and wooden shields floating above their heads.

"Why aren't we moving?" Hawkins growled, nudging Scorch who then bumped into me.

I couldn't even imagine how much hatred Hawkins harbored for Rainer. Most of her fingers were broken, her face had swollen to twice its size, her lip was split wide in half, and her right eye was hidden behind a huge blue lump for an eyebrow.

She hated Rainer so much that she was willing

to set aside her pain to kill her.

And then I thought of Zsasz and stared at the crowd of charging Northers. If there was anyone I hated as much as Hawkins hated Rainer, it was Zsasz.

This was it... this was my chance to take her out. She'd be too preoccupied hunting her attackers to even see me coming.

One arrow—that was all it would take.

"Come on!" Hawkins shouted, her voice exploding down the cavern behind us.

"Wait!" I hissed. "Let the archers finish and then we're going in."

One by one, women dressed in thick, protective gear ran away from the cabins and out through the wooden gates.

"They're everywhere!" one of them shouted, wild eyes searching the skies.

And we were—my people were surrounding the entire city. How had they pulled this off? How had they gathered enough numbers?

One of the Northers—no doubt a woman who'd once been a slave and brainwashed into becoming a mindless soldier—threw a pointed finger toward one of the cabins and shouted, "Stay inside!"

I couldn't see who she was talking to, but I was certain it was a pregnant woman. Several of them had run back beneath the safety of their cabins. Quickly, the space around us emptied as the soldiers made their way out of the wooden gates.

Then, from the trees beside the mountain, near the Northers' training grounds, came a dozen fire arrows whistling through the air. The flames twirled around the arrow shafts as they spun in the air, and one after another landed fiercely throughout the Northers' base.

Several of them crashed straight into the ground, extinguishing almost instantly the moment their flames touched the grass's morning dew. Others, however, penetrated the wooden gates and the colossal fence and landed pointing into the roofs of the cabins.

"Stay here!" I shouted, jumping out from the mountain's sheltering rock.

Sammy touched my back, but she didn't have the time to stop me. I ran in zigzag motions as more arrows rained down, one of them skimming my forearm—a hot, painful tingle equivalent to a poisonous bug bite.

When I reached the first cabin, I pressed my body flat against the exterior wall to protect my body beneath the overhanging roof. Arrows crashed around me, and one penetrated the side of the cabin. It snapped in half, but this didn't stop the fire from eating through the wood.

I reached for the handle, a strange groove in the middle of a long, sanded panel, and burst the door open. Inside, three pregnant women squealed like frightened mice, their partially cupped fists held up by their faces. They sat beside each other on the small, cotton-sheeted bed, their thighs touching and their plump bodies pressed together.

"The cabin's catching fire," I said. "Come with me. I'll keep you safe."

They hesitated, likely trying to figure out whether I was lying or telling the truth.

I must have looked like a complete wreck to them... like one of those dolls with growing hair left in the hands of a two-year-old—dark, uneven patches on my head and a horror-movie-style scar running down my face.

"Do you want to burn to death?" I snapped, and the shortest woman on the left—the one with the largest and roundest belly—squealed again and shook her head. "Then come on. Let's go."

They helped each other get up and rushed to the entrance door. Overhead, flames had already begun to lick underneath the rooftop and were now spreading to the door frame. I ran out, keeping my body as close to the cabin as possible, and signaled them to follow me.

"See that woman over there?" I said, pointing to Sammy.

She stuck her head out of the mountain's opening and turned it from side to side. Then, Hawkins's face appeared, and she did the same, before retreating back into the mountain. It was like watching figures pop out of a whack-a-mole game.

"Stay along the mountain and run there," I said. "Go, as fast as you can."

They ran as ordered, though it was more of a wobble, and I bolted straight for the other cabins, blasting open their doors and urging women to get out. By the time the final cabin was cleared, the first one was up in flames—a bright orange and yellow ball warming my cheeks from a distance. It cracked and snapped as the cabin fell apart, and I ran for Rainer's lair.

But as I neared Rainer's lair, a sharp, debilitating pain stabbed me in the back so deeply, I fell flat to the ground. The smell of earthworms entered my nostrils, and moist dirt stuck to my chin and lips.

What happened?

"Brone!" Sammy called out, sprinting out into the open.

I was too stunned and in too much pain to care that she'd used my real name. Slowly, I reached for my back, where the pain was quickly spreading, and the tips of my fingers touched a wooden arrow shaft.

CHAPTER 5

"Don't touch her."

"Back off."

"Mind if I look?"

"Who the hell are you?"

Groaning, I glanced up at the approaching pregnant woman. With a torch in one fist, she bent down, her belly sitting on her knees and half her face a bright orange color.

"I'm a doctor," she said, a thick accent rolling off her tongue.

I almost scoffed, but the pain in my back shot up along my spine, so I clenched my teeth instead.

What was a doctor doing on Kormace Island? Why wasn't she being used by the Northers as a Medic?

"I'd appreciate it if you all kept dat to yourselves," she then added, glaring at the women around her.

What was that accent? Polish? In high school, a new Polish kid had joined our class halfway through our semester. Kids started making fun of him for his accent, calling him Vladimir and

Dracula, and nearly every day, he'd shake his reddish blond hair that matched his bright cheeks and shout out, "Polish, *idiota!*"

She leaned in closer, her oily auburn hair dangling over one shoulder and her topaz wide-set eyes inches away from mine. She had a dimple in her chin, something that suited her nicely.

"Is not so bad," she said, poking at the fresh wound.

I winced and clenched my fist.

"It only penetrated the muscle tissue," she said. Raising her dimpled chin, she scanned Rainer's lair. "I need something to disinfect."

At once, the women around me stepped away as if I were contagious. What were they so afraid of?

A deep voice carried throughout the room, and I swallowed hard. "A-alcohol?" Eliot asked.

Had he been standing in there the whole time? Why was he still helping us? Why hadn't he run off to Rainer to help her fight? At that moment, I was in so much pain that it was easier to hate him than to be grateful for what he'd done.

The doctor nodded and reached for the leather flask held by long fingers twice the size of mine.

"Brone," she said, though it sounded more like a question.

Was she asking me my name? Did it even matter anymore? Everyone was dying. I'd probably die, too.

So I nodded, and she popped off the flask's circular cover.

"My name is Zofia," she said, taking a swig of the alcohol. She brought it to my lips and I pulled away.

The last thing I needed was alter my mind in the middle of a war.

"Suit yourself," she said calmly. Rolling me over onto my stomach, she poured some of the liquid over the wound. I let out a deep grunt, my fist clenching so tightly around Sammy's foot that something cracked.

Sammy sucked air in through clenched teeth and tried to pull away, but I didn't let go.

"This is going to hurt," she said. "Sure you don't vant any?"

When I didn't answer, she brought a piece of cloth up to my lips. "Bite."

I did as she told me and bit down on the small rag. It smelled of old water and dirt, but I didn't care. I'd seen women get arrows taken out of them, and the last thing I wanted was to chip a tooth while clenching my jaw.

Then, without warning, a blinding pain exploded in my back—it was like being stabbed all over again without the adrenaline to numb the pain.

"Here it is," she said, her finger digging inside

of me.

The next thing I knew, she was getting up with the arrow in her fist.

I tried to talk, but the cloth was still in my mouth.

"Rinse wound with alcohol," she said, pointing at someone.

What? How had she done it so fast? Why hadn't I felt it at all?

She turned around, crouched down so low it looked like she was about to sit on the stone ground, and stared me square in the face. "It vas very close," she said, showing me the arrow's bloody head. "It went through muscle but did not penetrate any organs. How are you feeling? You lost consciousness."

Too disoriented to respond, I reached for the wound on my back. At the same time, Zofia grabbed my wrist. "No, no... Don't touch. I will bandage you."

"So... I'm okay?" I mumbled.

She nodded.

At the same time, cold liquid poured over my wound and down my back and I let out a loud yelp.

"Fuck!"

"Disinfect," Zofia said.

"I know what it's for!" I snapped, clenching my fists.

I sat upright, and although Zofia tried to stop

me, I didn't listen.

"How long's it gonna take to patch me up?" I asked.

"Few seconds," she said, arching one of her red brows.

I made my eyes go big as if to say, *Well, what're you waiting for?*

What I should have done was thank her, but politeness was the last thing on my mind. Right now, our people and the Northers were at war, which meant there was no time to waste.

She applied pressure and wrapped a fabric material around my torso. It stung, but it was the pain inside that hurt most of all. How deep had it gone? It hadn't penetrated through my stomach, which I was thankful for.

"All done," she said. "I vould apply new bandage in—"

"Where's my bow?" I cut her off.

"Brone—" Sammy tried, but then I saw it lying on the ground next to a group of pregnant women. They all stared at me with petrified looks and protective hands over their bellies as if the sight of me were enough to harm their unborn children.

Obviously, they wanted nothing to do with battle.

"Give me that," I said, pointing at my bow.

When the pregnant woman closest to it hesitated and placed her second hand over her belly, I swung myself up with a grunt and limped toward my bow. "I'll do it myself," I growled, bending down to pick it up.

Everything around me went silent, and the women inside Rainer's lair stared at me as if waiting to see if I'd collapse. "What're you all staring at?" I snapped. "Grab your weapons and let's get out there!"

CHAPTER 6

The sound of battle was like something out of a historic movie.

Metal clanged against metal, wood collided with wood, pointed tips tore through flesh, bones snapped, arrows cut through the air, and women shouted at the tops of their lungs. The air smelled of death, if death itself had a smell.

It was a stale, hopeless scent that lingered in the air. It was also the smell of fire burning through wood—a smell that reminded me of the Village and the day we lost everything. Behind me, the entire gate, along with all the cabins that had once been tucked safely inside, were no longer visible. Instead, bright orange flames danced from side to side, engulfing the structures in their entireties.

Wood snapped as the fire crackled, and a blinding heat spread out over the battlefield. It warmed the back of my neck so much I had to run away from it and straight toward the battle to relieve the pain.

At the center of the city, tents fell apart, fire spilling through them like liquid. Several women—

some slaves and others Northers—lay lifelessly in the sand, their bodies mutilated by protruding arrows and spreading fire.

One arrow stuck straight out of a Norther's forehead, its stem so dark and curled it reminded me of an unashed cigarette.

Then, out from the forest came a dozen women—my women—with sticks and large stones held above their heads.

At the same time, one Norther held a sword high in the air and swung it down with all her might, decapitating one of the charging women. She jabbed her sword into the air again and let out a deep, rumbly cry.

A victory cry? A shout meant to intimidate her attackers?

Her shoulders, pads of long gray and beige fur, were covered in fresh blood. The armor on her chest, a metallic plate, made it impossible for the women charging at her to kill her. They would either have to throw something at her face—which was abnormally high—or attempt to cut off some limbs, which were also covered in plated armor.

Not all Northers had metallic armor, but the few who did walked about as if invincible.

This one, specifically, twirled through the air with her sword, slicing two women across the chest simultaneously. They froze with baffled looks on their faces, one carrying a spear and the other a large stone wrapped in a seaweed net.

And then, the blood came pouring out through large gashes in their midsections. The woman carrying the spear fell to her knees first, a horrified look in her eyes that told me she wasn't prepared to die. The other clutched at her spear and looked up at the Norther, almost pleadingly.

She tried to stay upright by jabbing her spear into the dirt and leaning her body against its shaft, but it was obvious she was losing strength. At the same time, the woman next to her collapsed to the ground.

The Norther carrying the sword raised her weapon again, prepared to stab her through the chest, and I fired an arrow straight for the back of her neck.

At once, she dropped her sword, both hands floating beside her hips as if trying to maintain balance. But she didn't last long—within a few seconds, she dropped to her knees and fell flat on her side, my arrowhead penetrating through the front of her throat.

I rushed toward the woman with the spear and dropped to my knees in front her of her. Her eyelids became heavy, and she looked up at me, her body convulsing as she fought to stay upright.

She parted her lips to say something, but a huge glob of blood spat out from her mouth, and all at once, her body went limp. I caught her midfall, resting her head into the dirt, and gently closed her eyelids.

"No!" cried one of her friends.

She came running so fast dirt flew into my face as she skidded beside her friend's dead body.

"Fuck, fuck, fuck," she said. "Watson... Come on, girl. Watson!"

Resting a flat palm on this woman's thigh, I shook my head as if to say, *She's gone.* Then, a small crowd of women wearing suede clothing circled us, legs trembling and teeth chattering.

Adrenaline. They'd never battled before.

"Where are you coming from?" I asked. "Who led you here?"

The women eyed each other, then stared at me from behind dirt-stained faces.

"Where are you from?" I snapped. Although I understood they were terrified, this was a matter of life and death, and we didn't have any time to waste. "The Cove?"

Several of them shook their heads, and at the same time, a familiar face made its way through the crowd. For the first time, it wasn't covered nor hidden underneath a hood. The melted skin on her head looked even more pink and bubbly underneath the sun's rays.

"Sumi," I said, not understanding how she'd found her way to us.

She'd left with Quinn and the other women—

the ones who had chosen not to battle. Why was she here? How had she found her way back?

"Brone," she said. "Sorry, I didn't recognize you right away with the—" she wiggled a finger in front of her half-melted face.

"Brone?" someone whispered.

"Is that her?"

"I didn't recognize her."

"She's alive!"

"She's fighting with us!"

The women whispered back and forth as if having been injected with a liquid form of self-esteem. Their knuckles whitened around their weapons and they nodded rapidly as if to say, *We can do this.*

Sumi raised her chin, exuding a confidence I hadn't seen since she'd worked as a Cook in the Village, and gripped the handle of her stone blade. "We gonna stand here like a bunch of sitting ducks, or are we gonna get out there and kill those motherfuckers?"

CHAPTER 7

"Watch out!" Sumi shouted, jabbing her knife under my armpit and straight into a Norther's stomach.

Our attacker froze midair with a battle-ax held in her grip. Then, as if in slow-motion, she dropped her weapon and fell to her knees with a loud thump.

"They're everywhere!" Sumi said.

I fired arrows at three Northers who charged straight into the forest, penetrating two in the back and the other in the leg. Many of them were moving inside the jungle now, on the hunt for my people who surrounded their city. A few others, however, remained at the center near the burned tents, slicing and swinging their weapons as poorly equipped women came running straight toward them.

Everything was so chaotic. Women ran in all directions, creating clouds of dirt and dust in the air. And nearly every time I raised my bow, someone bumped into me, causing me to lose my aim. I tore from my belt a knife I'd picked up in

Rainer's lair—it wasn't overly long, but longer than an average steak knife. Its handle was made of smooth, hard leather, cool to the touch. Its tip was pointed, though not overly sharp, and its edges were dull. It was the kind of knife used for penetration rather than cutting flesh, and had there been a better choice, I'd have gone with something else, but this knife was my secondary weapon and I'd simply have to make the best of it.

Sumi pressed her back against mine, and we moved like this, though I hadn't the slightest idea if she had any experience fighting. But, given the Norther she'd just killed, I was relatively safe knowing she had my back... literally.

"Who came for you?" I shouted over the sound of weapons clashing and women shouting. "How'd you get here?"

"Fisher!" she shouted as we stepped over a dead body.

Fisher? She was here? My heart rate sped up, and I searched the battlefield. She wasn't fit to fight, not with her injured leg. Oh God... If she was here, I had to find her.

"Is she here?" I shouted, turning my head sideways.

At the same time, a sharp pain shot up my back, but I ignored it. I couldn't allow the pain of my injury to interfere.

Sumi rotated her body to look at me, but

instead of answering me, she let out a quick grunt. It wasn't loud or long, but it was enough to tell me something was wrong. A cloudy glaze suddenly spread over her eyes, and rather than looking at me, she stared straight ahead into nothingness.

"Sumi?"

Nothing.

"Sumi?" I shouted, this time turning my entire body around to face her.

As I came face-to-face with her, she looked down at her chest, where a feathered arrow protruded straight out. She clasped it, and with slightly parted lips, looked at me one last time before collapsing.

The arrow's shaft bent sideways as she fell into my arms, blood squirting out from her wound.

"Sumi!" I tried.

But it was no use. Slowly, I bent down with her, allowing her body to rest in the dirt. With a lifeless gaze aimed at the sky, she looked at peace. I closed her lids, including her pink bubbly one, and let out a long breath through my nostrils.

At the same time, a similar arrow came whistling through the air, slicing a fine cut right across my cheek. The moment my eyes shot up, the amused smirk on Rebel's face was enough for me to drop my knife, load my bow, and fire an arrow so quickly she didn't have the time to wipe that venomous smile off her hideous face.

Her head shot back and her right eye exploded as my arrow penetrated her skull—a sound that was like pudding being stirred aggressively. Had she known it was me, Brone, who killed her? Probably not. She hadn't recognized me. I'd hated Rebel ever since she'd helped Zsasz capture us, and I wanted her to know that I'd been the one to kill her.

She'd never know, but I knew, and that was all that mattered.

Then, a dreadful feeling sank into the pit of my stomach. I couldn't quite put my finger on it, but for a split second, I knew something awful was about to happen.

Maybe it was the sound of women screaming around me, or, maybe it was the sight of Zsasz's mutilated body standing far away in my peripheral.

All of a sudden, a familiar voice carried louder than all the voices around me. It was a voice I'd come to think of as home; only in the middle of battle, it was the last voice I wanted to hear.

"Brone, watch out!" Ellie shouted.

Everything happened so fast that I didn't even have the time to see her running my way. She landed hard against me, her coconut-infused hair sweeping across my face and tickling my nose. The next thing I knew, we were standing face-to-face, her chest pressed up against mine.

"Ellie—" I blurted, unable to comprehend what

the hell was going on.

What was she doing here? Where had she come from? Why was she looking at me like that?

It was as if someone had thrown a bucket of polyurethane over her face and allowed it to dry for days—it remained frozen, her lips parted no wider than the width of a wool thread until finally, she sucked in a long, broken breath.

Slowly, she bowed her head and I followed her gaze.

Sticking straight out from her belly was an arrowhead—a sharpened seashell I knew belonged to the enemy—dripping with blood.

How...

"No!" I shouted, my voice sounding muffled.

Everything around me began to blend together in a swirling cloud. The only thing I could focus on was Ellie's bloodstained hands held firmly over the tear in her shirt.

"This can't be... How... Ellie... Fuck. No. Ellie," I rambled, hands trembling over hers.

This couldn't be happening. How the hell was this happening? Why the fuck had Ellie come out onto the battlefield? Why would she jump in front of an arrow for me? I wanted to scream and cry at the same time, but I couldn't move. Instead, I stared in horror as Ellie's lips curled up at one corner.

"It's... it's okay," she said, her eyelids fluttering.

No, it wasn't okay. This wasn't supposed to happen. I needed her. I wouldn't survive this island without her. A sickening sensation filled my stomach, making me want to vomit out my organs.

This couldn't be real. Any second now, I'd wake up in Rainer's lair with only a few hours left to live. I'd have chosen that over losing Ellie.

Ellie's head rolled forward and I shook her hard. "Don't you fucking dare. You hang on! There's a doctor over there." I pointed toward the mountain, but Ellie shook her head and smirked again—an angelic smile intended to provide comfort.

"I… I love you," she breathed, before collapsing into my arms.

CHAPTER 8

I screamed so loud I thought my vocal cords might rip apart, but I didn't care. Marching straight toward Zsasz, I shot an arrow, and then another, and another. It was almost as if everyone on the battlefield had spread apart like the ocean for Moses as I charged at her. And although I was certain everyone was still fighting, for a moment it seemed like Zsasz and I were the only two on the battlefield.

No one intervened, which was smart of them. The rage inside me was so intense I was prepared to tear someone's throat out with my teeth.

I'd never experienced so much fucking anger in my life—not even when I was first sentenced to serve time on this island.

Zsasz didn't appear threatened by my head-on approach. In fact, it looked like she was having a blast, swinging her sword and dicing my arrows into little bits as they flew straight for her. How did she manage to move so fast? It was clear, she'd spent her whole life training on how to fight.

Zsasz was a trained killer.

But I didn't care how good she was. All I cared about was that she'd killed Ellie. At this point, I'd die trying to kill her, and even after death, I'd come back time and time again to haunt her for all of fucking eternity.

I let out another loud cry and launched my fifth arrow, my few remaining arrows rattling in my nearly empty quiver. This time, her swing was a bit off and although she managed to hit my arrow, she stumbled backward, the smile on her face melting into a confused frown.

What's wrong, Zsasz? Think you're invincible? You ugly, mutilated fucking zebra bitch.

I took the opportunity to fire another arrow straight into her lower abdomen, right beneath the shiny metal plate covering her chest. Her bright eyes rolled up at me as if to say, *How is this possible?*

Where her smile had been only seconds ago, an ugly grimace took its place, making her look more hideous than she already was. The mutilated skin of her face loosened, resembling grated cheese left over on a cheese grater. Desperately clutching at the arrow's protruding shaft, she fell to one knee.

Although I didn't hear it with the sounds of battle surrounding me—the shouting, wood snapping, flesh ripping, throats being torn open— it was easy to imagine a loud thump as she fell. Leaning her body against her sword, she rested her forehead on its steel handle.

Her round, plate-covered back moved up and down as she breathed. Although silent, she was likely trying to figure out how to miraculously come out of this fight victorious.

By the time she looked up at me, I'd reached her side. With as much force as I could find within me, I kicked her in the face and something cracked against the pad of my foot. She swayed sideways but caught herself with a flat palm in the dirt. The kick had likely hurt me as much as it hurt her, and when my aching bare foot came down, I hopped sideways to catch myself.

I grabbed the handle of her sword right above her grip and side-kicked her in the face as hard as I could. Her head shot back, blood and saliva splattering onto my heel, the high bun on her head wiggling like a pom-pom, and she fell to her side. There was only one problem: she hadn't let go of her sword as I had hoped. Even with her one-handed grip, she was much stronger than me.

Trying to catch my footing, I stumbled on top of her. With a tight grip, I grabbed the arrow sticking out of her lower abdomen and pushed it in even deeper, causing her to yelp out in pain.

Her screaming was like music to my ears. After everything she'd done... after everyone she'd tortured and killed, Zsasz deserved pain more than anyone on this planet.

Warm blood poured over my fingers like running soap in a hot shower, weakening my grip around the arrow's shaft. It slipped and made squishing noises like the gutting of a Halloween pumpkin.

Without warning, her enormous sword came swinging at me, its long blade aimed right at my neck. I ducked in time to feel the cold metal graze the skin of my head, and little bits of dark hair sprinkled down onto her chest plate.

Great... a haircut, when all I wanted was for my hair to grow back.

The sword fell hard into the dirt on the other side of her. She was too weak to use it properly. In a panic, I lunged for her sword and bashed my fists against her fingers, trying to break her grip.

This did nothing—she held onto it as if her palms were superglued to the handle.

Instead, I stood up and stomped down as hard as I could. Something snapped, and a loud bellow came blasting out of her lungs.

"What's wrong, Zsasz?" I spat out like venom. "You can break fingers, but you can't take it?"

I stomped down again, feeling another snap under the pad of my foot.

She dropped the sword, but I didn't care. All I wanted to do was hurt her. When I went to stomp again, she pulled away and my foot landed in the dirt, a brown cloud of dust exploding up and around my calf.

In a hurry, I bent down to grab her sword, but something hard kicked me in the legs, and I fell flat on my face. Little rocks rubbed against my lips and scraped the front of my teeth; I held my breath, not wanting to fill my lungs with dust.

Shit. Where was the sword?

I reached around me, searching through the soft soil, when an awful sound warned me it was too late—the sound of metal being dragged through dirt.

My stomach sank.

The instant I rolled over to face my attacker, Zsasz climbed on top of me as if straddling a horse. She grinned—a look that said, *Thought you had me, didn't you?*

Although I managed to land a few good hits on her face, she didn't seem bothered by this. In fact, her smile spread even wider as if she were enjoying it.

I swung tight fists at her face, and still, she smiled.

The weight of her immense body was so overpowering that despite my squirming, I couldn't move. She held her broken hand up against her chest and with the other one, snatched me by the throat.

The second she did, I stopped breathing. Her grip was so strong that for a moment, I wondered if she was holding some sort of choking device—a metal clamp built by Smith.

Yet the warmth that spread across my neck told me it was her fingers doing the strangling, which was even more unnerving. I slapped her scarred, lumpy forearms, but she didn't budge.

My face swelled as if my skull were being pumped with fluid, and my peripheral vision began to darken.

Don't let her win.

Don't let her win.

Don't let her win.

"Get off 'er, ya fuckin' nasty wax face!" came a familiar voice.

In an instant, Zsasz let go of my neck and leaned her body backward in time to dodge the point of a spear. It slipped right in front of her neck, grazing her throat, and with the hand she'd been using to strangle me, she tore the weapon out of Flander's grasp.

As Flander stumbled forward, Zsasz spun the spear around as if she'd practiced that move a thousand times before and launched it straight into Flander's chest. The blow had been so mighty that it tore straight through, the point of the spear sticking out through Flander's back.

I tried to scream, but nothing came out.

Flander fell to the ground like a stringless puppet.

In a fit of rage, I growled out and swung a fist at Zsasz's face; a satisfying *crack* filled the air and her lower jaw wiggled slightly, but the next thing I knew, she was choking me again. As she strangled me and watched the life drain out of my body with her evil gaze, I wondered if there was even a soul in there.

My surroundings began to fade, and I thought of Ellie and wondered if it would be so bad to simply give up. What was the point of all this fighting? If I allowed Zsasz to kill me, it would all be over. And death by strangling was far better than being torn to shreds by some steel blade.

She can't get away with everything she's done.

She killed Ellie.

That's when I remembered something—I had a knife.

Without a second thought, I tore it out of my belt and with a stiff arm, swung its point straight toward Zsasz's unprotected neck. Her reflexes, however, were like a cat's. She raised her injured arm to block the blow, released my neck with her good hand, and reached for the knife in my fist.

But as she did that, I grabbed the arrow inside her stomach and tore it right out. She let out a shout but didn't have time to stop me from continuing my attack. Holding the arrow's staff near its fletching, I jabbed it straight up into her neck.

Fuck.

It didn't penetrate.

The arrowhead must have detached inside her body. Despite the lack of penetration, the blow had been hard enough to throw her into a coughing fit. Reaching for her injured throat, she gagged and coughed up a glob of blood.

If I didn't act fast, she'd finish me once and for all.

My arrows.

Shooting an arm straight above my head, I stretched as much as I could, grasping around for my crushed quiver, when my fingers touched the fletching of a loose arrow. It must have slipped out. I grabbed it near its sharp head, and when Zsasz turned back to face me, I swung the point right into her eye.

She let out a disturbing cry as a gooey fluid squirted out into my palm. Being that Zsasz was a goddamn cockroach, I didn't waste any time wondering if the blow had been enough to kill her.

As I tore the arrow out, she reached for her punctured eye, her disfigured face warping entirely. I'd never seen Zsasz like this before—for the first time, she was the victim.

Sucking in a deep breath of air to muster strength, I stabbed the arrowhead into her jugular as hard as I could. The point wasn't long enough to puncture deeply, but it was sharp enough to penetrate skin and cause damage to her throat. She was so preoccupied freaking out about her eye that I had time to do this over and over again until her throat looked like the bark of a birch tree.

Finally, she threw herself off and landed on her back, desperately clawing at her throat.

She was suffering, and she deserved every fucking second of it.

Weak and drained of all energy, I forced myself up and pulled her sword out from the dirt. As I approached her with it, she stared up at with primitive eyes, her torn nostrils flaring so fast they looked like damaged butterfly wings.

Her jaw, square and clenched, didn't open as I moved toward her.

I'd have expected her to maybe plead for her life, but she didn't. There was so much hatred in her eyes it was as if she were trying to murder me telepathically.

Finally, this was it.

Gripping the sword's handle as tight as I could, I raised it up over my head.

"If hell exists," I said, "you'll be spending the rest of your life cleaning up Lucifer's shit."

I took in a deep breath, prepared to deliver the last blow right into her throat, when a better idea struck me.

Why give her mercy?

Why end her pain and suffering after all the

pain she'd caused to countless people?

Instead of stabbing her sword down into her throat, I stabbed it into her leg, her femur bone causing the blade to shift. She screamed out so loud I didn't hear her flesh tear when I ripped it out and did the same thing to the other leg.

As she lay there, moaning and crying out in agony, I kicked her right arm away from her body and planted my foot down on her wrist. She was so weak she couldn't pull away, and I enjoyed it.

Did that make me sick? All I wanted was for her to suffer.

With a growl, I stabbed the sword down through her bicep, and as she screamed, her mouth opened so wide I saw her tonsils. Without removing the sword, I knelt to stare her in her one eye, allowing the weight of my body to shift the blade inside her arm.

Her breath was heavy and bubbly. How had she not passed out? How was she still even alive?

Then, I spat a glob of spit in her face and she winced. "Have fun bleeding to death, you fucking monster."

CHAPTER 9

I grimaced as a line of blood shot out of the Norther's chest and straight into my face.

"Got your back, Brone," Jack said. "Keep goin'!"

She looked like a demon pulled right out of hell. Her mouth, vivid red with blood spilling through the cracks of her teeth, opened and closed as she spoke, though I couldn't understand much of what she was saying.

Had she ingested drugs?

A long cut, probably as deep as mine, ran across her collarbone and her left shoulder. Her face was covered in dirt, so much so that it looked like she'd rolled face-first into it. Maybe she had. Her short, spiky hair was crimson red and gooey-looking, likely from running her bloody fingers through her hair over and over again.

Like a monkey, she jumped onto one of the Northers' backs, grabbed her by the head and chin, and snapped her neck. When the Norther fell, Jack landed on her feet and punched two fists into the air.

"I'm fuckin' alive!"

She ran off in the opposite direction and jumped high, kicking a Norther in the back. Next, she bounced away into the air as if performing a dance move and kept on running with two knives in her fists.

From where I was standing, it looked like she was enjoying the fight.

Unfortunately, her fun didn't last long. As she bounced up and down, slicing her small knives toward any Norther she saw, a set of familiar blades came violently thrashing toward her. It sliced through the dirt-filled air, leaving a clear streak floating above Jack's now headless body.

The moment Jack's body collapsed to the ground, Rainer stepped out into view with her two identical steel blades held by her sides. I'd seen these swords earlier that day—they'd hung on the wall inside her lair like nothing more than decorative pieces.

But it wasn't the swords my eyes kept gravitating to—it was her son, Isaac, who I couldn't stop staring at. He marched forward with huge, broad shoulders wider than two women standing side by side. His forearms were the size of my calves, and in his grasp was a massive battle-ax that looked like it weighed as much as a Great Dane. It was so heavy-looking that veins popped out through the golden skin of his arms, and his thick pectoral muscles bulged out to the point of resembling breasts.

The ax's handle was longer than the width of his body and constructed of dark cherrywood. The head was forged in steel, which came as no surprise. It was so filthy it looked like he'd murdered more than a hundred women with it.

Across his chest was a large metallic plate that would have likely glistened underneath the sun, but in the middle of battle, it was matte and covered with dirt and blood. A bone mask hid most of his face—both the top and the bottom—and from the skull's human resemblance, I could only assume it had been sawed off a gorilla.

When three of my people came charging at him from behind, Isaac raised the ax above his head and released a deep, animallike cry. He twirled it over his head twice, and though the women raised their weapons to attack, he swept the ax sideways, tearing through all of their torsos at once.

I turned away and winced, not wanting to see body parts fall to the ground.

No way could I take him out alone—I was out of arrows, my quiver was broken, and he was covered nearly from head to toe. I would have to get a perfect shot, and with the way Rainer was marching in front of him, it was obvious she'd fight to the death to protect her son.

I thought of Ellie's lifeless body and my throat swelled. But I couldn't focus on that. Women were dying... my women, and I had to stand up and fight. Turning around, I tripped over a dead body but caught my footing beside a dead Norther.

A sword.

I reached down and grabbed it, appreciating its light weight. I had planned to take Zsasz's sword, but the damn thing seemed built for a giant. Given how hard she'd strangled me, it was understandable that she'd managed to use it.

Glancing back at Isaac, I observed every piece of metal across his body. The only way anyone was going to kill him was with an arrow... or many arrows. Where were all of our archers? I peered toward the jungle's thick greenery, where women continued to fight near the trees.

Only one thing would have stopped them from shooting arrows: they'd run out, which meant all of their arrows were on the battlefield.

Then, like flowers blooming across a field of manure, dozens of arrows began to pop out at me. Some lay in the dirt, while others stuck straight out of our enemies like a frightened porcupine's quills. If I became desperate enough, I'd tear them out, but right now, I had plenty of arrows to choose from—and that wasn't counting all the full quivers lying in the dirt.

In a crouched position, I ran around as fast as I could, gathering both new and used arrows. One Norther lay in the dirt with two arrows sticking out of her—one out through her open mouth and the other out of her chest. In her large, dirt-stained hand, she held onto a longbow and underneath her, there appeared to be a crushed quiver full of arrows.

With my knees bent, I pulled upward on her arm, trying to roll her body sideways. It was like attempting to roll over a bag of bricks—the woman was huge. As I gave one hard tug, her body immediately rolled with such ease that I found myself questioning my own strength.

But, it hadn't been my strength.

"Two is always better than one," Johnson said, smirking sideways at me.

Her freckles were hidden beneath the dirt on her face, and across her chin was a gash so deep I could see a layer of fat and muscle.

"Some bitch's arrow almost got me," she said, no doubt noticing my stare.

"You okay?" I asked.

She nodded. "You?"

If I answered that, I feared I might give up my will to fight. So instead, I nodded, stuffed a bunch of arrows into the dead Norther's quiver, and pointed at the other arrows lying around. "Grab as many as you can. We need to get our archers back into this fight."

She bent down, her dirty blond hair looking like old rust at the base of her neck. Whether the blood was hers or someone else's was beyond me. If Johnson was here, who else had followed?

Although eternally grateful for their loyalty, I wished my friends hadn't come.

"Watch out!" Johnson shouted, throwing a loose arrow behind me.

The arrow didn't do anything but land in the Norther's face, distracting her for a brief second. I quickly picked up my new sword and, as the Norther's focus fell back on me, stabbed it straight through her stomach.

"Holy shit," Johnson breathed. "That was close."

I couldn't say anything, so instead, I kicked the woman off my sword and watched as she fell to the ground.

I twirled in circles, trying to catch a glimpse of my surroundings, but I couldn't. There was so much dirt I couldn't see anything beyond several feet. How the hell were we supposed to know when the battle was over? And with this much dirt clouding the battlefield, how were we supposed to kill Isaac? We'd never get a clear shot.

"Come on," I said. "Let's get out of here."

Guided by the high treetops, I charged toward the forest with my sword gripped firmly in my fists. For a brief moment, it reminded me of Halloween when I was fourteen-years-old. My mom had taken me to see our town's most haunted house, and to enter the house, we'd been forced to walk through a passageway so dark it was like I'd lost my eyesight.

It wasn't the darkness that scared me—it was the idea of something jumping out.

As I ran through the brown clouds of dirt, I couldn't help but tense up with every step I took. At any moment, someone could come charging at me with a pointed weapon aimed at my face. It was the strangest sensation in the world—I was surrounded by women left and right, yet I felt completely alone.

I spun around to make sure Johnson was still following me with her arms full of arrows, but when I looked back, she wasn't there.

"Johnson!" I hissed.

I backtracked a few steps, wincing to try to see clearly, but she wasn't there.

CHAPTER 10

The moment I entered the jungle, it was like a blindfold had been taken off.

Finally, I could see, though I wished I couldn't. Countless women lay across the jungle floor, their bodies tangled and piled overtop one another. Deeper into the jungle, the sound of battle cries and weapons clashing against each other filled the air.

Heartbroken, I stared at the lifeless bodies. The only reason they'd come out this way was because of Hawkins, and me. Their loyalty to me had led them to want to stand up against the Northers, and now, so many of them had lost their lives.

Northers, too, lay motionless over tree roots, dead bodies, and piles of rotten leaves.

Was this what Rainer wanted? She'd been so drunk off power she was willing to sacrifice everything to rule over the island. What was the point of being in charge if there was no one to rule over?

Suddenly, a soft moan caught my attention. I swung around and followed it. There were no words, only sounds.

Leaning against a large tree trunk was Arenas, her lips parted and her eyelids heavy. She stared at me as I approached, then winced in pain and with two trembling hands, covered the deep puncture in her abdomen.

"Br-Brone..." she mumbled. "Is... Is that—"

I hopped down into a crouched position beside her and dropped my overloaded quiver at my feet. "Shhh. Yeah, it's me."

A substantial amount of blood pooled through the cracks of her fingertips, further staining her suede top. Although usually golden brown, her skin was now as white as mine.

No way was she coming out of this alive.

"It... hurts. So... bad," she said, her lips forming an upside-down smile.

It was strange to hear Arenas speak without her usual Latina fierceness. I'd grown so accustomed to hearing her call me *chica* all the time that my actual name seemed foreign slipping off her tongue.

"P-please," she said. "H-h-help."

Pulling her in by her clammy neck, I pressed my forehead against hers. The last thing I wanted to do was kill one of my own, but I'd come to learn on this island that mercy was one of the greatest and most selfless things someone could do for another.

Had I been in her position, I wouldn't have

wanted to sit there for hours on end suffering horribly until my final breath. I reached for one or my collected arrows, not quite certain how I intended to offer her mercy. What was I supposed to do? Slit her wrists? How morbid was that?

The last time I'd offered someone mercy, I hadn't known the woman and I'd shot an arrow through her without her seeing me. Arenas was looking right at me. I couldn't stand in front of her and look her in the eye as I killed her.

I rubbed my thumb along the rough edge of the arrow's head, trying to figure out the most merciful way to end her suffering, when her eyes shifted from me to something behind me.

They widened, and I didn't waste any time turning around to see what she was staring at. I rolled sideways overtop my sword and loaded my bow. The moment I landed in a crouched position with my arrow pointed up, the Norther stood there with an empty hand held in front of her face.

What the hell was she doing? Trying to cast a spell?

Arenas gargled and blood came pouring out of her mouth. Right below her collarbone, at the center of her chest, was the head of an ax planted in her body—an ax that had been intended to stab me in the back.

The Norther, obviously realizing she'd missed her mark, took a step back and aggressively tore a short blade from her side. It was pointless, though; I fired my arrow straight into her heart. She clutched at the fur around the arrow and fell to her knees, a loud thump carrying throughout the trees.

Arenas stared ahead as if watching our attacker take their last breath, but she was already gone. Her gaze, a hollow look I'd come to know all too well on this island, remained fixated straight ahead. I shuffled toward her and with two fingers, closed her dirty eyelids.

My throat swelled. I couldn't do this anymore.

How the fuck was I going to survive this? Everyone I knew was dying. I thought of Ellie, and a sickening nausea crept into my stomach. My vision blurred and the next thing I knew, I was kneeling over a moss-covered tree root, emptying hot bile from my stomach.

"Hey!" someone shouted.

Utterly defeated, I turned around slowly without raising a weapon.

Kill me for all I care.

But to my surprise, it wasn't a Norther standing behind me.

"Brone?" Fisher asked, pointing what appeared to be a small crossbow at me.

Although I didn't respond, I must have made a face she recognized—immediately, she lowered her crossbow and quickly limped toward me, dragging wet leaves under her bad leg.

"Well, I'll be..." Biggie said, planting two large hands on her round waist.

"Girl, you don't look so good," Coin said, her lips pulled back over her golden tooth.

They were alive? They were all alive? Was I dreaming? I widened my eyes at them and craned my neck to see who else was standing behind them.

Out from behind Biggie came Rocket. She held a longbow in her small hands and smiled at me. Beside her was Elektra, looking even taller than she had the last time I'd seen her. Her hair, a ginger orange, looked like it had spent a day twirling around in a drying machine. It was chaotic and unkempt, yet somehow, it suited her.

Rocket wrapped an arm around her and pulled her close. "Kid here wouldn't take no for an answer. I even tried to tie her up to stop her from coming."

"You should've," Coin said, shaking her head. "She's a fuckin' kid."

"Language!" Rocket hissed.

Coin's jaw dropped, which meant something along the lines of *In what world is it okay for you to bring a child to war yet scold me from swearing in front of that same child?*

"Brone, you okay?" Fisher asked, crouching down beside me.

I swallowed hard, fighting the urge to burst into tears. This wasn't the time to mourn—it was the time to be the leader these women needed me to be.

Picking up my sword, I shot upright.

"Someone upgraded," Fisher said, eyeballing my steel blade.

"I could say the same about you," I said, pointing a finger at her crossbow.

She winked and jerked her head toward Hammer, who looked plumper than usual. "Hammer here hooked me up."

Hammer smirked and raised her round face the way someone would after winning an award.

I wanted to say something like *We're lucky to have you, Hammer*, but I didn't have the strength or the time to do it.

"Rainer and her son are out there," I said, pointing back at the city.

Coin took a step toward me. "Her son?"

"Where's Tegan?" I asked.

"Relax," Fisher said. "She's at the Cove. So is Proxy. A small group of women stayed behind. Tegan, well, 'cause she's pregnant. Proxy said she wasn't a fighter and refused to come, which is good for us. That girl's a walkin' encyclopedia. If we make it out of this, we need her around. Another woman stayed behind. Trish, I think her name was. She has severe sciatica and can't walk long distances—"

"Okay," I said, cutting her off. "We need to move."

"Her son?" Coin repeated, her voice jumping up an octave.

"Her sons," I corrected, and her eyes nearly popped out of her head.

Everyone broke out into bickering until I hissed, "Be quiet!"

"Is that why Tegan's—" Biggie started.

I nodded. "Rainer's using women to reproduce like fuckin' cattle. That's a conversation for another time. We can't sit around while they're out there slaughtering people. The guy's huge and he's armored from head to toe. And if we charge at him, we're going in blind. There's too much dirt flying around. We need to find a way to—"

"I have an idea," Rocket said, "but you might not like it."

CHAPTER 11

"I don't like this," Coin said, tapping her foot in the dirt.

Fisher shoved her out of the way. "Well, it isn't up to you."

"You understand what we're asking, right?" Rocket said, gripping Elektra's shoulders.

Elektra nodded as if she'd rehearsed this the night before.

Was Rocket seriously going to sic the kid on Isaac?

Rocket must have sensed my hesitation; she turned to me and let out a long breath through her button nose. "I'd never put her in harm's way. She'll be safe up there. The girl's a freakin' monkey. See that branch?" She pointed up to the largest tree in sight. "She could make it up there no problem and fire downward."

It was a solid idea, but what if Rainer ordered her women to shoot arrows up into the tree? What if Elektra lost her balance and fell to her death?

Then, I realized everyone was staring at me. What did they want? A decision?

"What?" I asked.

Rocket shrugged one shoulder. "Think it's pretty obvious that you're in charge now, Brone."

I'd grown accustomed to the idea of being in charge of those I'd rescued, but my own friends? It was a strange feeling.

But, Trim had sacrificed herself for me, and I wouldn't let that be in vain.

"Send her up," I ordered. "Rocket, Fisher, Biggie, you guys stay here. Coin and Hammer know the city—they'll come with me."

Everyone nodded like soldiers in rank and I turned around, prepared to make my way back into the city when someone's warm grip wrapped around my forearm.

"Brone," Fisher said.

She didn't have to say anything for me to know what she was thinking—her slanted brows and tight thin lips told me she was afraid this was a final goodbye. I wrapped my arm around her neck and pulled her in hard, my sweaty cheek sticking against hers.

"You guys stick together," I said, "and everything will be okay. You hear me? I'll be back. I promise."

I knew my promise meant nothing, but I needed to reassure her that I wasn't planning on dying.

Without another word, I turned around and ran

along the city's perimeter, ignoring the pain around my ankles from the shackles. Coin and Hammer followed close behind.

"Where we goin'?" Coin asked, jogging fast to catch up.

"If Rocket's plan fails," I said, "we need a plan B, and there's only one person on this island who stands a chance against Isaac."

CHAPTER 12

Voices erupted all around and women cowered in the corners of Rainer's lair.

"Relax!" Sammy shouted. "She's with us. They all are."

The pregnant women held onto their stomachs as if letting go would result in their child's death. They were afraid, and I didn't blame them. But the truth was, no one wanted to harm the mothers—not my people, and certainly not Rainer.

If anyone was safe, it was them.

"What's going on out there?" Sammy asked.

I shook my head as a way of saying, *It isn't good.*

The cavern had filled up quite a bit since I'd left. Slaves from within the city had found their way inside, no doubt looking to get as far away from the battle as possible.

"Where's Hawkins?" I asked, searching the torch-lit room.

Sammy shrugged. "She went after Rainer."

"Where's Murk?" I asked.

Another shrug.

With the back of my wrist, I wiped dirt and

blood away from my brow. Everything was so chaotic. I hated being unable to control anything, but I couldn't give up. Despite the mess we were in, I had to keep moving.

When something tapped me on the shoulder, I turned around to find BluJay standing still, her short blond hair sticking out in every direction. She forced a shy smile and waved to say, *Hello.*

"BluJay!" I said. "You're okay."

She nodded, the cute smile never leaving her childlike face. She made a few gestures, though I couldn't quite figure out what she was saying. At last, she placed a hand on either side of her body and threaded her fingers together over her stomach.

"You're pregnant?" I asked.

Smiling, she nodded.

I didn't understand what there was to smile about. How did anyone smile about being forced into pregnancy through rape? And how did she know she was pregnant? It had only been a few days. I clenched my teeth and glared toward Rainer's throne. From here, I could see Eliot's figure sitting behind it, and although I'd come here to ask for his help, all I wanted to do was kill him now.

The moment I marched toward him, BluJay grabbed me by the wrist and turned me around. With both palms facing upright, she brought her right one to her lips and pointed at Eliot.

What was that supposed to mean?

"Did he hurt you?" I asked.

She shook her head and made that same gesture.

"He's good?" I asked. "Kind?"

She nodded.

I stared at his dark hair floating right above the back of Rainer's throne. Around him was empty space, which meant the women in here were too afraid to sit close to him. Why hadn't he left? Why was he still in here? Was BluJay right? Was he kind?

I glanced back at Coin and Hammer, who were still catching their breaths. "Wait here."

Slowly, I made my way to the back of the room. Gliding my fingers along the throne's wooden arch, I reached Eliot's side. He didn't look up at me. Instead, he sat with his elbows on his knees and his head held in his large, veiny hands.

Dark curls sprang out between his fingers, and his massive back moved up and down as he breathed.

"Eliot?" I asked.

He flinched at the sound of his name and looked up at me with wet, bloodshot eyes.

"It's me. Brone." I leaned forward.

He stared at me, confused, with creases around his nose and eyes.

When I sat on the floor in front of him, he

pulled his feet closer to his body and wrapped his arms around his hairy legs.

"I heard you speak earlier. Can you speak English?" I asked.

At first, he didn't respond, but then, his bearded face moved up and down. I wasn't sure how well he spoke English, but it was a relief to know he understood what I was saying.

"I'm so sorry this is happening," I said. "I can't imagine how hard this is on you."

He sniffled and wiped his nose with the back of his arm. Right then, I didn't see hair on his chest or large bulging muscles—I saw a frightened boy who wanted nothing to do with this war.

"Are you okay?" I asked.

Slowly, his dark eyes rolled up at me. "Fight," he said, his voice deep and hoarse.

"Fight?" I asked.

"Pain is all I know," he said. "My mother... she trained me and my brother to fight. I hurt people. In many ways. I don't want to hurt anyone. I'm not like my brother. I don't want this life."

His last words came out as more of a squeal, and with his palms, he covered his tear-filled eyes.

"Eliot," I said softly, and he looked up at me again. "You don't have to live this life. There's so much out there that you know nothing about. You can help us stop this."

He lowered his hands, staring into me as if I

held a key to some magical world.

"Your mother and brother are out there killing innocent women. You can help us stop them."

His dark eyes narrowed into hateful slits. "You want me to hurt my mother?"

I swallowed hard. The last thing I wanted to do was turn Eliot against us. It was already a miracle he'd been willing to help. I had to go about this carefully.

"I would never ask you to hurt your mother," I said. "Maybe you can talk to them. Convince them to stop this."

I knew that would never happen, but it was the only thing I could say to calm him down.

His jaw muscles popped out and he shook his head. "No. I can't help."

Hearing those words was like breaking a completed puzzle apart—it stung.

"I understand," I said, standing. What I wanted to say was, *You're a goddamn coward*, but he was only human. How could anyone be asked to kill their own mother and brother? I must have been delusional believing I'd somehow convince him to fight with us.

"Anyone who can carry a weapon," I said, my voice carrying throughout the room, "gear up. We're going back out there."

CHAPTER 13

The heat of our bodies filled the cavern with dense air as we marched toward the cloudy opening. Outside and in front of the mountain where beautiful handmade cabins had once been lined up were planks of burning wood lying about and thick black smoke twirling in the air.

Half of the pike barricade had also tumbled over, pieces of smoldering wood lying about sporadically.

The plan was simple: if Elektra's arrows failed to kill Isaac, we would charge.

I turned around, trying to perform a head count of our Battlewomen. In total, we were ten or twelve, which, in my opinion, was more than enough to take down a man. Had it not been for his armor and his gigantic battle-ax and for Rainer standing by his side, I would have taken him down myself with a single arrow.

But with all his gear, it was like taking down a robot.

How were we supposed to injure him? We would have to aim for any visible skin.

In the distance, women continued to shout and cry out in pain, but the sound only came around every few seconds rather than all at once in a jumbled cacophonic orchestra. We were losing women—either that or we were winning; it was impossible to tell which.

"I see him!" Sammy said, pointing a stubby finger into the cloudiness in front of us.

Although barely visible, I saw him, too; he stomped his way through the battlefield, swinging his ax over his head and around him as he'd done right in front of me. Even if we were outnumbering them, this bastard alone would continue reducing our total population.

Beside him, Rainer's blades sliced through the air, clear streaks appearing through the dirt. With fewer feet scattering across the battlefield, the dirty air was slowly clearing up. Now visible, women with weapons held over their heads emerged, moving one at a time toward Rainer and Isaac. Why were they charging at them one at a time? They were going to get themselves killed.

Isaac prepared himself, tightening his grip around his ax.

And then, as if perfectly timed, the arrows came raining down, their pointed heads landing hard against his plated armor. The sound of stone clinging against metal spread through the battlefield, and quickly, he turned around and slouched his shoulders to shield himself.

It was pointless. Elektra's arrows were hitting him, but they weren't *hitting* him. All they did was ricochet off his back, which was basically a giant metallic shield. How was anyone supposed to take this guy out?

The moment the arrows stopped, Isaac swung his ax again.

"I have an idea," I said. "But I need you guys to move fast."

Everyone nodded, including Coin and Hammer. Although I didn't want them to be a part of this, I needed them. They both held fighting sticks close to their chests, gripping and regripping the handles.

Coin bowed her head, nostrils flared as if prepared to tear someone's throat out with her teeth. "Just tell us what needs to be done. Can't wait to take this son of a bitch down."

I stared at Isaac's swinging ax and swallowed hard. Admittedly, my idea was a bit suicidal, but I didn't know what else to do. If we stood any chance of taking him down, we needed to disarm him.

"I'm going to charge at him," I said, and everyone looked at me as if half of my brain had been surgically removed. "Relax," I continued. "I'm not taking him out. I only need him to miss his swing so I can cut the ax's head off."

"With that sword?" Hammer asked, pointing at

the weapon in my grasp.

I nodded.

Without even asking, she pulled it out of my hand, raised it up under her nose, and inspected it. She then shook her curly-haired head and dropped it into the dirt.

"Hammer—" I started.

"That sword's edges are too dull. You'll swing it and it'll either bounce off or get stuck in the wood. You, with the red-handled sword—" She pointed at a small woman who looked too weak to even be carrying a sword and made a gesture that meant, *Give that to me.*

The woman offered me her sword without a fight.

Hammer patted me hard on the shoulder. "Don't fuck this up."

"Wait," Sammy cut in. "Why can't we go with you? Won't distracting him work better?"

I arched an eyebrow. "Have you seen the guy? He swings that thing like it weighs no more than a feather. If we all show up at the same time, he might get worked up and start spinning around. I'll never get to the ax if he keeps swinging it over and over again."

It was obvious they didn't want me risking my life to end the battle, but that was precisely what had to be done. We were out of solutions, and right now, Isaac and Rainer were the ones causing the most casualties. With them gone, maybe we stood a real chance.

Closing my eyes, I let out a long breath through my nostrils.

"You sure you're ready?" Hammer asked.

"No," I said, and I bolted straight toward the armor-plated Beast.

CHAPTER 14

It was like something out of an action movie—slow and calculated. Had I actually been starring in a movie, loud ominous music would have been added to the soundtrack for dramatic effect.

But this wasn't fake, and it didn't go as planned like some perfectly outlined script.

Just as I appeared in front of Isaac, he swung his massive weapon over his head. I didn't stop running; instead, I charged straight for him. As the ax came swinging toward me, I dodged, a warm gust of wind hitting me in the face.

Had I not been wearing my stupid ankle shackles, I'd have probably run faster.

As he brought his weapon back to his body, I raised my sword, prepared to slice through his ax's wooden handle. Unfortunately, it didn't work out as I had planned. In one quick swing—a movement so fast I didn't have time to anticipate it—he elbowed me square in the face.

It was like having a cement block thrown at my head.

Crack.

I flew up in the air before falling flat on my back. The landing was less than pleasant, and a burst of air blasted out of my lungs as I hit the ground.

For the first time, I understood why cartoons often included little birdies around someone's head after an injury. My surroundings became blurry, and all I could see were bright, pixelated dots floating in front of my eyes. My ears rang so loudly I couldn't hear anything else.

Was he coming at me?

If I didn't get up, everything would soon fade to black. I'd seen the way he used his ax—his kills were instant. In a panic, I felt around for my sword, dirt accumulating underneath my fingernails. It had flown right out of my hands when he'd hit me.

Where the hell was it?

Slowly, my vision began to return. Isaac was still blurry, and now, there were two of him. Why wasn't he charging at me? Then, I realized that the second Isaac wasn't Isaac at all.

I sat upright and reached for my cheek, immediately regretting doing so. It felt like someone had taken a hot iron to my face; the pain was so sharp that I pulled away. He'd likely torn my cut right open and possibly even fractured my cheekbone.

"What are you doing?" came Rainer's harsh voice.

Finally, my hearing returned.

I blinked repeatedly until the three of them came into focus: Isaac and Eliot facing each other with weapons in their hands, and Rainer throwing herself between the two of them like any concerned mother would do.

What stood out most of all, however, was that Rainer wasn't trying to stop the fight—she was standing in front of Isaac, knowing all too well Eliot wouldn't kill his own mother.

How could she pick a side? They were equally her sons, yet she protected Isaac over Eliot.

"Put that down, now," she ordered.

Eliot grimaced and tightened his grip around a sword that looked like it had been forged specifically for him—it was at least four feet in length and nearly as wide as my face.

"This is not what you were trained for!" Rainer shouted.

For the first time, she looked out of control. The high ponytail atop her head swung from side to side as she shouted, her sword waving through the air in front of her. Her skin, typically an olive color, had darkened to a deep plum.

Had I known any better, I'd have thought she was threatening to kill Eliot herself.

Would she? Would she murder her own son if he got in her way?

She jabbed her sword again, nearly reaching

Eliot's bare, muscular torso. He hadn't worn any armor, which probably meant he'd changed his mind last minute about helping us, picked up a sword, and came bolting out of Rainer's lair. His feet, too, were bare, his large toes hidden in a pile of dirt and ash.

What was he thinking? How was he going to win against his fully armed brother?

He breathed rapidly, his chest heaving, and stared at the two of them. "This is not... not right," he said. "You are killing women. Why, Mother? For power? Like you have spoken of since we were boys? And you..." He pointed his mighty sword above Rainer's shoulder and at his brother's face. "You are a coward. Look at you. You are a giant beside these women. Does that make you feel powerful, brother? Powerful like Mother?"

Although strained, his English was surprisingly good.

"Don't make me choose," Rainer said, eyes narrowing on her son. "Because I will."

Eliot's sword fell a few inches, as if a broken heart had weakened his muscles. I couldn't imagine what he was experiencing. His own mother was basically admitting that she'd kill him if necessary.

Using my sword for support, I slowly got up. Their argument was so heated that not a single one noticed me getting back on my feet.

I stared at Isaac, prepared to attack him from behind and penetrate my sword right beneath his body armor, when Hawkins came running out into the open. Her broken hand, a mangled mess, lay flat against her chest as she ran straight toward Rainer with the Ogre stick held high above her head.

She let out a monstrous shout, her face distorting beyond recognition, and threw herself at Rainer. Together, they collapsed to the ground, a cloud of dirt engulfing them entirely.

At the same time, Isaac roared, swung his ax over his head and aimed it at his brother. But before the ax came down, Eliot charged toward his brother and tackled him to the ground. Isaac's ax flew out of his grasp and he fell with Eliot on top of him, causing the earth beneath my feet to tremble. More dirt floated into the air as the two struggled, throwing heavy blows at each other. With bulging shoulders, Eliot tore off his brother's metallic headpiece and gorilla skull mask, then started bashing his fists into his face.

Together, they disappeared behind an enormous brown cloud, while beside them, Rainer and Hawkins came into view. They lay there, Hawkins atop Rainer, yet no one moved.

Why weren't they moving? I took a step toward them but stopped when I noticed Hawkins's limp hands resting on either side of Rainer's body. Out from her back was Rainer's sword aimed straight at the sky.

With a grunt, Rainer pushed Hawkins off and tore her sword out of her stomach. Dark blood stuck to the blade like maple syrup on a butter knife. She didn't bother cleaning it off; instead, she swung around in a panic, her hateful gaze fixated on her sons.

Without hesitating, she ran behind Eliot and raised her sword, prepared to sever his head.

"Eliot!" I shouted, but he was beating his brother so hard that he didn't hear me. Was this Rainer's doing? Was it the abuse? It was as if he'd kept a lifetime of rage bottled up inside, and now, it was coming out on his brother.

Rainer bared her teeth, about to strike the blow, when I did the only thing I could think of: I threw my sword right at her the way one does a hunting spear. The throw was awful, but it miraculously managed to hit her. She winced in pain, dropped her sword, and clutched at her hand.

Her bright eyes rolled up at me.

At first, they were animallike—ferocious and hungry for blood. But then, something changed. She pulled her face back and her lips parted as if she'd come face-to-face with a ghost.

"You," she breathed.

The shocked look on her face didn't last long at

all. Within seconds, she was glaring at me so intensely I could have sworn hot, invisible lasers were shooting from her eyes. She reached down into the sand and grabbed two swords—hers, and the one I'd thrown at her.

Shit.

"You have no idea how long I've been waiting for this day," she said, walking toward me.

Both swords hung by her sides, their sharp tips dragging in the soil. She walked with her head bowed forward, creating shadows over her high cheekbones. Had she not been so tan, with her black leather clothes and her tall boots, she'd have resembled an angry vampire. But with the brown and gray fur sitting over her shoulders and the metallic armor plates across her chest and forearms, she looked more like a Viking warrior.

Her nostrils twitched as she moved toward me, and I took a step back.

How was I supposed to fight her? I didn't have a weapon. I searched the ground, prepared to pick up anything I could find when I tripped over a dead body and landed awkwardly over someone's bloody stomach. My elbow hit something soft, causing a squishing sound, and I jumped back up onto my feet.

My knife, I remembered. It wasn't much, but it was better than nothing. From my belt, I pulled out my small knife and held it up near my face. This seemed to amuse her—she smirked as if I were nothing more than a two-year-old trying to defend herself with a gummy worm.

I swallowed hard, prepared to fight to the death.

CHAPTER 15

First, I saw Sammy, then Coin and Hammer. Behind them, another dozen women came running onto the battlefield with various weapons held by their sides, over their chests, and above their heads.

Clenching her jaw, Rainer turned toward them.

Although it may have been a coward's move, I took this opportunity to charge at Rainer with my knife held firmly in my fist.

At the same time, the battlefield seemed to shrink in on us. A few nearby Northers saw my women charging and took it upon themselves to do the same. Within seconds, everyone was running toward the same spot—toward Rainer— with weapons bouncing in the air.

No matter what happened, I couldn't lose focus on Rainer... not now. This was it... this was the end. If I killed her, the fight was over.

Sammy was at the front of the line. With eyes fixated on Rainer, she let out a hoarse scream, her tomato-red face jiggling as she ran.

At this pace, both Sammy and I would reach Rainer at the same time. Would this work to our benefit, or was Rainer trained for this?

As I prepared to throw myself at Rainer, Sammy jumped upward with a sword in both hands and swung it in a downward motion. But as she came down from her jump, Rainer stabbed one of her long, shiny swords upward, penetrating Sammy's chest midair.

High off the adrenaline pumping through me, I couldn't comprehend what had happened. The only thing on my mind was the image of me killing Rainer; and in that split second, Sammy wasn't a friend or even a human being. She was a distraction I could use to my advantage.

Sammy's limp and heavy body forced Rainer back a few steps, and at that precise moment, my knife came sweeping through the air, its pointed tip aimed at Rainer's unprotected neck.

Yet she knew I was coming. With Sammy's body still stuck on her sword, Rainer threw her right elbow out, knocking me square in the nose. My head rocked back, and warm blood trickled into my mouth, filling it with a rusty taste.

I reached for my bloody nose, took a few wobbly steps backward, and fell to the ground.

Rainer tore her sword out, the sound reminding me of an old wet rug being pulled off the ground.

Only then did it hit me.

Sammy.

She'd killed her.

She'd fucking killed her.

I wanted to scream out, but I was too disoriented. Rainer's blow, coupled with her son's earlier hit, was enough to give me a concussion. I blinked several times, trying to get the two Rainers in front of my face to merge into a single person.

At once, as if pressing the play button on an action-packed movie, everyone crashed into each other in front of me. Blades swung through the air, axes came crashing down, and women screamed at the top of their lungs.

I wanted to stand up and fight, but I couldn't. Instead, my head rolled in every direction as I fought to stay alert, and I held onto my knife as if it would somehow be enough for protection. Eventually, Rainer would find her way over to me and finish what she'd started.

This time, I wouldn't be able to stop her.

The sound of flesh tearing and bones breaking slowly faded until finally, everything went black.

CHAPTER 16

"Give her some space."

"Get out of her way!"

"Move!"

The moment I opened my eyes, hot searing pain shot up my nose.

Awesome. First, a possible cheekbone fracture from Rainer's stupid son, and now, Rainer herself had likely broken my nose.

When Zofia, the doctor I'd met earlier that day, leaned in uncomfortably close to my face, I tried to squirm away. Her eyes were so far apart, she reminded me of an ant, but somehow, they suited her. Her auburn hair looked even redder than it had earlier, and that's when I noticed all the blood smudged on her neck, shoulders, and hands.

She didn't seem injured, though, which meant the blood wasn't hers.

"You have several fractures," she said, brushing a gentle finger along the bridge of my nose and across my swollen cheek.

I winced and pulled away.

"Relax," she said, her thick accent soothing me.

"I fix your nose."

I made my eyes go big. What the hell was that supposed to mean?

"When you were passed out," she said. "I fix it."

Oh, thank God.

"She okay?" came a familiar voice.

At first, I thought maybe I was hallucinating. But as she came closer, her sconce's orange glow lit up her bloody face, and I knew I wasn't hallucinating.

"Hey, kid," Murk said.

Why was she looking at me like that? Like she knew me?

"Murk?" I asked.

"Brone," she said, a sly smirk on her lips. "I was right about you."

I tried to sit up, but Zofia pressed on my chest and told me to lie back down.

"I thought you didn't recognize..." I tried.

"I was only trying to protect you," Murk said.

Sighing, I closed my eyes, relieved to know that Murk hadn't lost her memory.

Rainer, I remembered. Shooting upright, I searched the cavern.

Murk must have known what I was thinking— she knelt by me and slowly pushed me back down. "You have a lot of injuries," she said. "You need to rest. Don't worry about Rainer. I finished this once and for all."

I stared into her bright, crystal-like eyes that matched her icy hair. "You killed her?"

Murk nodded. "It's over, Brone."

One by one, faces emerged from behind Murk. Biggie, Rocket, Elektra, Fisher, Hammer, Coin... My friends who had survived. Then, beside Biggie appeared another familiar face—Quinn.

She forced a smile, her septum piercing barely moving on her face. Her colorful hair that had once reminded me of Harley Quinn was now a filthy, bloodstained blond. She was nearly as tall as Biggie, through much smaller now. Her tattooed arms, which had once been thick and flabby, were as small as mine.

She cast her eyes to the ground, and there was no doubt in my mind that she'd lost countless women she cared about in battle.

"We did it," I said, staring at everyone in Rainer's lair. "Are there others?" I asked. "Where are Fran and Pam? Where's Scorch? Dibs?"

Murk solemnly shook her head. "The last stretch was rough... They didn't make it."

A sinking feeling sat in my stomach, and I swallowed hard. How had I lost so many people in a single day? If I allowed myself to start thinking about all of those who'd lost their lives... Flander, Sumi, Johnson, Arenas, Jack, Fran, Pam, Scorch, Dibs, Ellie... I feared I might fall into a depression so deep I'd never find my way out.

"We have several women outside," Murk said. "They're searching for more survivors."

I nodded without saying anything. My throat was so tight it felt like Zsasz was strangling me again.

"Watch out," came someone's voice.

The crowd of women around me broke apart as a tall, fur-covered figure entered the cave. She was carrying someone, but I couldn't see who it was.

"Zofia," the voice said, moving closer.

The moment I caught a glimpse of her face, I slapped Murk's hands away from me and sat upright.

"What the fuck is this?" I snapped, staring the Norther in the face.

"Relax," Murk said, no longer able to hold me down. "That's Iskra. She was one of their medics."

"And what the hell's she doing here?" I growled.

"Iskra isn't like them," Murk said. "She's with us."

Iskra... I remembered that name. Olga, the old Russian woman, had told me that Iskra had always been the sweetest of the Russian orphans. I also remembered her face. Iskra was the one who had come to my defense when I'd jumped on Georgia. If it hadn't been for her, Georgia and I would have been forced to fight to the death.

She looked the same as she had that day—lanky, pale, and with puffy bags that sat under her eyes and over her cheeks. Unlike the other Northers, she wasn't wearing any metallic armor or carrying any weapon. She stared at me as if seeing an old friend for the first time in years.

"You," she said, still holding onto the limp body in her arms. "I saw your sadness for this girl."

Sadness? Who was she talking about? A few women stepped farther away from Iskra, allowing the sconce's warm glow to illuminate the body in her arms. The woman's hair, dark and wavy, hung so low it nearly touched the ground. Underneath Iskra's fingers and over the woman's shoulder was a blue and yellow butterfly tattoo I'd have recognized anywhere.

I parted my lips to breathe Ellie's name, but nothing came out. My throat swelled and I turned away. I wanted to step closer, kiss Ellie's cold forehead, and tell her that I loved her, but I couldn't move.

Footsteps shuffled behind me, but still, I didn't look. Instead, I stared at Rainer's old throne, wondering if my heart might explode. This was worse than anything I'd ever experienced in my life... worse than being sentenced here, and even worse than being dragged away by police officers while my mom cried out for me, a petrified look on her face.

"Let's put her down. Right here. Perfect. Ah. I see what you did there," came Zofia's voice.

"Where did you learn to do this?"

"Olga," Iskra said. "She was a nurse in Russia."

No one said anything, undoubtedly because they had no idea who Olga was.

"You did well," Zofia said. "The wound is clean, and it looks like you pulled the arrow out perfectly."

The wound? Why were they talking about her wound being cleaned? I swung around to find Ellie lying on her side with Zofia crouched behind her. She squinted, examining Ellie's puncture wound, and smiled up at Iskra.

"Let's bring her somewhere comfortable until she vakes up," Zofia said. "Continue to monitor her. We need to be careful of infection."

Wakes up?

I ran to Ellie's side and dropped to my knees. Still smiling, Zofia looked up at me.

"She's... she's... she's..." I sputtered.

Zofia reached for my shoulder, a touch as warm as a hot mug of cocoa on a crisp winter day. "Because of Iskra, she is."

I gazed at Iskra, my throat so tight I thought I might stop breathing. My bottom lip trembled, but no words came out. It was like I didn't have to vocalize how I was feeling. She smiled sweetly at me and nodded as if saying, *You're welcome.*

And then, the tears came pouring out. I threw my arms around Ellie's body and pressed my face against hers. It was warm, not cold, and her skin became slippery with all of my tears.

"You're alive," I breathed.

CHAPTER 17

Leaning against the entryway, I stared at Ellie's peaceful face. She lay on the bed I'd sat on earlier that day, half of her body lit up by a ray of sunlight coming through the hole in the wall. It was strange to think that only hours ago, I'd been standing in this very room, preparing myself for death.

"She will be okay," came Iskra's voice.

I turned my head sideways.

"Iskra..." I said.

She raised an open palm and shook her head somberly. "After everything my people have done to yours, this was the least I could do. I will spend the rest of my life trying to make up for what happened."

"This wasn't your fault," I said.

She cast her dark brown eyes to the cave's solid floor. "I should have spoken up... When I was young, I felt it wasn't right. But I was too shy... too quiet, to question Rainer in front of everyone. I wasn't the only one. Zsasz wasn't always so bad, you know."

I clenched my fists, finding that incredibly hard

to believe, but reminded myself that at one point, Zsasz had been nothing more than an innocent child—an orphan thrown into the system against her will.

"She was the funny one," Iskra said, smiling at the memory. She had a large smile—the kind that reveals every tooth in one's mouth. Luckily, hers didn't appear to be rotten. They weren't white by any means, but they weren't any worse than other teeth on this island. She leaned her head against the stone wall behind her and sighed. "She used to make jokes all the time, especially when Rainer would turn away. But Rainer was always so angry. All she ever spoke about was this *Murk*, and how one day, she would get her revenge. So when Zsasz made jokes and Rainer heard them, she'd grab Zsasz by the hair and throw her face-first onto the ground, filling her mouth and eyes with sand and dirt. Zsasz cried every time but didn't stop her jokes, even when Rainer started burning her skin with hot metal or hitting her across the face." Iskra sucked in a long breath and let it out through her nose. "The jokes only stopped when Rainer started forcing Zsasz to kill people. When she and her other women caught someone running wild in the jungle, they'd capture her, tie her up, and get Zsasz to stab a knife into her heart."

I swallowed hard, sick to my stomach. How the hell could anyone do that to a child?

"Hold old were you guys?" I asked.

"I was six, and Zsasz was nine. I think that's why Rainer picked on her the most—she was the oldest of us all."

Iskra's smile returned. "You know her name wasn't always Zsasz. It used to be Dominika. Rainer, when she wasn't beating us or yelling at us, spoke of super villains around fires at night. She said a dark creature by the name of Batwoman brought chaos to cities in the real world. She said she could fly and climb tall buildings... taller than trees. She then spoke of a hero by the name of Zsasz. I think she spoke of her to make Dominika feel better about her scars. Some days, Rainer was like a mother to us, and when she told that story, tears filled her eyes as if she felt awful for what she'd done to Dominika. It didn't last, of course. But her story was powerful enough to convince Dominika that her scars were something to be proud of."

"So she kept cutting herself," I said, matter-of-factly.

Iskra nodded.

"And killing," I added.

She nodded again.

I hated Zsasz—the last thing I wanted was to have any sort of sympathy toward her. But after hearing Iskra's story, it was hard not to acknowledge that Zsasz, too, had been a victim in all of this.

In a sense, everyone was a victim of their circumstances. No one was born evil—events and situations were what changed people. But then I thought of Eliot and how he, now a young man, knew right from wrong.

How was it that some people, despite their heinous pasts, were able to overcome it all and bring good to this world while others continued down a dark path of self-harm and violence toward others?

Neither one of us spoke, and instead, I watched Ellie's chest move gently up and down.

"Are you sure she'll be okay?" I asked.

Iskra's thin pale lips curved up at one end. "I promise you that I will do everything to make sure she survives this."

I reached for Iskra's shoulder and she flinched.

"I'm sorry," she said. "I am not used—"

"Hey, it's okay," I said. "You don't have to explain yourself to me. But I do have to explain something to you."

She blinked, her lips sealed tight.

"Rainer lied to you," I said.

Iskra tilted her head. "About what?"

"About Batman."

"Batman?"

I let out a soft chuckle. "The story is actually about *Batman*, not Batwoman, and Zsasz wasn't a woman, he was a man. And Batman was the hero, not Zsasz... Zsasz was a murdering bastard who worked for Penguin."

Iskra cocked an eyebrow. "Penguin?"

I shook my head. "Never mind. The point is, forget anything Rainer ever taught you other than English. She had serious problems." I tapped my temple. "If she couldn't even be honest about a story everyone knows, she probably lied to you your entire childhood."

Iskra stood there, biting her bottom lip. It looked like it was sinking in.

"And Batman isn't real," I said.

She let out a breath so loud I thought maybe Ellie might wake up. "What a relief. She made us fear the real world with that story... She told us Batwoman... Batman, I mean, entered the homes of people and tore children apart limb by limb. She said that she alone was the only one capable of protecting us from her... him, I mean."

"I'd be willing to bet that Rainer said Murk was a lot like Batwoman," I said.

Iskra looked away from me as if embarrassed for having ever believed anything Rainer said.

Slowly, I reached for her shoulder again. This time, she didn't flinch but instead rounded her back and smiled shyly.

"You're with us now, Iskra."

She parted her lips to say something when Ellie

let out a soft moan.

CHAPTER 18

"Ellie?" I said.

She moaned again, rolling her head from side to side. Large beads of sweat slid down her forehead, which was cold to the touch.

I turned to Iskra. "What's wrong with her?"

Iskra planted two balled fists on her waist. "Probably a fever. Her body is trying to fight an infection. Don't worry. Zofia will gather medicine for her. You should rest, too, Brone."

Only when she said those words did the sickness sink in. It was as if I'd been so pumped with adrenaline I'd forgotten how grave my injuries were.

"I'm... I'm okay," I lied.

"Why don't you lie down with her?"

I smiled at the thought, then bent down and kissed Ellie's clammy forehead. As I pulled away, Ellie's plush lips stretched into a faint smile.

"Ellie?" I asked.

Slowly, she opened her honey brown eyes. They were narrow and bloodshot, but they were the most beautiful thing I'd seen all day, like a sun making an appearance after a devastating hurricane.

"Did... did we win?"

I let out a relieved laugh and kissed her lips. "We did."

She swallowed hard and winced. Beside her head, atop a small wooden table, was a stone bowl with water in it that Iskra had left for her. I picked it up and gently tilted it against Ellie's lips. She slurped it up as if she hadn't had a lick of water in days and nodded rapidly when she'd had enough.

"Are you okay?" I asked.

"Are you?" she said.

"Are you waiting for me to thank you for saving my life?" I asked.

Her eyes turned into little moons, which I knew was a translation for, Yes.

"I thought you were dead," I said, trying hard not to let my anger show. "Why would you have done something so stupid like that? I could have lost you, Ellie. What the hell were you—"

"And I could have lost you," she said. She reached for my face—a delicate caress—and stared at me intently. "I wouldn't survive this island without you."

"You survived it before—"

"That was before I met you," she cut me off. "It isn't all about you, Brone. It was either me or you, and at that moment, I wanted you to live. You can be pissed off all you want—"

"I'm not pissed off. I was terrified—"

"I get that," she said. "But had you been in my shoes, you'd have done the same thing."

She swallowed hard again and her eyelids became heavy. How was I supposed to argue with that? She was right. I'd have jumped in front of an arrow for her time and time again.

"You need to rest," I said.

She cleared her throat. "Aren't... Aren't you going to thank me?"

I smiled, staring at her perfectly symmetrical face. I brushed my thumb along her jaw and across her lips, then slowly bent forward and kissed her again. Her hot breath slipped out through her nostrils and onto my face.

I pulled away, but only briefly, before kissing her nose, her soft cheeks, and her clammy forehead.

"I love you," I said.

With eyes still closed, she whispered, "I love you, too."

"I'll be back soon. I promise."

When she didn't respond, I knew she'd fallen asleep.

I got up, a throbbing pain shooting down my back, and made my way down the cavern. Iskra followed close behind without saying a word. Every muscle and bone in my body was hurting so badly I thought I might pass out, but after all that had happened, I needed to go out there and see what was going on.

As much as I wanted to lie against Ellie and escape this reality, I wasn't finished.

The moment I stepped out into open air and onto the desolate remains of the battlefield, my throat swelled. The sight was absolutely devastating—bodies lay everywhere, both Northers and my people. The solid wooden cabins that had once been lined up against the mountain were nothing more than cracked wooden planks and piles of ashes. The tents, too, along with the entire gate, had burned to a crisp. All that was left was an open field full of bodies, bloody weapons, and dust.

Women walked about, stepping over bodies with heads tilted forward as they searched for survivors. The sun was slowly beginning to set, which was likely why so many women were scavenging through the battlefield. If there were any other survivors, it was important we find them as soon as possible.

At the center of the open space, where the tents had once been, I caught a glimpse of something I wished I hadn't. With a metal brace fastened around her ankle, Smith lay beneath large slabs of wood, covered in ash. Half of her body, including her face, was burned away.

Poor woman.

She'd been trapped as her tent went up in flames.

I breathed in a long, calculated breath, wondering if I'd ever get over a sight like this. It was even more disturbing than seeing our Village burn down. I'd never seen so many dead bodies before. The smell was enough to make me want to vomit—it didn't smell like decay, at least not yet, but it was a smell I'd come to associate with death. Maybe it was the combination of ash, smoke, and blood.

I didn't remain focused on the destruction for much longer. One by one, women began pointing my way and calling to their friends. Slowly, a crowd formed before me, and women knelt down—even those who weren't my people.

At the front of the crowd was Snow Face and her women—tall, lanky figures with white dots splashed all over their dark skin. With a spear planted in the dirt by her knee, Snow Face bowed her head.

"We did it," came Fisher's voice.

I turned sideways to find her standing next to me. She gave me her walking stick, but I shook my head.

"Take it," she said, her tone harsh and authoritative. "You need it more than me right now."

I took it from her, allowing it to absorb some of my body weight. I couldn't understand how I hadn't collapsed by now, but I wasn't about to allow myself to.

"Looks like they've chosen their leader," Fisher said.

Murk appeared to the left of me with gashed arms crossed over her chest. "A solid choice."

"Murk," I said, regripping Fisher's walking stick. "What do we do now?"

She looked up at the cloudy sky, the wrinkles on her face fading as she stretched her chin upward. She breathed in as if breathing for the first time. "That, Brone, is up to you."

I almost laughed but thought it might be inappropriate considering what we'd gone through.

"Up to me? You're the leader," I said.

She shook her head like a parent trying to explain the meaning of death to their child. "Don't you get it, Brone? The people have chosen." She leaned into me then, her lips tickling my earlobe. "Besides, I'm too old for this shit."

Then, she pulled away and with a pained grunt, slowly knelt on one knee.

One by one, everyone raised a solid fist in the air with their thumbs tucked in. Their eyes—expectant, glossy balls filled with anguish—remained glued to me.

What were they waiting for? For me to take charge?

I was about to turn away when an unusual sensation came over me, tightening my chest. As I stared at the grisly scene and the women who, despite having gone through hell and back, still looked to me for guidance, realization hit. I was *exactly* what they needed.

For the first time, I was confident I could make their lives worth living; I didn't view myself as unfit to be a leader. I thought of Trim, and rather than feeling inadequate or unworthy of her sacrifice, I imagined her smiling down at me from wherever she was now.

Standing tall, I drew my shoulders back and smiled at my friends beside me, sensing nothing but love and gratitude. Then, turning my attention to my people, I raised Fisher's walking stick into the air.

"Today," I shouted, my voice carrying across the wreckage below, "we defeated the enemy!"

Voices erupted so loudly I felt the vibrations underneath the pads of my feet.

Bringing my stick back down, I focused on every face, one at a time. "I know there are many injuries, and I know we've all lost people we truly care about."

The excitement and celebration dissipated, only to be replaced by an inconsolable sadness.

"For years, you have all suffered at the hands of Rainer. You have either been attacked, imprisoned, or abused. I promise you that all the lives we lost today won't be in vain. Your friends and your loved ones sacrificed themselves so that you could live the best life possible on this island."

Women nodded while some wept into the arms of others. I knew that pain—it was enough to bring anyone to their knees.

"Today," I said, my voice growing louder, "your fight has ended!"

A loud uproar shook the entire city and women blasted their fists into the air.

Smiling down at everyone, I raised my chin. "And tomorrow, we live."

Visit **shadeowens.com** for more works by Shade Owens.